The Heart
of Aleppo

The Heart
of Aleppo

Ammar Habib

THE HEART OF ALEPPO

Copyright © 2018 by Ammar Habib

Cover Art by Fiona Jayde

Printed in the United States of America
ISBN: 978-1724216380

First Edition: July 2018
First Printing: July 2018

For more information, please visit:
www.ammarahsenhabib.com

Other works by Ammar Habib include:

DEDICATION

This novel is dedicated to the brave people of Syria.

TABLE OF CONTENTS

LIST OF CHARACTERS

SETTING:
Aleppo, Syria in the summer of 2012

PROTAGONIST:
Zaid Kadir – a 13-year-old boy living in Aleppo

MAIN CHARACTERS:
Fatima – Zaid's neighbor; a 13-year-old girl
Salman – Fatima's brother & Zaid's best friend; a 15-year-old boy

ZAID'S FAMILY:
Nabeel – Zaid's older brother by 12 years; an officer in the Syrian Army
Abbi – name Zaid calls his father by
Ummi – name Zaid calls his mother by
Aisha – Zaid's sister-in-law; Nabeel's wife

SUPPORTING CHARACTERS:
Jari – a former soldier of the Syrian Army
Faisal – a 17-year-old boy
Amaan – Faisal's brother, a 16-year-old boy
Ethan – a humanitarian worker trapped in Aleppo

INTRODUCTION

Thank you for picking up a copy of *The Heart of Aleppo*. Before the story begins, I would like to briefly explain why this novel was written. I personally believe that the Syrian Civil War is one of this generation's greatest tragedies. With the way it is proceeding, it'll be remembered by future generations in the same manner that we remember the Rwandan genocide and the Bosnian War of the 1990s.

The motivation for writing this story was simple: I wished to bring more global attention to this crisis. Although the characters are fictitious, this novel accurately depicts the events that transpired in Aleppo during the summer of 2012. I hope that reading this will lead readers to have a greater understanding of the plight those in Syria face, as well as those in other war-torn regions. If this work helps garner more attention for those in Syria, then I will have considered this project a success.

In an over-politicized world, my wish is for this work to humanize those we call "refugees". This book is not about the politics of the Syrian Civil War or any other conflict. Its aim is not to convince readers to support any faction or political party. Instead, this story is about the unbreakable spirit of humanity. It is about how humanity often shows its true strength during the darkest times.

Your friend,
Ammar
July 2018

1

CHAPTER 1
DAY OF RECKONING

The sky rains fire down onto Aleppo.

Gunfire surrounds me. Bullets whiz through the air, striking anything in their path. Running through the street, I hear bombs falling from the heavens. They grow louder with every passing second.

Then it starts again. Deafening explosions rock the city. Men and women topple over as the bombs and missiles erupt. Buildings go up in smoke. Chunks of debris are blown into the air before spilling down on the city, crushing anything in their path. I feel the heat of the blasts crash against my skin. I witness walls and entire buildings ferociously collapse, kicking up enough dust and smoke to rival a sandstorm.

A building's wall creaks as I run under its shadow. It breaks off in the next instant. Avoiding the falling debris as I leap over rubble, I witness the city that I call home—the city I grew up in—again turn to ashes. But I can do nothing. Like the rest of them, I can do nothing but flee. Some flee to shelter. Others flee away from the battle. However, there is no escape from this. My mind continues to scream one thing through all the madness: *run! Run and don't stop! Run until your feet fall out from under you!*

The Judgment Day that the *Imam* always spoke of is upon us. It is the end.

I hear nothing but the ringing of the earsplitting destruction all around, sense nothing but the insurmountable heat. Black ash covers me. I wipe my eyes of the dust, desperate to clear my sight. My vision is tunneled ahead as I try to escape the bombs. My feet are numb, but

2

I don't stop. My heart pounds against my chest like a mad drummer, threatening to burst out at any moment. But I don't slow down. I can't.

It's chaos. Madness. The rockets are plummeting onto the street at random. Homes and shops go up in a blinding blaze. The explosions are everywhere: in front, behind, and on either side. There's just chaos as the bombs strike the city. Blackness shrouds the heavens. I can't see ten feet ahead of me. There's so much thick, toxic smog. I w—

I'm suddenly sent lurching forward before crashing on my side. My head is spinning. The ringing is louder than ever before. I lay there a moment longer, unable to muster any strength. What just happened?

My thoughts still in disarray, I stagger to my feet. I almost topple over immediately, but I maintain my balance. The ground is shaky, and I can barely keep it under my feet. Was that a bomb? It almost hit me. A few more feet to the left and I would have been caught in the eruption. Instead, a truck was set ablaze. The fire is scorching. That could have been me in it.

A man dashes right by me. Then a boy who's nearly my age. Neither one gives me a second glance.

Keep running, Zaid. Don't stop!

The explosions aren't slowing down. Neither is the gunfire. Continuing to retreat from the bullets, I shake my head in an effort to diminish the disarray. The endless barrage almost drowns out the screams. Some are of the people—my fellow civilians—being engulfed by the explosions and debris. I hear their thunderous cries before they are cut short. Others are of those like me, those fleeing their homes in terror. People run right over one another.

The gunfire grows closer with every second. A bullet shoots right by me. Then another. Followed by a third. *Don't slow down, Zaid.*

Keep running! The smoke is so thick now that I can barely even see where I'm stepping. However, it only makes me run faster.

But the firefight is moving too quickly. It's catching up. I can't outrun it. Vehicles are riddled with bullets before their engines catch fire. The bombs continue rocking the street, leveling anything or anyone they hit. Shockwaves and heat crash against me from every side. Black smoke keeps rising up to the heavens.

My foot hits something, causing me to stumble. I hardly pay any attention to what it is: a corpse, a woman. Catching my footing, I keep dashing for my very life. I can't slow down. Not even two steps later, I run right over another body. A third is to my right, but I don't even look at it.

A rocket slams into a high-rise building directly in front of me. The scorching explosion cuts through the smoke. I react on instinct. Shielding my face from the blast and the dust, I take cover behind a broken-down car. There's another figure hiding on all fours. It's a man. He's not even twenty, hardly seven years older than me. His head is pressed against the concrete and his hands cover the back of his skull. He's cowering, too scared to even move.

The roar of the blast dies off. By the time I look back up, the building's wall breaks off and falls toward the road. I leap back to my feet. But then I stop. Hearing a cry above the destruction, I whip my head around and see a woman. Her foot is trapped under a chunk of debris.

I don't think—I can't think. Not now. Sprinting to her in a frantic dash, I crouch down beside her. The debris has her left foot and calf pinned. Her gaze locks with mine, eyes consumed by a fearful terror. It's the same terror I've now seen too many times. They're begging for any help.

What can I do? Will she even be able to walk after this? Don't think about that now, Zaid.

Her foot might be shattered under the concrete. But it doesn't matter. I have to try something. There's a gap between the slab of concrete and the ground, and I find a place to grab the debris from underneath.

They're almost here. The gunfire is closing in.

The concrete debris is thick and appears heavy, but I don't let it sway me. I can't leave her here to die. With a deep breath, I try raising it up. The weight doesn't move. Squatting down, I lift up with all my might. Using my back and legs, I pull with every ounce of strength I can muster.

The fighting is drawing closer. The gunfire sounds louder than ever.

I can't lift the debris, but I don't give in. I feel my veins showing as I try to move it. All I need is a few inches, just enough for her to move her foot out from under it. My arms are shaking. My body trembles. My ears go deaf as another explosion erupts on the other side of the street. Its heat crashes against my back, but I don't waver. The concrete is still not moving.

The shooting is nearly on us.

I look up at the scorching heavens. With a roar, I give it everything I have. I muster all that I can rally. I don't stop. My fingers are in pain and feel like they're going to break off, and I cannot feel my arms. But the concrete doesn't move an inch.

A bullet strikes the debris directly to my left. They're upon us. It's too late.

CHAPTER 2
ALEPPO

Days earlier:

"Zaid… Zaid…"

Hearing Fatima's whisper, I am abruptly yanked back to reality. Once again at my school desk in the back of the class, I notice that the entire classroom is silent. The teacher stands a few feet away. Her condemning gaze is on me. So is the entire class's. Oh God, not again.

"Well, Zaid?" the teacher obviously repeats. Her eyes are daggers. "Are you still with us?"

She asked me a question, didn't she? "Well, Ms. Farooq… uh—the, uh…"

"Please save yourself the embarrassment." Turning around, she starts making her way back to the front of the room. "It would be good if you kept your mind in the class and not in the clouds, Zaid. Perhaps your test scores would start to reflect that as well."

There are a few chuckles from around the room. My cheeks redden as I sink into my chair a bit more. Looking a bit to my right, I catch Fatima's gaze. She shakes her head in amusement before looking away. That's the second time today I've been caught daydreaming.

Ms. Farooq arrives back at the blackboard. "As we were discussing, after spending time in the military during the 80s and 90s, President Assad came to power twelve years ago in 2000, succeeding his father."

Didn't she say all this yesterday? I look up at the clock. You've got to be joking. It's only been two hours since classes began, meaning that it's still another two before our break.

"And like Ahmed brought up earlier," Ms. Farooq continues, "since the civil war began last year, it brought about some major things in our city. For the past couple of months, there have been several large protests in Aleppo. The first one was this past May. Some are pro-Assad while many are against. And then there were the bombings—"

A hand goes up.

"Yes, Ahmed?" Ms. Farooq says.

"Why are so many people against our president? My father says that he is a great man and that he's helped our country's economy and infrastructure. Civil servants like you, Ms. Farooq, and my father have benefited because of him."

Oh, Ahmed. Ever the know-it-all. Everyone was just waiting for his "valued" commentary. I exchange a quick smirk with Fatima.

As always, Ms. Farooq is the only one who appreciates his thoughts. "Very good, Ahmed. Although the people in our city primarily support him, there are many outside of Aleppo that view him as a tyrant."

"Why?" Ahmed asks.

I look down at the handout that sits on my desk. All the words on there are just blurred together. With a sigh, my gaze drifts to the window. It looks so nice outside today. Why can't time move faster?

"Because he came into power unelected. As was his father." Ms. Farooq pauses for a moment. "And before you ask about the 2000 and 2007 elections, Ahmed, many regard those as rigged. So no matter how much good he may do in power, the fact that President Assad gained his power without an election makes many dislike him."

Another girl's hand goes up. "Is that why the fighting is happening? And the bombings?"

"It's very complicated, Maryam, since there are a lot of reasons. But you could say that the direct cause was President Assad's handling of the wave of protests that swept over our region in 2011, the Arab Spring. I'm sure many of you remember all the commotion about those last year. But…"

She goes on. I don't even know how she got on this subject. The last thing I remember was her talking about the Treaty of Sèvres. We have a test coming up on it, but I don't even know how to pronounce it, let alone know what it is. But Ms. Farooq always forgets what she's teaching and somehow starts talking about the news.

As the class's self-appointed "know-it-all" keeps conversing with Ms. Farooq, I steal a quick glance at Fatima. She doesn't notice. She's wearing a green *hijab* today. I don't think I've ever seen it before. It looks nice on her, making her face almost beam. She's already a little fairer than the average Syrian girl, but the green headscarf makes her seem a bit more today. I wonder if she ever notices how I look—

"Zaid!"

Ms. Farooq's voice cuts through the air. Looking at her, I feel everyone's gazes back on me. Not again.

***

"Ali."

Hearing his name, Ali leaves the line of boys and joins Mansoor's team. Only five boys left now. Please don't let me be the last one picked.

With a football curled up under his arm, Salman looks over the remaining options. The sun beats down on all of us as we stand on the grassy field, but he's hardly sweating. At fifteen, Salman is two years older than me, but he honestly looks like he's seventeen. He possesses the kind of build that would make him good at nearly any sport, and he has the brains to go with it.

8

"I'll take Jamal."

Jamal hustles out of the line and joins the other six boys on Salman's team. *He didn't pick me? Seriously, with everyone watching? Come on, Salman. We're neighbors.*

It's Mansoor's turn again. No way is he picking me. Not after I cost his team the game last time in such an embarrassing way. He doesn't even waste a moment with his choice. "Amir."

Salman's turn again. It's my last chance for salvation. He looks over me and the other two remaining boys. Behind us, many of the class's girls are settling under some shade to watch the match. Fatima is there too. *Please, Salman, don't let me be picked last in front of her.*

His eyes stop on me for a long moment. This is it!

"Ahmed."

Are you serious?

Mansoor doesn't hesitate with his last pick. "Dawud."

Dawud runs off, leaving just me.

"Looks like you're with us, Zaid," Salman says as his hand beckons me toward his group.

Before I even take a step to join them, the rest of the boys turn around and start running toward the center of the football field. I weave through the pack, nearly out of breath by the time I catch up with Salman at the front of the group.

"Thanks a lot for picking me last," I mutter to him.

Salman goes along with the sarcasm. "Don't worry, Zaid. There was an even number of us today, and I knew nobody else would pick you."

I playfully hit him on the back.

He laughs with a smile. "My sister told me you were daydreaming in class again today."

"Fatima told you?"

Salman nods. "Keep your head in the game, not in the clouds. Do that long enough and maybe you won't get picked last next time."

9

***

Like every other school day, it ends with me making my way down the sidewalk alongside Fatima and Salman. The walkway is not very busy, but the roads are packed with more cars than usual. Up ahead, we can see the bus stop in the distance.

To our left is a beautiful, green garden protected by a metal fence. The most prominent tree there is the Turkey Oak. You can always make them out because the full-grown ones have an orange streak around the base of the trunk and possess glossy leaves. It was the first tree I ever climbed. Nabeel was cheering me on the entire time. He said it's the best tree to learn how to climb because it's sturdy and has plenty of branches. The hardest is the Mediterranean Cypress. It's so weak that it often bends if you try climbing it. The only person I've ever seen climb it is Nabeel. Not even Salman or any of Nabeel's friends could best it.

Continuing down the sidewalk, Salman is carrying his and his sister's book bags, leaving Fatima's hands free. He carries them both with more ease than I have just carrying mine. How does he always do it?

Aleppo's summers are always hot. But July is the worst. At the Friday prayer in the *masjid*, the *Imam* sometimes talks about how hot it will be in Hell. I have a hard time imagining how anything can be hotter than this. Not that I'd ever tell him that.

Looking back toward the garden, I think I see something sitting in the branches of one of the taller trees. It looks like a… golden eagle. I haven't seen one of those in a long time. Within a few moments of seeing it, the bird suddenly takes off toward the blinding sun, forcing me to look away.

"What did you keep daydreaming about, Zaid? In class today, I mean." Fatima asks, bringing me back to reality.

"About being a world-famous doctor." Salman nudges me. "Right?"

"Yeah. That and other things," I reply.

"I kept trying to get your attention, but you never heard me until it was too late," Fatima comments. "You know, Ms. Farooq would quit picking on you if you would just pay attention while she's talking."

"But if you do that then the entire class would lose their entertainment," Salman jokes.

Fatima swats his shoulder. "Be nice, Salman!"

Salman laughs it off as he puts his strong arm around me. "Zaid knows I'm kidding. With Nabeel gone so much, I have to fill in as his older brother and this is all part of it."

I smile as I playfully push him off.

"Do you know when Nabeel will be back?" Salman asks me.

"He keeps saying 'soon' every time I talk to him. But soon never seems to get here."

"I miss him." Fatima pauses. "Did you notice how empty the school was today? I counted nine students missing from the class."

Salman rolls his eyes. "You would be the one to count that."

***

The dry heat is unbearable. I should have taken *Ummi's* advice and worn my *thobe* today. It seems that nearly every man and boy was wise enough to do that, except for me and Salman. Instead, I insisted on wearing jeans and a western shirt to school. Now I'm paying the price.

You can hear the bus from a mile away. Just like every other public bus here, it's loud, old, and worn down. It was once painted green and white. However, now the green has faded and the rest looks more brown than white. None of the windows are broken, but a few are cracked and a couple of them look like they've been replaced. The vehicle reeks of oil. It's probably older than even my parents. But the driver, Nasir, claims it's never broken down or stalled on him. I guess that's worth something.

Along with us, there are always a handful of adults waiting for the bus at this stop. As it arrives at a halt, the bus's door swings open, allowing a few people to unload. They hastily make their way off before we come aboard.

The bus driver is my father's age. Like always, he's dressed in a long and loose, ivory white *thobe* that holds a few stains. His messy hair and beard are relatively trimmed. He knows us by name and usually greets us. But today, Nasir doesn't even acknowledge us as we climb onboard, failing to even look our way.

The grim expression on his face doesn't suit him. He's listening to the radio. It's low enough to where I can't hear what the host is saying, but it sounds like the news.

The bus is full as usual. Nasir always reserves the front row for us. Taking our seats, we sit in our normal order: Fatima by the window, Salman in the middle, and me closest to the aisle. Looking back as I place my bag on my lap, I recognize most of the passengers by their faces. Normally, the bus is a little loud. Not today. The people with smartphones are looking down at them while the other passengers mirror Nasir's bleak expression. A few have their hands raised as they make a silent prayer. I wonder—

"Zaid, ask your *Abbi* if you can come by after *salat* and dinner. I want to show you the new football my father gave me yesterday. I didn't want to bring it to school until you got to play with it first."

Hearing Salman's voice, I turn to face him. "Sure thing."

***

The actual bus stop is about a half mile from our street. But Nasir always goes a little off route and drops us off only a block away from our homes. He's always been kind to us. Most people in the city are.

Shops line up the street as far as the eye can see. They're all at least three stories high. There is an assortment of stores, selling everything from jewelry to furniture to food. Mirroring this part of the city, the buildings are all old. But I guess it's all relative since Aleppo was founded over 7,000 years ago. I remember Nabeel once saying that the city has over two million people living here.

Outside of Salman and Fatima, there are not any other kids our age living in this neighborhood. Nonetheless, the sidewalks are congested with people. It's always loud this time of the day, and the streets hold the same oily smell of the bus. Many of the shopkeepers know me because of my parents, but I don't know most of their names.

Just down the road, the large *masjid* stands tall. My *Abbi* takes me there for at least one prayer every day, and we go there every Friday for the weekly sermon. The building's cobalt dome and tall minaret loom above all the surrounding buildings, always making it easy to find no matter where you are.

Our home is three stories tall. The bottom floor is my father's rug store. He sells everything from simple prayer rugs to more decorative tapestries. We've lived here for as long as I can remember. Even Nabeel was born here and he's twelve years older than me.

Arriving through the shop's front doors, I'm immediately hit by a wave of cold air that drowns out all of the heat. I see my *Abbi* entertaining a customer interested in a tapestry. The tapestry is black with decorative gold embroidery, displaying an image of the Holy Kaaba in Mecca. Our shop is larger than most rug stores I've seen. It's also the oldest one on the street.

The rugs are an assortment of various colors. From darker navy and black shades to brighter crimson and cobalt colors and everything in between, coming here is like walking into a multi-colored work of art. I think *Abbi* arranged all the hanging tapestries so it would have that effect. He's always possessed an artist's eye.

Hearing me enter, the customer and my father turn to see me before I greet my father in the traditional greeting.

"*Assalam-O-Alaikum, Abbi.*"

"*Walaikum Assalam,* Zaid," my father replies.

The customer smiles and nods. I don't know his name, but I recognize his face. Looking to my left, I see Bilal cleaning off a few of the prayer rugs that have been on the shelves for a while. He's worked for my family longer than I've been alive. Sitting on the floor, Bilal is going through each shelf as he checks every rug. He greets me in the same way as my father.

Glancing back at my father and the customer, I notice that they're actually not talking about the tapestry. The smile that greeted me is no longer on *Abbi's* face. Instead, he's wearing an expression that I've never seen him show before. He looks almost… worried.

That can't be right. I see the expression of the customer. It's the same. Turning back to Bilal, I notice him wearing the same look as he continues with his work without paying me any heed. First the bus and now this. What's going on with everyone?

Arriving at the back of the shop, I reach the wooden staircase. I hustle up the steps one after the other. The floorboards creak as I climb each one. I pass by the photos hanging from the crimson wall. The first picture, an older one, shows *Abbi and Ummi* on their wedding day. The next one is a family photo that was taken when I was hardly a week old. The third displays Nabeel in his military uniform. I think that photo was taken at the ceremony when he was promoted to the rank of captain. The final frame holds a photo of Nabeel and Aisha from their wedding ceremony.

14

With the book bag hanging off my shoulder, I'm out of breath by the time I reach the top of the stairs. As soon as I make it to the second floor, a lighthearted voice cuts into the corridor. "I think I hear a handsome boy coming."

Hearing Aisha's voice, I see her emerge out of the kitchen and into the corridor. Wearing a mostly plain, black *abaya* with a bit of gold embroidery, her long black locks hang freely.

She smiles as her eyes focus on me. "I knew I recognized those footsteps."

Running up to her, I greet her like I always do. "*Assalam-O-Alaikum*, Aisha!"

She responds with a warm hug. I only met Aisha two years ago, which was shortly before she married Nabeel. However, it seems like she's been a part of the family all my life. She's barely a decade older than me but has become my second mother.

"How was school today, *Dr. Zaid?*" Her voice is as cheerful as ever. She sounds like Nabeel every time she calls me that.

"It was boring. Why is everyone looking so worried?"

Her expression turns inquisitive. "Who's looking worried?"

"*Abbi*, Bilal, and everyone on the bus."

"It's just politics, Zaid. Nothing for a young man like you to worry about." She glances back toward the kitchen. "I went shopping earlier and got some things for Ramadan since it's starting on Saturday. We'll be having a feast just for you."

I feel my smile grow.

"Nabeel called about an hour ago. He wanted to talk to you."

My eyes light up, much to her amusement. "Really!"

She playfully flicks me on the forehead, just like Nabeel always does. "If you hurry up and call him, you can catch him before he leaves the base."

Before Aisha even finishes her words, I am running up to my room.

***

I take a seat on my bed as I hear my brother's voice spill out of the phone.

"Father says you didn't do very well on your last test."

I knew he'd say that. "Maybe I should have studied harder."

"Or pay more attention in class." Nabeel's slight smile is displayed in his voice. He's always smiling around me. Him and Aisha both.

"I'll try." I pause for a moment. "Everyone's seemed worried today, but nobody is saying why."

"It's probably just boring politics, Zaid. Nothing for a strapping young guy like you to worry your mind about."

"That's exactly what Aisha said."

Nabeel lightly laughs. *"I guess we both think alike. Ramadan is starting this Saturday. Are you excited about trying to fast every day this time?"*

"I guess. Salman says the first three days are the toughest. After those, you get used to waking up early to eat. But I don't know if I'm ready yet."

"Well, you got two days left to get ready." He pauses. *"I wish I could be there."*

Looking out the window, I see the clear skies, reminding me about going over to Salman and Fatima's house later. "So when are you coming back? You still need to take me to the park and show me that wrestling move you were telling me about."

It takes him a moment to respond. *"I don't know, Zaid. With everything that's going on, the army has been sending me everywhere. But it'll be soon. I promise."*

"You're not in any danger with all the fighting that's happening, are you?"

There's a slight pause on his end, but his light tone doesn't diminish. *"...of course not. You never need to worry about me. Just worry about*

16

your studies. I need a good doctor to take care of me when I get old, God-willing, so I'm counting on you!"

I laugh.

"But I promise, when I get back, we'll spend a whole day at the park."

"You always say that."

"This time, I'm telling the truth. We'll be at the park so long that you'll be begging me to take you back home. Just wait and see, Dr. Zaid... just wait and see."

***

I find the kitchen empty when I come down. Even Aisha isn't here finishing up cooking dinner like she normally is. Neither is *Ummi*. In fact, I haven't seen my mother since arriving back home.

Hearing a sound, I make my way down the hall and into the sitting room. Here's everyone. *Abbi* and *Ummi* are sitting on the couch while Aisha and Bilal stand behind them. They're all watching the news. It's a breaking report about something, but I don't pay it any attention. The words on the screen seem a bit jumbled in my head when I try to read it, just like the words in books usually are.

I step into the room. The floorboard creaks under my feet, but none of them seem to notice. Why isn't *Abbi* downstairs? The shop is normally still open at this time. The news anchor is going on about what President Assad said this morning, reassuring Syrian citizens about something.

With *Abbi* distracted, maybe this is as good a time as any to ask him about going over next door. He usually answers 'yes' whenever he's preoccupied. I walk around the couch until I'm visible in his peripheral vision. I wait there for a few moments. Then a few more. He doesn't look over at me.

"...*Abbi?*"

He still doesn't glance away from the television.

"*Abbi?*" I speak up a little louder.

He suddenly turns and looks at me as if he didn't notice I was there before.

"*Abbi*, after *Asr Salat*, can I go and play with Salman?"

Abbi and *Ummi* exchange a long glance before he looks back at me. "Not today, Zaid."

There's something in the way he looks at my mother, something in both of their expressions, that seems off. It mirrors everything else that's been happening today. However, I don't argue or show my disappointment. "Okay."

"Go ahead and make your ablution, Zaid. We'll eat after *salat*."

"Are we going to go pray at the *masjid?*"

Abbi thinks for another short moment. "Let's pray at home today, Zaid."

We almost never perform our afternoon prayers at home. I nearly ask him if something is wrong, but I stop myself. His eyes are already telling me… and their answer frightens me.

CHAPTER 3
NIGHT OF TERROR

Hearing a sound, my eyes slowly open. The first thing I feel is soreness. My bedroom is dark as only a bit of starlight spills in through the window. Enveloped in my bed's warmth, I almost don't want to look up. But I force myself to do so and notice a silhouette in the darkness. She's rummaging through my closest and is tossing some items and clothing into a bag.

"*Ummi...*"

The silhouette turns around, revealing my mother's face. I can barely keep my heavy eyelids open and can hardly make out her features, but I see her eyes clearly. They seem concerned... more than they were before. My weariness is so intoxicating that half of me thinks this is a dream.

"Go back to sleep, Zaid." Her voice is a soft whisper.

"What are you doing?"

"Please, Zaid. Rest."

My body doesn't want to argue with her. Leaning my head back, I let the fatigue drag me back into a slumber.

***

"Wake up, Zaid!"

Feeling a hand shaking me, my eyes wake with a jolt. For a long moment, I'm in a daze of confusion. I can't even see straight as my mind goes wild. My gaze slowly settles on my mother's face. The nightlight reflects off of her gentle features. A look of concern is

19

washed over her. It's the same expression she and my father wore all evening. Except now it's much worse.

"It's time to get up."

"A—already?" I must be hearing her wrong. Is this a dream too? My head feels even heavier than before. Wiping my eyes, I look over at the clock as I let out a yawn. "It's only 10pm, *Ummi*."

"You have to go to your *ammu's* home." Gently putting her hand behind my head, she doesn't allow me to lie back down. "Get up, Zaid."

My uncle's house?

She takes a step back as I sit up and release another exasperated yawn. My eyes are begging to close, but I fight it. She turns the bedside lamp on with a click. I'm suddenly shielding my eyes from the light, trying to shake off my confused stupor.

"I've already packed your things, Zaid. Bilal is waiting outside with everything."

"What's going on?"

Her voice. It's as sweet as always, but tonight it holds something else: urgency. She sets out some clothes on the foot of the bed. "Come on, Zaid."

"*Ummi*—"

"Get dressed, Zaid. Quickly now."

***

I'm slow getting dressed. No doubt, all this weariness is from playing football under the scorching sun. I wear what my mother left for me: a pair of jeans, a thin but nice collared shirt, and dark blue sneakers. My mind is still waking up, still half clinging to the hope that this is just a dream.

I've hardly even tied my shoelaces when *Ummi* knocks on my door.

"I'm ready."

She opens the door, allowing the bright hallway lights to spill into the room. *Ummi* walks over and takes my hand in a motherly way before guiding me out of the room and into the corridor.

"Quickly, Zaid."

How many times has she already said that? Holding her hand, I follow her down the corridor and onto the creaky staircase as I let out another long yawn. We hastily descend down to the lower level. It's a struggle just to keep my eyes open. We're on the second floor within moments, but we keep going down. We continue past the photos and into the empty shop. A few lights are dimly illuminated, but it's mostly darkened. The shop's doors are open, and I see Bilal's rickety car rumbling outside as it waits.

Stepping out of the shop, I see Salman and Fatima standing next to the car. They're awake too? Their mother is hugging Fatima. Is she... crying? Their father has his hand on Salman's shoulder and is telling him something. What's that look on Salman's face? I've never seen him look that way before.

I suddenly notice *Abbi* and Aisha waiting for me as well. Why does Aisha have tears welling in her eyes? Is this a dream? But it feels so real.

Stepping out onto the sidewalk, my mother again speaks, "You'll be going to your *ammu's* house. You'll be safe there, Zaid."

Safe from what? I'm so confused and tired that I can't even talk right now. We stop right by Bilal's car. He's already in the driver seat, both hands on the steering wheel. I look back at my mother, finally able to speak. "*Ammu...* he lives close to Salaheddine, doesn't he?"

"It'll be safe there, Zaid."

"Safe from—"

Letting go of my hand, *Ummi* gently kisses my cheek before clasping both hands around my face. Why are there tears in her eyes

21

too? Have they been there this whole time? Leaning forward, she rests her forehead against mine. Her touch is cold. I've never felt it like that. She's trembling. I hear her whisper a prayer: *Ayatul Kursi*. She's asking for *Allah* to protect me. For what feels like a long moment, everything is at peace as she holds me like that. It's like I'm wrapped in a warm blanket of protect—

The sensation vanishes when she pulls away and takes a step back. Everything returns to the way it was. Aisha tightly hugs me next. But it's different from before. There's a coldness in her. I can feel her shivers too. Is this some sort of hallucination? She whispers something, but I can't understand her trembling words. She says Nabeel's name.

Just like *Ummi*, she finally lets go after kissing my forehead. *Abbi* puts one hand on my shoulder and the other on my opposite cheek. His powerful hands are so warm. "I know you're confused, Zaid. I am sorry. Know that we're doing this for you. Don't be afraid, Zaid. Never be afraid. We will see you soon, God-willing. Be strong for your friends. Watch over them."

My gaze locks with his. His words and voice are strong, but I see what rests behind his eyes: fear.

"God-willing, we will see you soon," he repeats. "And remember that *Allah* is always with you. Those who put their trust in Him always fulfill their purpose. Do not lose faith, Zaid, no matter what."

"...yes, *Abbi*." It's all I can say.

He squeezes my shoulder. "Go, Zaid... go. And have no fear."

***

I watch my family as we pull away. They start off right outside my window, close enough for me to reach out and touch. All of their eyes are locked with mine. The longer my gaze stays with theirs, the

22

more fear courses into my veins. Am I really suddenly leaving them? I see the tears they're holding back. Something tells me to reach out, reach out and grab ahold of them all one last time. A voice compels me to embrace them and refuse to let go

But then we begin to leave. With every second, my family begins to grow smaller, more distant. I keep my gaze trained on them: father, mother, and Aisha. *Ummi* suddenly clutches *Abbi's* arm. She's shivering. As we continue to pull away, something washes over me. A weight drops onto my heart that's too heavy to bear. And with each passing moment, it crushes down on me with more unrelenting force.

I watch as they grow too distant for me to see their tears. A pit forms in my stomach, as if there is something I should have said, something I should have *done*. My hand begins to quiver.

Then they're too far for me to observe their faces clearly. The knot grows tighter, the fear taking a stronger hold of me. I grab my trembling hand, trying to stop it. Tears begin to form in my own eyes. Why am I feeling this?

Soon, I can't tell them apart. It's too late now—too late to say anything to them. Too late to hold them. The weight is heavier than ever and the knot is about to make me throw up.

And then they're gone.

***

Bilal drives down the streets under the cover of night. His car constantly shakes as it moves, the uneven road and lack of shock absorbers only making it worse. Its engine rumbles. Nobody has said a word. Not Bilal. Not Fatima. Not Salman.

Salman is in the front passenger seat. Sitting next to Fatima and behind Bilal, my gaze stays aimed outside. The streets are never deserted, but there are more people out than usual. A lot more. And they all seem to be in a hurry. Normally, the only people out at this

23

hour in this part of the city are those making their way to or from the *masjid*. The part of the city where the nightlife exists is far from here. However, tonight is different. Swarms of pedestrians crowd the street and many of them are carrying bags or luggage.

I tear my eyes off the scene and focus on the back of Bilal's head. "What's going on?"

Salman and Bilal exchange glances. After a long moment, Bilal looks back at me. "It's the rebels. There's a threat that they are going to finally attack Aleppo itself."

…what? No. The civil war is happening far from here, isn't it?

"There have been rumors that they will attack soon. But we recently found out that they overran a military base and now have more artillery power. If they attack, rumors are that they will first invade through the north side, close to Ballermoun. There is a warning that they might invade your neighborhood before dawn today. That's why your parents want to get you out of there. Your uncle is at the southwest part of the city in Salaheddine. You will be safe with him tonight until your parents are ready to evacuate. Then we will figure out what to do."

"Th—they're going to attack Aleppo?" Words overflowing with disbelief, I barely hear anything else Bilal says.

"Don't worry, Zaid. You'll be safe with your uncle. Then, when your parents join you before morning, God-willing, we will all get out of the city together before anything happens."

I hang on to Bilal's words as they echo in my head again and again. It all starts to make sense: the absence of children at school, the strange behavior of everyone today. Is this what it was all about? The rebels are preparing to invade?

"But *Abbi, Ummi,* and Aisha… what about them?"

"They'll join you before morning, Zaid," Bilal repeats. "Along with Salman and Fatima's parents. Don't worry about them. They are only a few hours behind us. You will all be fine."

I look over at Fatima. Her hands are clasped in her lap and her gaze is aimed down at them. Did she know about any of this today? Did Salman and Nabeel? If they did, why didn't they say anything?

"But I don't want you three to be worrying about anything." His words full of a brotherly authority, Bilal pauses. "As long as we're together, we'll keep our trust in *Allah* and everything will be alright."

Confident as he sounds, Bilal's words are of little comfort. The more I let them echo in my head, the heavier the weight on my soul becomes. *The rebels are attacking Aleppo? The rebels are attacking Aleppo. The rebels are attacking Aleppo!* I feel my soul go from disbelief to shock and fear. Did I leave them all behind without even knowing it? Will I ever see them—I can't even say that.

There is complete silence in the vehicle. I can't stop replaying Bilal's words in my head again and again and again. Each time I do, I feel the burden on my soul grow more taxing. If this was a dream, I would have woken up by now. It's really happening. But it can't be. How can everything change so quickly?

If the rebels are invading, won't the army stop them? They've been fighting them everywhere else. They'll come here and protect us, won't they? There are already security forces in the city. They'll keep everyone safe. I know it.

"…Bilal?"

"Yes, Zaid?"

"What about—"

Everything goes up in smoke.

***

The peace ends. Deafening gunfire lights up the darkness.

The roar of bullets cuts through the stillness of the night. My eyes widen. I can't move. I can't do anything. I'm paralyzed. That's… that's gunfire. In the distance. No, it's closer. It's loud—so loud.

Bilal swerves the car in a sudden move, barely missing the car in front of us as it suddenly stops. We ride onto the sidewalk with a heavy bounce. Lurching forward, I'm thrown off of my seat when we crash into something. I roughly fall onto the car's dirty floor. I hear Salman hit the dashboard and Bilal yell something as we come to an abrupt halt.

My eardrums are ringing. The shrilling roar of bullets is growing. It's growing louder and louder with every passing second. It's drowning out everything else—everything but the screams of people as they flee. I can barely see out my window. The people trying to escape are chaotically retreating back from where we came.

I try to climb back onto my seat. My breaths are quick. I watch the men, women, and children fleeing down the road, right over one another. Bullets are flying in between them. They—they're being shot at.

Everything suddenly slows down as I horrifically watch the scene unfold. Something explodes. It's a vehicle. Its shockwave crashes against the car as I jump back. My ears fall deaf. I hear nothing but a loud ringing. The blast lights up the street in a blinding blaze. Even behind the window, I feel the heat and sense the flames coming from my left. Whipping my head around, I see a truck only twenty yards away erupt into an explosion. It lights up the night and is set ablaze with a thunderous blast. But I can't hear anything. Nothing but the ringing.

Were there… people in there?

Keeping my wide-eyed gaze on the wreckage, I witness hundreds of people spilling out of their cars and trucks before running away from the shooting. Bullets whiz right by us faster than I can see them. We… we have to—

Something metallic crashes through the window. I impulsively turn away. But I feel it rush right by me, barely missing my ear before

26

burying itself in the seat. Was that a—a bullet? I look at the others. Have they gone deaf too? Do they hear the ringing?

Salman is yelling something, but I can't understand. Bilal is too. I can't hear anything. Fatima is frozen.

Suddenly, the deafness vanishes like it was never there. The ringing is replaced by gunfire. It's rancorous. So are the chaotic screams. There's another thunderous explosion down the road. Kicking up dirt and gravel into the air, it drowns out everything else for a moment.

This is really happening.

"Get out! Get out!" Salman shoves his own door open. "Get out!"

Bilal does the same. Fatima frantically follows suit. I spill out right behind her and onto the hard concrete. I fall to my knees. Fatima is next to me. I look up at Salman. He's crouched down behind the car, watching the scene behind us unfold. His wide eyes are consumed with fear.

My body is shivering. Sweat runs down my face. I keep my eyes locked on him. I still hear the gunfire. It sounds like firecrackers are going off right beside me. It's not ending… it's not ending. A battle has erupted out of nowhere.

Salman rips his gaze off of the scene and looks down at us. Grabbing Fatima and me by our shoulders, he forces us to stay low to the ground. I barely hear him above the bullets. "Stay down! Don't move!"

Fatima falls flat on her chest. Still on my knees, I come onto my elbows as well. Tucking my head in, I clasp both my hands around it. The vociferous gunfire shakes the very ground. Metallic bullets piercingly slam and break against buildings, metal, and glass. It's endless. The sound of shattering windows and clanging metal surrounds us. The bullets strike Bilal's car, one after another.

My heart is going to burst out of my chest. It's beating so fast. I feel Salman hunch over the two of us, his hand staying on our backs. His breaths are quick and heavy. Does he know what to do? Does anybody? Fatima shrieks as a bullet hits the ground only a few feet away from us. The concrete beneath us trembles harder than ever before. Are they feeling this too?

Another explosion goes off. Its heat crashes against my side. For a moment, it puts out the shooting and seemingly sets off an earthquake. I pull closer to the ground, hardly able to keep my balance. Then there's another blast. It's louder and stronger. It's followed by a third. Are those vehicles exploding? They're going off like dominos. I can feel their shock waves. They're so close.

We're next to a vehicle. Is it going to explode too!? I need to move. We need to go. Why can't I move? I'm trying, but I can't move a muscle. All I can do is shiver. My own body has shut down. What's happening!?

Salman's yelling again, but his words are barely audible above the gunfire and eruptions. "Whatever you do, don't stand up! Stay down!"

A few bullets again clang against Bilal's car. I hear one rip through the window. Where is Bilal? Is somebody shooting at *us*? I pick up Salman's voice again, but I can't make out his words. And I can't look up. Quivering more feverously than before, I can't do anything but listen to the endless barrage.

There are screams—anguished screams. Screams that momentarily cut above the chaos before dying out. Are... are people dying? Are they dying all around us?

A rifle fires off above the rest of the chaos. It's closer than anything else, closer than the rest of the shooting. I cover my ears without thinking. It goes off again, louder than before. And then again.

"Over here!"

It's the voice of a man, one that I don't recognize. It's coming from straight ahead.

"You three! Get out of there!"

More bullets bang against Bilal's car. Is the voice talking to us? I feel Salman look in the voice's direction.

"Zaid! Fatima!" Salman's words are louder than ever. "Run straight ahead! Now!"

Salman grabs me by the shoulder and forces me up with a running start. I don't resist and dash alongside him. Fatima is half a step ahead of us. I see the man who's been yelling. He's standing at the entrance of a darkened shop. One hand holds a rifle while the other urgently beckons us onward.

My vision is tunneled, and I see nothing else but the man and shop. I hear my heavy breaths and feel Salman's hand on my shoulder. The bullets whiz all around us. One strikes the ground right behind my feet. I don't look back. I sense something pumping through my body. I'm running faster than ever, barely able to keep my balance, but Salman holds me up as he stays right alongside me.

Stumbling into the shop's entrance, we're ushered inside by the man. He doesn't even glance at us as he keeps his gaze on the chaos outside. I step into the shop, followed by Salman and Fatima.

Smash! One of his shop's windows suddenly shatters as it's shot up. I instinctively duck, but the man doesn't move. Instead, he takes aim and pulls his weapon's trigger three quick times. Its roar makes me go deaf again. I shield my ears and hear Fatima's shriek.

With his back to us, the stranger takes a step out of the shop. "Are any of you hurt?"

"N—no. I don't think so," Salman stutters.

"You three go into the far back room. Close the door. Don't open it unless it is me."

"W—what about—"

"I'm going to go and get others."

29

Without another word, he disappears into the night.

CHAPTER 4
PROTECTOR

Salman closes the room's heavy door, shutting it completely before he latches the strong bolt. His face is red and covered in sweat. Mine feels no different. He takes a deep breath. Then another. His palm presses against the door as he bends over a bit. Staring at the ground, he runs his opposite hand through his hair.

Standing next to Fatima, my breaths remains quick. I can barely keep myself from keeling over. My body wants to shut down again, but my heart is still pounding like a drum—still throbbing. I still sense the energy pumping through my veins. Is this adrenaline? I didn't know it was real.

We can't hear anything in this room, not the gunfire, explosions, or screams. It's as if nothing is happening out there. But... but we all know the truth.

Looking from Salman to Fatima, my mind won't stop replaying what occurred. I'm stuck in the loop. I feel the explosions. The ringing of the bullets remains in my ears. The ground still trembles underneath me. That all happened, and I was in the middle of it.

After what feels like a long minute, I refocus on Salman. He stands upright, leaning his back against the wall. He's desperately trying to get his breathing under control. Fatima is on her knees, her face in her hands. She's saying something, but I can't hear it.

Two ceiling lamps illuminate the room. It's a large storage closet. The walls are as thick as the door. It's mostly empty outside of a shelf that is pushed up against a wall. Its racks are lined up with an assortment of books.

Turning away from my surroundings, I look back toward my friends. Fatima's eyes are shaking, but Salman has calmed himself, at least somewhat.

"Bilal… where is Bilal?"

Hearing my words, Salman looks at me. He tries to say something but stops himself short before turning away. His eyes are trying to hide tears, tears that can only mean one thing.

No. No. *No*… it can't be. I feel my eyes widen. Bilal was with us in the car. Not even ten minutes ago, I was sitting right behind him. Talking to him. Looking at his face. His voice still echoes in my head. He was alive right in front of me. He said—he said that—

I collapse onto my knees. Then my hands. My face loses its color. My arms are trembling. Without thinking, I begin to violently cough. The images of what just happened outside are burnt into my skull. I see and hear it all. I can't push it away. I try to control it, try to hold back all the emotions, but I can't.

My face grows red as the coughing continues. It won't stop. I sense it coming. I suddenly throw up what little food rests in my stomach. It coarsely exits in the form of a dirty yellow and orange liquid, spilling out onto the floor. My body convulses as it all erupts.

A hand comes onto my back. Fatima is crying behind me. Every syllable is consumed by an ocean of sadness. I've never heard her sob before. Not like this.

I stay down on all fours long after I let it all out. Staring down at the vomit, I smell the foul stench but don't possess the nerve to move. This can't be happening. It was only ten minutes ago… ten minutes ago… ten minutes ago…

Somebody is in the shop. Heavy footsteps press into the floorboards. Each step is louder than the last. They're slow, as if the person is carrying something. Salman and I look up at the heavy door.

Just when the steps arrive at the closet's door, they turn and go somewhere else. There is complete silence for a few moments, but then they're back outside the room.

There are three quick but powerful knocks on the door. "It's me."

Salman exchanges a glance with me. He recognizes the voice too. Arriving at the door, Salman unbolts it before yanking it open with a heave, revealing the shop owner.

His breathing is a bit heavy. The first things I notice are his hands. They're bloodied. There's some dirt on his face that wasn't there before. The shop owner is my father's age, maybe a few years older. His face looks weary and his eyes appear old. They don't hold any of the fear that I've seen on everybody else's faces. Standing in the doorway, he looks down at the vomit and then at Fatima as she continues crying.

"Is she alright?" the man asks, his voice strong.

Salman nods.

"Do any of you know anything about nursing a wound?"

After a long moment, Fatima softens her weeping enough to reply, "I—I've taken some classes."

"Good." He looks over at Salman. "Are you her brother?"

"Yes."

"You two, with me. There's a boy. He's been shot. I have him in the other room. I know how to treat the wound, God-willing, but I will need some assistance. He's nearly unconscious from blood loss. We need to work fast." His gaze focuses on me. "I need you to try the phone lines. See if you can get ahold of the police. Let them know where we're holed up. If you can't reach them, try any other number you know."

I somehow manage a nod.

"There's a phone upstairs. It's in the first room on your left. Stay away from the windows no matter what you hear." With those

33

words, he motions for Salman and Fatima to go with him. Following him, Fatima glances back at me for a quick second before disappearing.

***

As I step out of the room, I hear low moans. It must be the boy. He's calling out for his mother. He's calling out to *Allah*. His voice is desperate. He's not screaming. In fact, he is barely loud enough to be heard. But his wails drive a stake through my heart. With each syllable I hear, it's like something has grabbed ahold of my heart and is crushing it. The shop owner's voice rises above the boy's as he instructs Salman and Fatima on what to do.

I quickly find the staircase in an attempt to escape it all. Climbing them, I arrive in a brown-walled corridor. I don't go near the windows as instructed, but I still see the bright flames cutting through the darkness outside. One of the windows is shot up, its glass lying scattered on the ground. I hear gunfire. I hear yelling… and I hear screams. It's distant now, and it's almost drowned out by the hungry fires.

First room on the left. The open door leads into the kitchen. I don't switch on the light, but my eyes adjust to the darkness. It's smaller than ours, and I immediately locate the phone attached to the wall.

Not wasting any time, I punch in the police's number just like the shop owner instructed. My heart is excited as I put the phone to my ear, expecting the ring.

It's dead.

There's not even a sound. That can't be right. I must have dialed it incorrectly. I try it a second time. Again, nothing happens. No, something must be wrong. I hastily dial the number again. And again. And again. Each time is quicker and more frantic than the last.

34

My heart pounds almost as violently as it did on the street… but nothing happens.

I bang the phone back down against the receiver. With my hand still on the phone, I stare at the framed picture next to the receiver. I can't make out the details, but it shows a man holding a newborn baby. I pause for a long moment.

That's it! Without thinking, I dial the phone number of my home: 21-789-5485. With each digit, the hope in my heart grows stronger. I can almost hear *Abbi's* powerful voice in my ear. Pressing the last '5', I put the phone tightly against my ear.

Not even a sound.

This can't be happening. Not them too. I frantically attempt a redial. 2. 1. 7. 8. 9. 5. 4. 8. 5. My sweaty fingers quiver as they hit each button longer and harder than before. Again… no sound. Please, *Allah*. Please, don't leave us here abandoned. I dial the number one more time, faster than before. Nothing happens. The phone won't connect. It's either our line or theirs. And if it's theirs, then that means…

I can't even think that!

My entire body shivers. I start punching the phone's digits so rapidly that I might break it, but I don't care. I need to get in touch with somebody, anybody. *Abbi, Ummi*, Aisha… please, somebody. 2! 1! 7! 8! 9! 5! 4! 8! 5!

We can't be trapped here alone. Please let me hear their voice, God. Please let me know that we're not here alone. I'll do anything. Anything.

But the line stays dead.

Trembling, I let go of the phone. It falls toward the ground, hanging on its cord. I slump down alongside it. The realization of the truth finally washes over me. We're alone. I'm alone. Here in this dark room, as I hear the chaos outside, I finally face the truth: there is nobody coming to rescue us.

***

I return to the room long after dialing the last number. When I arrive, they're all back here as well. The vomit is cleaned up. Salman and Fatima are sitting in a corner as she holds one of his arms. The shop owner is on the other side of the room. With his back to me, he rummages through a chest that was not there before. Salman's head is hanging low. Fatima glances up at me and I see the look in her eyes. Her cheeks are wet. I don't hear the wounded boy in the other room. I know what it means.

Hearing me enter, the shop owner looks back. "What happened, son?"

"The phone lines were down." My voice barely above a whisper, I close and bolt the door behind me.

"How many times did you try?"

"I lost count."

He thinks for a long moment before nodding. "You did what you could. What's your name, son?"

"Zaid."

"Jari."

Why does that name seem familiar? I finally see what Jari is digging for as he pulls it out: a pistol. He takes hold of the weapon as if he knows how to use it. I watch him pop out the magazine and inspect the gun before reloading the weapon and tucking it into his belt.

"What's... what's that for?"

"I lost my rifle when I rescued the boy. Until we get someplace safe, we'll need this for protection."

"From what?"

"I'll do everything I can to make sure you never find out." He looks over Salman and Fatima. "Are you three okay?"

Salman looks up at him and slightly nods.

"I'm sorry you had to go through that with the boy. Having your help was the only way I could give him a chance."

"I... understand." Salman's voice is bleak.

"You three must be hungry."

Nobody answers.

"Stay here. I have some food in the kitchen."

CHAPTER 5
VALOR

Jari brings in three bowls of food on a tray. They're filled with lukewarm, yellow lentils and pita bread. He hands us the bowls one by one. I finally realize how famished I am when I take mine, triggering my stomach to go wild. I don't care about the bland taste as I scoff it down.

All of the shop's lights are turned off, save for one of the dim lamps in this large closet. The light softly reflects off of all our faces, and the closed door keeps the light from spilling into the rest of the shop.

As he watches us eat, Jari takes a copy of the *Qur'an* from the bookshelf behind us along with some rosary beads. The holy book's cover is black and gold. It's a worn out copy, its edges folding in. Even the pages have turned brown.

We eat in silence as he sits in front of us, reading to himself. Nothing is heard except for the faint whisper of his recitation. He looks up every now and then, as if trying to ensure that we're eating the food wholeheartedly.

I devour the lentils using the bread and my hands. It doesn't take long for me to wolf it all down. I'm eating so fast that I start sweating a bit, but I can't stop myself and am nearly tempted to lick the bowl clean.

"You're not hungry?" Fatima asks, noticing that Jari doesn't have a bowl for himself. "You can have some of mine."

He looks away from his reading and at her. "I'm fine. I'm sorry that's all I have for right now."

38

"Thank you," Salman says as he puts his bowl down. He glances down at it for a quick second. "What happened out there?"

Jari closes the holy book and sets it on his lap. "People thought the rebels would hit Ballermoun first, but they've invaded the city through Salaheddine. Where were you three headed?"

"To Salaheddine," Salman answers. "Zaid's uncle lives there."

"I pray that he's safe."

A silence falls over us, but it's short-lived before Salman breaks it. "Thank you for helping us."

Jari faintly nods.

"Why did you do it?"

"Why would I not?" Something about him reminds me of my father. He looks and sounds nothing like him, but he emits the same presence. After a long moment, he continues. "Do you three go to school?"

We all nod. Is he trying to change the subject?

"You seem like bright children." His looks over at Salman. "You look like an athletic boy. What sports do you enjoy?"

"Football and wrestling."

"Is that what you want to do when you grow up?"

"I…" Salman hesitates. "I want to play on the national team."

Jari smiles and nods before turning toward Fatima. "And what about you, young lady?"

"A nurse."

"You must be a smart girl."

"I'm at the top of my class." Unlike she normally does, Fatima utters those words bleakly.

"Well done." His gaze finally sets on me. He pauses as he stares into my eyes. "…and what about you?"

"I want to be a doctor—a surgeon."

"Really? And where do you plan to study?"

"Here at the University of Aleppo."

"A very wise choice, Zaid. I don't doubt you will make it." Jari takes a deep breath, his eyes not leaving me. An abrupt growl consumes the room. Is… is that Jari's stomach? He must be starving. Did he really give us all the food he has? Jari goes on, acting like he didn't hear it. "Hold fast to your dreams, young man. Hold on to the hope of a better tomorrow. Protect it with your life."

There is another awkward silence, but I soon break it. "Were you a police officer?"

"Why do you say that?"

"The way you knew how to shoot."

He lightly folds his arms. "I was in the army up until a few years ago."

"The army? My brother is a captain."

"What's his name?"

"Nabeel Kadir."

Jari nods. "A brave man no doubt. I'm sure you are no different, Zaid."

"I—I'm not the brave one." I'm almost afraid to say the next thing. "I'm scared."

"All brave men are."

"Are you?"

His eyes grow more focused. "I will never show it if I am. Not when there are people depending on me to be brave."

I mill over his words as another stillness washes over us. This time, Salman is the one to end it. "Will the army come?"

"I'm sure security forces are already engaging the rebels. By tomorrow, the army will begin their offensive. But the fighting will likely…" Jari stops himself. "Get some sleep you three. Tomorrow will be a long day. If we can't reach anyone by phone, we'll have to make our way out of here at dusk."

"Why?"

"The fighting in this neighborhood will likely become heavy."

"Won't the army protect us?"

Jari looks distant for a moment. "Don't worry. I'll keep watch over you three." Rising to his feet, he picks off four small prayer rugs from the top of the shelf. "But before you sleep, it is time for the late night prayers. I think we should do them all together."

I forgot all about that. This is usually the time *Abbi* and I would do our late night prayers whenever we did them together. But tonight, for the first time in my life, I don't hear the call to prayer echo through the city.

***

Outside of the air conditioning's low rattling, the room is silent. But my thoughts are far from peaceful. The quieter the room, the more chaotic my mind grows. With my eyes shut, I keep reliving all the chaos. I see the car exploding over and over again. It's just as hot as it was then. The bullet barely misses me. I hear its rush before it plunges into the seat with a loud thump. A few more inches and I would have been the boy in the next room. The visions and the sounds won't stop. They won't leave me in peace, no matter how hard I try.

And I keep seeing Bilal.

He's gone. He's really gone. It feels so surreal, as if it's a dream. How can he be dead when he was just speaking to me? Maybe, at any moment, he'll come knocking on the door. Jari will open it, and we'll see his smiling face.

But I know that's nothing more than a false hope. Just like everyone else on that street—everyone else who was around me—he's gone and he's never coming back. The more I think about him, the more I see his face, the more I begin to accept the reality. This is no dream. The people out on that road are gone… forever.

Now I'm lying here on a cold floor in this strange place. And my thoughts keep revolving around my home and the people there: *Abbi, Ummi, and* Aisha. Bilal is gone. What about them? If Bilal could disappear in the blink of an eye, then couldn't—

I shiver at the very thought.

They would know what to do, wouldn't they? They would be able to keep themselves safe from everything. I know *Abbi* owns a few guns. He would protect *Ummi* and Aisha like Jari protected us.

But maybe—maybe they are looking for me. I truly hope not. If something happens to them because of me, if they get hurt or... I don't know what I would do. I don't know how I could live.

Just the thought of it nearly drives me mad.

***

"Are you having trouble sleeping?"

Lying atop the prayer rug, I slowly roll over to come face-to-face with Jari. A few feet from me, he's sitting with his back against the wall. He's writing something down on a piece of paper. Fatima and Salman are a little ways away from me. They seem to be heavy in slumber. Only one of the storage closet's lights is still dimly illuminated.

I look back at Jari. I've only known him for a couple of hours, but his presence gives off a sense of protection. It's as if I'm safe as long as he's around me. "Aren't you going to sleep?" I ask.

Jari shakes his head. "Not tonight."

"Every time I close my eyes, I keep seeing it." My voice starts shaking. "I keep see—seeing... all the..."

"It's okay." His tone is reassuring. "It'll all be fine."

"How long do you think this will last?"

"The fighting?"

I nod.

"Longer than any fight should. But *Allah* knows best." He pauses. "Do you live with your parents?"

"My father owns a rug store."

"Does he now? Maybe I can pay it a visit when all this is over."

I slightly smile.

Jari glances down for a moment. "She's a nice girl, you know."

"Who?"

He smirks. "How long have you known her and her brother?"

"All my life."

"They say closeness often brings about fondness. It was true for my wife and me."

I sit upright. "You and your wife grew up together?"

He nods. "She moved next door when I was a little younger than you."

"Is she in the city?"

Jari's smirk slowly vanishes. "She's far from it. Too far to be in any danger. For once, I'm glad she's not with me."

He again glances away before my words bring his attention back to me. "Can I ask you something?"

"Anything, Zaid."

Hesitating for a brief second, I finally ask the question that's on my mind. "Why didn't you eat with us?"

"I'm not hungry—"

"I heard your stomach growling."

Jari pauses, slow to reply, "I don't have much food, and I need to save it for you three."

I almost ask him 'why' but stop myself.

"I've lived most of my life, Zaid. But you and your friends are just beginning yours. I don't believe in happenstance. You were brought to my doorstep, and it's my responsibility to look after you." He falls silent for a moment. "So you want to be a doctor, Zaid?"

"I've wanted that all my life."

"Why?"

"Because I want to make the world a better place. I…I want my life to matter. I want to save those around me, do something meaningful."

He warmly smiles. "Will you promise me something, Zaid?"

I nod.

"No matter what happens, don't forget who you are. And never abandon hope. Start making the world a better place now by never letting hope die in yourself or in anyone around you."

I don't reply right away as I notice what's lying on the floor beside him: a book. It's not the book that gets my attention; instead, it's what he is using as the bookmark. It's a gold medal with a red, white, and blue ribbon. The metal is rusting, but I immediately recognize it. Nabeel received one just like it after his first campaign. "That's the Order of Bravery."

He follows my gaze to see what I'm looking at before picking up the medal with his free hand. "Yes, it is."

"But you're using it as a bookmark?"

"And that surprises you?"

"It's just that I've always seen it framed," I reply.

"The people framing it must have valued it."

"And you don't?

"Some lives for medals." He pauses. "Others find their gratification in living for an ideal."

I don't understand what that means. There's another awkward silence before I think of something to say. "When did you earn it?"

"December 1990. During The Gulf War. A convoy of Syrian and American soldiers was ambushed and pinned. I led the rescue operation. Through *Allah's* allowance, my men saved over fifty lives. I'll never forget what my superior officer told me afterward. He said there'd be a place for me in the army until the day I die."

"But you left?"

As he nods, I see a distant look briefly enter his eyes.

"Why?" I ask.

Taking a deep breath, Jari looks at the ground in front of him. "I took a stand, Zaid. I stood my ground and went against my superiors over something that I knew would cost me my career. But I still did it because there are some things worth surrendering your wealth, honor, and life for. Things that matter more than my own life."

I stay silent.

"When the masses are against you, when fear is on every side, and when it seems like you're alone, that is when you should stand the tallest. That is when you plant yourself like a mountain, and you do what your heart knows is right. Even if death will be your only reward." He pauses before looking back toward me. "It's getting late now, Zaid. Try and get some sleep."

"I don't think I can sleep."

"Close your eyes at least. If your mind won't rest, let your eyes do so. I'll switch off the light." Jari rises to his feet. "You have a long day tomorrow with your friends."

With a nod, I slowly resume my previous position as the room goes dark. Taking a deep breath, I shut my eyes, hoping that my dreams will allow me to escape reality.

CHAPTER 6
SACRIFICE

A prayer echoes in my head while I sleep. The voice sounds like my *Abbi*. No, it's Jari. His voice is low, barely above a mutter. It's softer than before, as if he's holding something back. Am I dreaming this? It feels too real.

"...forgive me, Lord... I promise to protect these children with my life. I've... I've made mistakes... I've been trying to make it up since that day... trying to do the right thing even... it's only led to ridicule and dishonor... and... I'm being punished ever since...

Is he crying? The weeping is faint, but it consumes every word.

"...I lost... Fiza... and... I take an oath... I won't fail these children... through Your strength, I never go back on my word... never."

***

It still feels like nighttime when I drift out of my slumber. Of course, there's no real way to tell in this darkened room. It's not as warm as before. Maybe it's because the lights are off. Sensing Jari laying near me, I turn to face his direction.

It takes a few seconds to adjust to the darkness. Everyone appears to be asleep. Jari is resting on his side. I squint my eyes to get a better look at him. He... he's tightly gripping his stomach. Even in the blackness, the anguish painted on his slumbering face is obvious. His stomach releases a rumble longer than any I've ever heard before.

The realization of his earlier words begins to dawn on me. There's food upstairs. I saw it when I went to use the phone, but he's starving himself to ensure that we have enough. For a moment, it seems so surreal that a complete stranger would do something so— so… I can't even find the word.

What kind of a person does that? What kind of a person starves themselves so that a stranger will have enough? The thought of it leaves me with goose bumps.

His stomach growls again. And then once more, louder than ever. Is it minutes or seconds between each one? As I stare at Jari's grimaced expression, it's as if I am literally feeling his pain. A part of me believes that this can't be real. He would put himself through this torture for us?

I focus on his face for a long time, as if searching for a sign. What is it about him that's so familiar? What gives a person this selflessness?

There are scars behind Jari's eyes. I don't know what created them, but they're undeniably present. I noticed them when I asked him about the army, the medal, and why he left. Is that what he was praying about? Did they do something to him?

Continuing to look at his face, I finally remember the answer to the question that has been eating away at me all evening: where did I hear Jari's name before? Jari was the name of the hero in a book we read for school. I don't remember much, but I recall the meaning of the name: one who God will set free.

***

I hardly even slip back into sleep before I jolt up. Somebody is banging on the shop's front door. It's thunderous enough to shake the building. I shoot up to my feet, everything a blur. The knocking is still ringing in my ears as I wipe my face.

My vision starts to focus. Salman and Fatima are standing as well. The storage closet's door is open just a crack. Jari is peering out into the rest of the shop, pistol in his hand. The banging continues, louder with each passing second. The three of us exchange confused and dazed glances, but Jari doesn't look back at us. What could that be?

Without thinking, I take a few steps toward Jari. Looking through the doorway's crack from afar, I see the sunlight spilling into the shop. A loud, haughty voice cuts through the air. "We know you're in there!"

That voice sounds angry and dangerous. I again look at Fatima, but she keeps her eyes glued to Jari's back. So does Salman. Shrilling gunfire breaks the stillness, and I instinctively wince as my heart skips a beat. But Jari doesn't move an inch. His strong jaw is clenched, his eyes unwavering. The grip around his gun remains tight and his other hand is formed into a fist. I don't hear the bullets hit anything. Maybe they were fired into the air.

"Come out!" Every syllable is mixed with a vile intent. Are those the rebels? "Come out and face the consequences of betraying your country!"

What is he—

"Any soldier who served a tyrant is a coward! And they will all receive a coward's death!"

Soldier? Nobody here is a soldier except... Jari glances back at us. My eyes widen at the realization of what's occurring. Those rebels want him. They want to execute him! Jari wouldn't—

"If you don't come out, we'll come in and drag you out like a dog!"

I see the look in Jari's eyes.

"Don't go!" Those are the only words I can blurt as I suddenly race toward him. Stopping at Jari's side, I stare up at his face.

48

He finally looks at me. "If I don't go, they'll come in here and take me anyway. But if that happens, they'll find you three. And God knows what they'll do."

"Bu—but we need you!" My voice is frantic. "I—I need you!"

"You need nobody but your Lord."

I'm shaking, trembling. So are my words. "We can—we can fight them. You have a gun!"

Jari smiles down at me as he puts his strong hand on my head and lightly ruffles my hair. *How—how can he be smiling like that?* "I would be honored to fight at your side, Zaid. Anyone would." He places his pistol on the floor. "But only one of us will have to leave today."

Is—is he really going to do this? This can't be happening too! How can he just walk out there? He's hungry. Weak. They—they'll kill him, and he doesn't even have the strength to defend himself! My heart beats against my chest. My hand starts to shiver.

"Don't come out of here no matter what happens. Hide in here until nightfall. Avoid traveling in the day when you can." Jari glances over the three of us. His eyes hold no fear. They possess nothing but... peace. "Protect each other. Don't let this darkness consume you. Remember this city as it was. Remember its beauty. Its heart is in its people, not its buildings. Fight to keep the heart of Aleppo inside of you."

There is dead silence as Jari thinks for a moment.

"It was nice to finally share a meal with somebody after so long. I never thought that would happen again. Thank you. Thank you for giving me something that I am willing to give my life for. I wish I could have known you three longer."

"I—I—" My eyes begin to water. "I can't lose you too!"

Jari takes a deep breath, his gaze locking with mine. "I spent years trying to live a good life. But this death... it'll be good enough."

Helpless, I watch his hand leave me as he turns toward the door.

49

"*La Illah Ila Allah.*"

I have never seen a taller man.

He doesn't look back. Jari opens the door without missing a beat, pausing for only a moment. Walking out of the room, he quickly disappears out of sight. The sound of his heavy footsteps reverberates through the entire shop with every step he takes. Hearing him grow further away, I tremble faster. The voices outside abruptly stop. His footsteps also arrive at a halt. But then I hear him unlatch the front door. It opens with a loud creak.

This can't be happening! This can't be happening!

There's a long pause. However, the violent voice breaks it. "You are a soldier!"

"I was a major colonel in the Syrian Armed Forces." Jari's voice is calm. I hear him step onto the sidewalk without faltering.

"A traitor!"

Jari's words don't waver. "I betrayed none, least of all my Lord or my people."

How is he not scared? Is his heart not pounding like mine? Maybe he has a plan! Maybe—maybe—

"You are a traitor to your nation! To this city! Get on your knees and beg for forgiveness."

There's no response.

"I said get down!"

There are two sudden and powerful thuds before a body hits the ground. I instinctively cringe, as if I feel the blows too.

Stop it! Please stop it!

Fatima grabs a tight hold of her brother's arm. They're both as terrified as I am.

Allah, please save him!

"Now beg for forgiveness, traitor."

Silence. There are two more violent thuds. They're louder than before, and I flinch with each one. But Jari doesn't make a sound.

50

"Beg!"

Don't let him die, God!

"Kill me if you wish." Jari's words are tired, yet powerful. "But I won't ask forgiveness for something I have never done."

There is a long pause. My quivering fist is curled so tightly that my nails dig into my palm. A gun's trigger is cocked back. "Then look down, traitor."

No response.

"I said look down!"

"If you're going to pull the trigger, be a man about it. Look me in the eyes when you do."

There is a stillness. *Please—please save him. If You're listening God, don't abandon him. Do something! Please!* The scene is frozen in time. Everything stops. Everything grows so quiet that I can hear my beating heart and my quivering breath. A hope creeps into my heart. Maybe… maybe something will—

Bang!

CHAPTER 7
STEPPING INTO THE ABYSS

Did… is Jari really—first Bilal, now him? I can't believe it. I won't believe it. Not even when the foul stench enters the shop. Not even when I hear the dispersing footsteps growing further away. Not even when the blast of the gunshot echoes in my head over and over again.

I don't shiver. My heart isn't pounding. My breaths aren't quick. I'm simply paralyzed. I keep staring at the door's opening, half-expecting to hear Jari's heavy footsteps and see him rounding the corner.

Please. Please don't be gone.

Salman is the first to move. He quietly closes the closet door, once again encasing us in a dead silence. After a long moment, he looks back at me. Is he holding back tears?

"Jari…" My voice is weak. "…he's…"

Fatima looks at me and then her brother. "What are we going to do?"

"We have to stay here." His words are a whisper. "Just like he said. We stay here until dusk no matter what."

"What about Jari?"

"We have to leave him."

Fatima's voice rises. "We can't just leave his body there."

"We have to." Salman's palm leans against the wall as he slumps down. "It's the only way."

"Salman—" Fatima begins.

"We don't have a choice."

Another stillness consumes the room for a few moments. But then a horrific image enters my mind, one that nearly makes me vomit. "They shot him because he was a soldier. Called him a traitor. Nabeel… he—he's a soldier." My voice grows frantic. "What if they go after *Abbi! Ummi!* Or Aisha!"

"They will be safe, Zaid," Salman replies.

"How do you know that!?"

"Because we have to believe in something, and I'm going to believe in hope! I choose to believe that Jari did not die for nothing!"

That silences me. For a moment, Salman sounded just like Jari. I glance over at Fatima before looking back at Salman. I take a deep breath and wipe my brow, calming myself down.

"Where are we going to go?" Fatima's question is aimed at her brother.

"Go back the way we came from, back toward our homes."

"What about the police station?"

"If the rebels overran this district, then chances are that'd be one of the first places they attacked. They'd also attack the hospital so they can use the medical supplies to treat their wounded. I read that's what invaders do."

"Do you know the way back home?" I ask Salman.

"Not exactly," he replies. "But I know the general way back to the district. Once we're there, it's easy to spot the *masjid's* blue dome. That'll lead us back home."

"What if they're not home, Salman?"

Salman's voice is calm, his expression stoic. "We'll figure it out. We have to take it one step at a time. As long as we stay together, we'll make it through this. We'll make sure that Jari's sacrifice is worth something."

***

I'm trapped in a dungeon.

This room doesn't have a clock, and I don't have a watch. The longer the day grows, the warmer it gets in here. The A/C worked fine last night, but it is now beginning to sputter. I soon find myself wiping my forehead every few minutes. Thankfully, Jari brought us some jugs of water and more bread during the night. I drink a sip of water every now and then but hardly nibble on the bread, unable to bring myself to eat.

The walls are thick enough to keep us secluded from anything happening outside. However, every once in a while, we hear a faint explosion or rumble. About a few hours into our wait, we hear one louder than any other. The entire room trembles as the eruption occurs. Glass chaotically clatters and a couple of books fall from the quaking shelves. The very walls tremor with a rage. For a moment, it feels like the entire shop is going to collapse on us.

Salman puts a reassuring hand on both Fatima's and my shoulders. He's so calm. He's always been the best of us.

I fall asleep a little after the explosion. I don't know if it's exhaustion or slumber. Either way, I pray that it will be my gateway to escaping this nightmare. However, it's a restless sleep. Every few minutes, I wake up to see Salman still by my side, deep in thought, and Fatima lying down on the other side of him.

At one point, all sleep suddenly vanishes from me and I awaken wide-eyed. I know why. Normally, *Abbi* takes me to the *masjid* around this time for the afternoon prayers. Rain, shine, sickness, or health, we always went. It's in my blood now. But not today. Today, it is just the three of us. Today, for the first time, I don't say my prayers.

But even in this silence, there is no peace. I can't stop hearing the blast that ended Jari's life. I can't stop hearing the attack from last night: the screams, explosions, gunfire, pounding. It's all there. And I will never un-see it—never forget the chaos and destruction that surrounded me on all sides. However, most of all, I will never forget

54

the look in Jari's eyes before he turned and willingly walked to his certain death. Behind that gaze was something I have never seen a person encompass before: true courage.

***

Waking up from one of my short sleeps, I find Fatima sitting next to me. I don't know the time. It feels like we've been in here for days. My mind and body feel worn out and I don't know why. The more I sleep, the more exhausted I become. Maybe it's this heat.

Fatima's dark pink *hijab* is a bit disheveled, but she is quickly fixing it. It's all muscle memory, as I imagine she can barely even think about that right now.

Her eyes look tired, begging to sleep. Maybe her mind is keeping slumber out of reach. She keeps her gaze aimed above but notices that I am awake. There's a copy of the Qur'an and a set of green rosary beads in her lap. They're the same ones Jari used last night. Next to her is a prayer rug that looks like it was recently used.

"Are you okay, Fatima?" I know she's not. None of us are. But I ask anyway.

She takes a deep breath before responding, "Yesterday, we were in school. We were sitting in class. We were in the fields. We walked to the bus. Now... it's like we're suddenly trapped in a nightmare." Her hand is lightly shaking. In her eyes, I watch her relive last night. "And now Jari's gone." She pauses as her gaze slowly drifts down to the holy book in her hands. "Why is this happening? To us? To our city?"

I look away from her and utter the only thing that comes to mind. "...I don't know."

"Do you think God is hearing our prayers?"

55

"I would like to keep thinking so."

"Why doesn't He answer?"

I don't reply. What can I say?

"People are—they're dying, Zaid. Bilal. Jari. I don't know what we'll find when we step out. And…" She turns to meet my gaze. "I'm scared."

For the first time in my life, I wish she wasn't looking at me. Not like that. I see the dread consuming her face, and I don't know how to take it away.

***

I'm not sure how long it's been since I've bowed my head. It's a haze between my dreams and reality now. My eyes scream for rest, but my mind forces me awake. Drifting in and out of consciousness, I resign to watching the sweat run down my arms as I wait for the hits of sleep. When I finally do glance back up, I find Salman and Fatima both fast asleep.

It's so hot. Hotter than it would be outside. Beads of sweat are running down my face, and my clothes feel drenched with it. My shirt is glued to my body. The A/C is now dead silent, which can only mean one thing.

Maybe there's a towel on the shelf. Slowly staggering to my feet, I stumble my way there. My legs are numb after sitting down for all this time. I grab ahold of the shelf to keep myself steady.

The first couple of shelves are lined up with books. I look between them but find nothing of use. However, something on the edge of the third rack catches my eye.

It's a note. It's been folded up twice and appears somewhat familiar. Glancing at it for a moment, I slowly take it into my hands. There's writing on one side of it. Is that… my name? I look it over a few times, thinking that I must be hallucinating. But there it is: Z-A-I-

D. Wait… this is the same piece of paper that Jari was writing on last night when I couldn't sleep.

Below my name is another scribbled line. The words appear jumbled at first, but I am able to figure them out:

Read this when you need it the most.

What does that mean? Holding it with both hands, I turn the folded note to examine it from all sides. Why would Jari write a message for me of all people? A part of me wants to open it now, but the instructions echo in my head. *When I need it the most.* As bad as things are right now, I don't think this is the time he intended it for.

A bead of sweat drips off of my face and splashes onto my hand, reminding me of what I'm here for. I hastily stuff the note into my pocket and yank out the first small towel I find on the shelf. I wipe off my face in one go. The white towel is cool against my face. It's the closest thing to a breeze I'm going to get today.

I take a deep breath, savoring the moment for as long as I can. It must be close to dusk now. A part of me is scared. This room is like a safe haven. Even without Jari, his presence is still here. Nothing can touch us in this room. But out there, out on the streets of Aleppo, it will be a different story.

There, no place will be safe.

Looking down at Salman and Fatima, I remember the last thing I heard Jari utter in his sleep: he never goes back on his word. Ever since he said those words, I can't let them go. They echo in my head, louder each time. My hand curls into a tight fist. No matter what happens, I *will* honor what he said before walking out to his death. I *will* protect Salman and Fatima with my life… that's my oath.

And just like Jari, I will never go back on my word.

***

Salman gently pushes my shoulder, throwing me out of a light doze. "It's time to go."

I stagger to my feet alongside Salman and Fatima. My eyelids lose their heaviness, but my mind is a mix of weariness and dread.

"Zaid, go back up to the kitchen. See if you can make a food bag. Take as much as you can carry. I'll see if there's anything in the closets that we should take. Fatima, see if you can gather up any first aid supplies."

I don't understand why he always does this, making decisions for the three of us without ever asking our opinions. But, as always, I don't voice my objection.

Stepping out of the storage closet, the first thing I see is the evening sunlight spilling in through the broken and cracked windows. It'll be nightfall within half an hour. I finally get a good look at the shop. I didn't even notice last night, but this is a bookstore. Pausing for a moment, I examine my surroundings. One side of the shop has neatly organized religious texts and books sitting on wooden shelves, while the other side is dedicated to novels. It's small and quaint, possessing a cozy aura. Jari owned a bookstore? I would never have guessed.

Quickly going upstairs and onto the second floor, I stay away from the windows like before. More of them have been shot up now, and the glass on the ground crunches under my feet. I hear the distant chaos. It's all the same: endless racketing gunfire and booming explosions. It sounds further than last night. God-willing, the fighting will be far from here when we depart.

Stepping into the kitchen, I see the picture by the phone again. There's enough light this time for me to see the details. The photograph is encased in an old frame. The man in the photo is… is Jari. He's so much younger, but it's undeniably him. Holding a newborn baby girl, he proudly looks at the camera. His eyes are the same as I saw last night when he watched us eat, and his smile beams with joy.

I take a deep breath before tearing my gaze off of the picture. I need to gather supplies. There's not much in the fridge, but I hurriedly go through the cabinets one by one. The kitchen's window is broken, so I do my best to not make much noise. I don't want anybody who might be outside to know that somebody is in here. I feel the heat coming in through the opening. Even when I have the chance, I don't dare look outside.

There's a large sack with sturdy straps that I can hang off of my shoulder. I take whatever food I can that's easy to carry: a few pieces of large pita bread, some mangos, and a box of dates. Packing it all in the sack, I then fill a few canteens with water. It's not much, but I pray to *Allah* that it will be enough.

When I arrive back down, Salman and Fatima are just finishing their searches as well.

"I found some wrapping and disinfectant," Fatima says. She has a similar, but smaller, sack slung over her shoulder.

Salman nods in approval. "There were some flashlights and batteries in some of his drawers. Anything in the kitchen, Zaid?"

"I bagged anything that will be easy to carry and eat."

"*Alhumdulillah.*" Uttering the thanks to God, he takes the canteens from me.

I finally notice what he is wearing around his waist. My first reaction is disbelief. I've never seen Salman wear something like that. However, after a few quick blinks, I realize that I'm not hallucinating. "You're taking Jari's pistol?"

Fatima sees it too, her eyes widening. Salman simply nods.

"If a soldier sees you with it, they might mistake you for a rebel."

"It's not only the army and rebels that I'm worried about," he replies. "When bad things like this happen, sometimes the worst sides

59

of people reveal themselves. And God forbid if that happens, I'd rather have this with me than not."

***

We step out of the shop together with Salman half a step ahead of us. The first thing that hits me is the odor. It's the foul stench of smoke and flames mixed with something else. It's so thick that I can hardly breathe. The next thing is the heat. The summers of Aleppo have never felt this hot, this… dry.

Coming onto the street, I cough a few quick times and instinctively try and shield my nose and mouth from the stench. But it's more than smoke. The smoke reeks and is blended with an odor that I've never smelt before. It nearly makes me throw up.

What has happened to this city?

My gaze is drawn to the shop across the street. Or, what's left of it. The three-story building is now just a pile of bricks, stones, and ash. It lies there in a mountain of blackened rubble. It's as if the shop was never even built. The building on its left now has half of its wall blown to bits. I can see its decrepitated insides. It's slightly leaning to the side, threatening to topple over at any moment. It's not the only damaged building. Most buildings lining up the street are only damaged by the gunfire, but a few are as bad as this one. Some are still on fire. I hear the faint crackling of flames and feel the heat coming from all sides.

Fatima gasps and turns away, but Salman and I observe what's left of the street. The road is littered with the remains of vehicles. Many are shot up and riddled with bullets. I doubt even their owners would be able to recognize them now. The ones not ripped to shreds from gunfire were lit up in explosions. Many of them are still smoking. Their metal is covered in ash, their windows blown to bits. Their insides are burned out, and their engines are now just debris.

Trees are uprooted and poles are knocked over. Several have collapsed onto the road, wrecking vehicles. It's like the scene from those pictures we'd see in the textbooks. The pictures of World War II. The pictures of Rwanda during their civil war. The pictures of Baghdad after it was invaded.

There's no sign of life anywhere. It's as if the apocalypse has come.

I finally see Jari. I see the man who saved us from becoming a part of this scene. He's only a few paces away, next to a streetlamp. With his back to me, his limp body is lying on his side as if he's sleeping on the dirt road. His outstretched arm covers his face, and there's a dark red stain on the sleeve over his forehead.

We don't say anything. Not a word. We don't even look at each other. Instead, we keep our gazes on him as the dim rays of the evening sun reflect off of our savior.

For a moment, a part of me thinks that he'll wake up at any second. But I know better now. I inhale a deep breath. Without thinking, I take a few steps toward him. Salman and Fatima follow. I crouch down right next to his body. There are some flies buzzing around his head. I want to swat them away, but I can't move a muscle.

Jari's arm still covers his face, almost tempting me to reach out and move it out of the way. But I don't want to remember his dead eyes. I want to only remember the courageous ones I saw step out of that door to face certain death.

Behind me, I hear Fatima make a low prayer for him. She whispers the words always said when we learn of a death. "To God we belong, and to Him we all return."

Salman crouches down next to me and lays his hand on the corpse. His head hangs low for a moment as he whispers something too. Being right next to Jari, I now know what that foul odor is. It's death. After what feels like a long time, I kiss my right index and middle finger before touching Jari's grizzled cheek with them. He's cold, much colder than he looks.

As I slowly rise back to my feet, I hear Fatima behind me. "Shouldn't we find Bilal?"

"We need to move," Salman answers.

"But—"

"It's what he'd want." Salman pauses. "Whatever you do tonight, don't look at any of the bodies you might see. Especially their faces."

I don't reply as I keep my eyes on Jari.

"Understand?"

After a moment, I slightly nod, still not breaking my gaze from Jari.

Salman turns to his sister. "Fatima?"

"…ok."

CHAPTER 8
VALLEY OF SHADOW

The foul stench is everywhere. It floods the buildings and road. It's in every crevice. It's soaked into the very brick and mortar of these streets I used to know.

We walk in a single file: Salman up front and me in the back. The sack quickly grows heavy on my shoulder, soon seeming as if it's filled with bricks. But I trudge on. The weight of the sack is nothing compared to what my heart is feeling right now as I see the city I call home—a city that has stood for over 7,000 years—suddenly turned into wreckage.

Not long into our journey, the last rays of sunlight disappear over the horizon and leave the forsaken city shrouded in darkness. The few street lamps and lights still standing are not illuminated. With smog encompassing the city, the stars and moon are nowhere to be seen tonight. Neither is a single stray animal. Surrounded by a thick forest of smoke and fog, I can't even see ten feet in front of me.

But the night is not a peaceful one. The only constant reassurance that the city is not abandoned is the echo of far-off chaos and nearby flames. Thunderous explosions sound off like clockwork in the distance as they rock the city. We can't even go a block without hearing one or feeling the ground lightly tremor beneath our feet. The first few cause me to flinch, but I slowly grow immune to the tremors. However, even with all the smoke, we almost constantly see the dim light of carnage coming from the direction of the Saif Al-Dawla District.

July nights were always warm in Aleppo, but the smoke and smoldering ruins make it all the more unbearable. The heat goes right through me. I was wise enough to bring a small towel from Jari's kitchen and am forced to use it every twenty minutes or so to wipe off my face.

Every now and then, there is a burning vehicle, trash can, or building that provides some illumination. I usually hear the crackling flames moments before the bright fire cuts through the smoke. But even in the darkness, even when there are no flames to provide any light, I make out the silhouettes of all the destruction around us. Some buildings are completely obliterated like the one across from Jari's shop. They're nothing now but a mountain of brick, mortar, and ash. Others have a damaged portion or have been shot up. Debris and rubble spill onto the road. Some buildings tumbled onto one another, creating even more destruction. It's everywhere you look. You can't escape it.

The streets are dead silent, but the silence is not without a sound. It's the sound of desolation. The sound of destruction. The sound of terror.

Not even a day and a half ago, we walked from school to the bus stop. The roads were crowded with cars, trucks, and buses blaring their horns. The sidewalks were packed with pedestrians and merchants. Now, it's a ghost town. It's as if there was never any life here.

The city is… hollow.

A wall of smoke and smog surrounds me on all sides, preventing me from truly seeing anything clearly. Is it a blessing or a curse? I don't see any of the destruction until I'm right on top of it. If Salman was even five more steps ahead of me, he would be lost behind the wall. We're out on an open street; yet, it feels as if I am trapped in a prison. The dark walls of this prison follow me, not allowing me to escape their grasp.

We're not alone. Walking through the darkness and smog, we cross paths with another group within the first fifteen minutes of the sun setting. I hear their footsteps first. It's faint, almost inaudible. I think that it's just my mind playing tricks on me. But then they step right out of the thick smoke, walking toward us. My heart instinctively spikes up in fear before I realize what they are: a father and his daughter. The girl is maybe a year younger than me. She's holding her father's hand as he keeps her close.

The father's clothes are covered in dirt and dust. He does not pay us any heed. His downcast eyes are red and his beard appears a bit wet. He acts oblivious to everything around him, except for his daughter. He holds her as if he would die before ever letting go. My gaze locks with the girl's as they pass right by us. Her eyes are just as tired as her father's, and her gaze is still wide-eyed as she looks at the abyss around her. I witness countless emotions in them: confusion, fear, sorrow. They're the same eyes as mine.

At that moment, I feel something. A connection. We're strangers, yet comrades. I've never met her, but I know what she has been through. I know she witnessed her city suddenly torn apart.

I look away from her as she and her father continue on their path and we continue on ours. With every passing second, the echo of their footsteps grows fainter and fainter until they have again disappeared in the black smog. Without uttering a word, I pray that God keeps a hedge of protection over them.

Each street we come on to is the same as the previous one: buildings have been turned to ashes, vehicles are blown to bits, wreckage is everywhere, and the innocent have suffered. I do what Salman ordered: look straight ahead and ignore any corpses. Don't even glance at them. They're on every street, nearly littering some roads. I see them in my peripheral vision. Sometimes, a fire is reflecting off of them. Other times, it's just their silhouettes. I try to make avoiding them into a game. But my mind is too aware of the

65

reality to do that. I think Salman purposely goes around as many as he can so that we don't walk over them.

The foul stench of carnage is strong on nearly every street. The vile odor follows us no matter where we go. If I had any food in my stomach, I would have thrown it up long ago. Every half hour, we see somebody cut through the fog and appear into view. Sometimes it's a traveling group. Other times, it's a person sleeping in an alley or sitting with their head in their hands. Hardly any of them give us a glance.

Every step is harder than the last. My feet become weighted stones. I almost can't feel the uneven and cracked concrete underneath me. It's as if I'm moving in a trance. I don't know where I am or where I'm going. I'm simply walking through the abyss and listening to the only sound: my soft footsteps.

The longer we travel and the heavier my sack becomes, the more a fear grips me. The fear that we don't know if we're fleeing danger or walking into a den of hungry wolves. The fear that by the time we do reach home, what happened to Jari may have already happened to everyone.

We keep moving. We stay on the side of the road. Every once in a while, we climb over or go under some debris. Salman and Fatima don't slow down a bit. I don't know how long it's been. However, after a while, I start having a hard time keeping up with them. It must be at least two hours before my feet begin feeling numb. And another half hour before I completely lose sensation in them. They're so tired now that it hurts just to take another step. But Salman and Fatima don't stop or complain and neither do I.

Every time I look up above, hoping to catch some sight of the heavens, all I see is smoke. It's blocking out any light from the stars. There will be no relief tonight.

I notice a silhouette up ahead. It… it appears to be the minaret of a *masjid*. Hope is suddenly injected into my heart. With every step, the minaret breaks out of the smoke, and I can better perceive the *masjid* itself. I see its domed roof. It's standing tall above all the destruction. If it's still standing, it'll be safe inside, right? Nobody will come into a *masjid* and harm us.

But then I see the entrance. The wall has collapsed in on itself. It's been blown into a pile of rubble, completely blocking the front doors. One of the minarets has broken off and fallen straight down, smashing into the marble tiled courtyard. The minaret lies broken and scattered, no more recognizable than any of the other ruined buildings.

As the flames of another wreckage reflect off of the minaret and *masjid*, I stare at it in disbelief for a long moment. I almost ask Salman and Fatima if we should try to go around the *masjid* and look for the women's entrance, but they hardly even give it a glance before continuing down the broken road. And so, without a word, I follow.

We keep trudging through the darkness, not knowing what lays even twenty feet ahead of us. For a little while, I think I hear some gunfire a few streets down. It spikes up for a moment, breaking the silence. We all stop. But then it dies off… and we keep moving.

There is a slight nighttime breeze long into our journey. The wind blows through the hollow streets, but it's barely strong enough to be felt. However, as soon as it hits me, I look up and thank *Allah*. Just this drop is enough to quench my thirst for a while.

A few blocks later, I think I hear some sirens not too far away. They sound like police sirens. Or maybe an ambulance's. Salman and Fatima don't seem to react to it. However, the noise disappears as if it was never there, just like everything else tonight. Maybe my mind is playing tricks on me. We march on.

The longer and further we go, the louder the sound of silence becomes. It grips my soul like an unrelenting leech. It speaks into my heart, letting me know just how forsaken these streets have become. Is the entire city as desolate as here?

The silence is faintly broken by the crackling of a fire. It sounds like burning debris. I see it up in the distance as it dimly breaks through the mist. A few steps closer and I notice that it's coming from an alley up ahead.

There's a large heap of wreckage between us and the fire. Salman nearly runs into the debris before stopping. It's about twice as tall as him. The mountain is made up of a bunch of bricks from a toppled building that's overrun onto the road. He looks to the right and then the left. There's no way around it.

Salman expertly climbs it. His movements are slow. The higher he goes, the more loose pieces of debris he unintentionally knocks down. With each move, he makes sure to find a stable footing before taking the next step. He arrives at the top with relative ease. Finding a firm area to plant himself, he turns around and offers Fatima his hand. After she takes it, he pulls her up and over to the other side. It's almost effortless for him.

He firmly takes my hand next. As he pulls me with a heave, I grab a piece of debris that is jutting out and kick off of another to help push myself toward him. He lets out a groan as he yanks me upward. The heavy sack isn't making it any easier. I sense it pulling on my shoulder, forcing a pang of pain to run through it. My arm feels like it's going to break off. As soon as I'm at eye-level with the top of the wreckage, I grab it with my free arm and help pull myself up. I groan in pain, my face turning red. My entire body is shaking as I dig deep to find my strength. Going up a few more inches, I throw my chest onto the mount and quickly worm myself onto it. As I do, a jutting brick's edge sharply jabs into my side, but I barely give it a wince.

Salman hops down to join Fatima. I follow him. My feet hit the ground hard, shooting a shot of pain up my legs. The sack violently smashes against my sore upper knee, and I almost fall over before Salman catches me. That hurt more than I thought it would. As I rise back up, the foul odor immediately hits me.

Finally on the other side, we take a moment to catch our breath before moving on. Passing the alley with the light, I look into it. There's a trashcan on fire, dimly illuminating the narrow lane. Not far from it is a woman. She's sitting with her back against the brick wall. Her head hangs low and her knees are up to her chest. There is a child with her, no older than three. He's clutching her shoulder as the woman weeps and shivers. Even out on the main road, I think I can faintly hear her whimpers above the low flame.

I stop, turning to fully face her. I hear Salman and Fatima do the same before looking back at me. Staying there for a few moments, I keep my eyes on the woman and child.

"Zaid, what are you—"

Salman quiets when he sees me reaching into my sack. I feel his gaze go back and forth between me and my sack a couple of quick times. I hastily rummage through it until I pull out a loaf of bread and a small bottle of water. Without a word, I leave Salman and Fatima behind as I start making my way to the woman.

"We need that, Zaid."

Salman's voice is as authoritative as ever, but I don't care. With every step, the heat of the fire grows a bit warmer and my footsteps seem to echo loudly. The closer I get to her, the more I feel my heart tremble. I don't know why. Maybe it's because she could very well be someone I know.

When I'm a few steps away, she suddenly looks up, as if just hearing my footsteps. The crackling of the small fire becomes inaudible. So do my footsteps. Her cheeks are damp, and I can see her face clearly as the flames softly reflect off of her. Her long black hair is uncovered and a mess while her headscarf is wrapped around her neck. She freezes upon noticing me, not sure my intentions.

But then she sees what I'm carrying. I take the last steps to her. Her gaze stays locked with mine. She doesn't say anything and neither do I. I hand her the items one at a time. First the bread. Then the

69

water. She takes them into her slim, quivering hands. Behind her tear-filled eyes is an ocean of gratitude. I see a sliver of light slowly break through the blackness. It's as if life has returned to her.

The woman takes the last item. I pause for a second, thinking of what I can do for her. Reaching back into the bag, I carefully pull out a long carving knife I found in Jari's kitchen. I put it on the ground next to her before turning and leaving.

As I walk away from her, my bag seems lighter. However, at the same time, it weighs heavier than before. I can feel my feet, at least a little bit. For perhaps the first time since this nightmare began, my soul senses something besides fear and despair. A short-lived gust hits me and takes away the odor for a brief moment. I sense the woman's gaze on my back. It was filled with dread a few moments ago. Now, there is a hint of something else: hope.

I will never forget those eyes.

Fatima and Zaid watch me the whole way back. His arms are crossed. "What are you thinking? We needed that."

"Not as much as she did. I have more food, but she didn't have anything and has a child with her."

"It's not your decision to make, Zaid."

Turning away from them, I look straight ahead as I switch the sack onto the opposite shoulder. "It's what Nabeel would have done."

Salman doesn't argue with that.

"Let's go."

***

"We'll stay here."

I hardly even noticed that we stopped. But sure enough, we're standing outside of a double-story building. There's a burning car a little ways down the road. It's far enough that we barely feel its heat, but its light reflects off of the structure. The building's windows lay

70

shattered on the ground, and the door is barely hanging on its hinges. However, it seems mainly undamaged. Less than the others at least.

Fatima's voice cuts into the air. "I think we should keep—"

"No," Salman snaps. "We're stopping here."

"How long has it been?" I ask.

"Since we left the shop? Nearly five hours."

I can't feel my feet. The stench is soaked into my soul. And this sack is heavier than the rest of the world combined. Even my eyes have to fight to stay open. The more I try to keep them awake, the harder they struggle to sleep. It's as if I've been sleepwalking for the past couple of hours. Salman takes a step toward the shop's door. "Wait here a moment."

My dull gaze follows him in as he enters the shop's blackness without another word. As I see him vanish inside, I don't feel anything. I think I'm too exhausted to be worried.

Grabbing ahold of the guardrail that leads into the building, I lean against it to hold myself up as I readjust my sack's thick strap. Within a few moments, I hear his voice cut outside. "Come in."

I let Fatima go first and trail in behind her. Moving up the brick steps, my shoes crunch down on some broken glass, but I don't even give it a glance. I hear Salman trying to turn on a lamp. He flicks the switch a few times. It's to no avail. Entering the building, my eyes slowly adjust to the darkness inside.

It's a restaurant. Several tables are flipped over or turned onto their sides. A lot of glass cups lay cracked, chipped, or shattered on the ground. Some chairs are knocked over along with scattered silverware, plates, and dark tablecloths. People must have been in here when all the shooting began. Seeing the mess, I can only imagine the chaos that likely ensued when the attack occurred. God-willing, they all got out safe.

Now inside, my legs start to tremble a bit. They're threatening to collapse in on themselves. It's beyond soreness and pain now.

Salman flicks on one of his flashlights. He keeps it aimed at the ground so that it doesn't attract any unwanted attention.

I'm the one to break the silence. "Do you know where we are?"

"I didn't see any landmarks while we were walking," Salman replies. "But I know we're far from Ballermoun. God-willing, we're far from the fighting as well. It will be easier to tell when the sun comes up."

"What if all the landmarks are destroyed?"

Salman ignores the question. Using his light, he scans the area until he finds a staircase at the back of the restaurant. He then traces a path from it to us and then back to it. "Let's go upstairs and see if there's anywhere we can rest."

I follow Salman and Fatima through the mess and toward the stairs. We avoid as much of the broken glass as we can, stepping between the tables and over the fallen chairs. Salman kicks any of the debris in his path, clearing the way for me and Fatima.

We climb up the creaky staircases, hearing them sound off beneath our feet. With the gradual and heavy steps they're taking, I think Salman and Fatima are just as tired as I am. Every movement is a battle. Everything from my joints to my muscles to my very bones wants to shut down, but I won't let it. One more step... one more step... one more step...

Arriving at the top, we find ourselves in a narrow corridor. It's completely bare, except for a couple of frames hanging from the walls. It's too dark to make out what they're holding. I hear a sound. It's a faint scurrying not too far away. I see the fat rat just as it darts into another room. No doubt, Salman scared it with the light. We slowly enter the hallway.

But then there's a sound—a loud one—and it doesn't belong to any of us.

A floorboard creaks. They both freeze with me. Salman almost immediately snaps out of his trance and steps in front of me and Fatima, blocking us from whatever may be in the abyss. Salman yanks out his pistol before aiming the flashlight and weapon in the direction of the sound.

There's somebody standing in the shadows. Peering from behind Salman, I see the stranger. Not even ten feet away, he shields his face from the bright light.

"L—let me see your hands," Salman orders. His grip around the weapon is tight.

Slowly, the figure raises both his hands, revealing his weary and dirty face. It's a boy. He looks to be Salman's age, which means he's probably two years older than Salman. The hand that he used to shield his face is covered in a bit of blood. His clothes are as dirty as his face and hair. Breathing quickly, his body is trembling a bit and his eyes are as red as ours. There's a long moment of silence as his gaze goes from the gun and on to each of us before he breaks the silence. "My brother's in the other room. He needs help. Do you have any medical supplies?"

Salman doesn't make a sound or move. He keeps the gun trained on the newcomer, holding it perfectly still.

"His leg is hurt," the boy continues.

Salman continues to stand his ground.

"...please."

Those eyes and that voice. They can't be lying.

"How was he hurt?" Salman's tone is authoritative, more than it's ever been before.

"We were caught in the crossfire. A bullet hit his leg. I don't know how to stop the bleeding."

"Are you being followed?"

"I don't think so."

The corridor grows tense with every passing second. Salman keeps staring down the boy, unsure if he is friend or foe. The stillness is frightening. After a long moment, Salman lowers the gun, but he keeps it in hand. "We have some supplies. Show us to your brother."

"He's right in this room." The boy motions to the room he just walked out of.

Salman's gaze remains focused on the boy, but he speaks to me and Fatima. "Fatima, come with me. You stay here, Zaid. Watch for anybody that might be following them."

I nod.

Salman and Fatima follow the boy into the room. I notice Salman still hasn't put away the gun as he goes in before Fatima. They disappear into the doorway, but I stay there in the hallway for a long moment, not moving a muscle. My mind is so tired that I barely even registered what happened. One moment we were alone, and in seemingly the next moment, they're assisting some boy and his brother.

Shaking my head, I stagger into the room opposite of the one they went into. I hear a moan come from their room. It's not a voice I recognize. Fatima tears off some of the wrapping from her bag. There's a spray. Sounds like an anesthetic. The foreign voice immediately sucks in some air, quelling a yelp. I hear the boy from the hallway whisper something, but my ears are too tired to pick up what he says.

Looking out of the broken window, I find myself staring into the thick fog we came out of. I can't see clearly past the dense wall of smoke and smog, but I hear the distant blasts and see the flames that dimly cut through the mist. And I can certainly distinguish the shadows of the wreckage, rubble, and ashes. Even up here, the stench of destruction and the odor of the dead reaches me.

It's hard to stand, let alone move, with as numb as my legs are. I'm quivering. The adrenaline is gone. My legs finally give in. I desperately grab ahold of the wall and barely keep myself upright. My drowsy eyes stay aimed at the desolation outside.

The street is forsaken. The *city* is forsaken.

If there was ever a time I missed the warm embrace of my mother, it is now. I crave it more than anything else. What I would give to be held by her loving arms right now. Closing my eyes, I see her face. It's warmly smiling at me. I feel her touch—the touch that always filled me with a sense of protection. But tonight, it causes a shudder to shoot up my spine. Tonight, she's not here. Nor will she be tomorrow. A tear slowly runs down my cheek.

The fear-striking silence surrounds me once more. It's my only companion. The hollow sound of silence is worse than gunfire and explosions. Worse than screams. Worse than terror. Because mixed into this silence is abandonment and suffering.

And more than anything else, this silence is the silence of the unknown.

CHAPTER 9
NEW COMRADES

This is a dream—a memory. I know that. But it feels so real, and I wish it would never end.

One... two... three... four. With the fourth skip, the rock plops into the pond with a loud splash. Standing at the edge of the water, I still hold the position I threw the rock in. Seeing it finally go under as its ripples spread in every direction, I turn around and shoot Salman and Fatima a smirk.

"That's four!"

Fatima shakes her head, now having lost her title.

Salman chuckles as he takes a step closer to the lake with a rock in hand. "Congratulations on being able to throw better than a girl, Zaid. I'm truly impressed."

I roll my eyes. "Let's see how you do, Salman."

He gets into position. The sun is high, but we're protected under the shade of an ancient tree. Even so, I'm sweating a bit as I watch his eyes grow focused. I know that look all too well. Salman gets into position so casually, as if he's hardly even thinking about it. How is he always so cool under pressure while I can't hold a decent conversation without getting nervous?

Salman cocks his arm back. Without wasting another moment, he sends his rock sailing. It gracefully soars through the air with more elegance than any rock should before striking the water with a splash. One... two... three... four... five! As the rock sinks into the pond, he turns around with a victorious smile.

Salman shoots me a wink. "Can you beat that?"

The burden of pressure immediately begins crushing my heart. Crouching down, I start rummaging through the stones at my feet. I look for the perfect one. Flat but not circular. The size of my palm but the weight of a tennis ball. And triangular. After a few moments, I find the perfect stone buried underneath some useless ones.

Holding it with my right hand's thumb and middle finger, I firmly hooked my index finger along the stone's edge. I remind myself that my thumb goes on top of the stone, not the edge. Don't want to make a fool of myself like I did last weekend.

I stand up straight, facing the pond at a slight angle.

Keep this position, Zaid. Don't lose it during the throw. The lower your hand, the better. I wind back. *Throw out and down at the same time. Strength isn't the key. Speed is. Don't mess this up. Not in front of Fatima.*

With a quick snap of my wrist, I launch it with as much spin as possible. The stone cuts through the air, heading straight at the water. It strikes the pond perfectly.

One...

Two...

Three...

Four...

It sinks down. So do my hopes.

"And the still reigning champion: Salman!" Salman cheers behind me.

My shoulders slump as my hopes of victory vanish. I thought I had him. It looked so perfect. But, like always, my aspiration plummets away. Fatima pats my back as she speaks to her brother. "Be a good sport, Salman."

"Sure, sure." He comes up from behind me. "Good try, buddy."

"Yeah. Thanks."

"Well, it's a good thing your dream is to be a doctor. Even with your grades, you have a higher chance of becoming that than being a professional rock skipper."

Is that supposed to make me feel better?

"Don't worry. Your day will come, Zaid."

I turn and look back at his smiling face. He's not more than a step away. There's a devilish look in his eyes. No, he wouldn't—

"But it's not today!" With a laugh, he suddenly shoves me. My arms are flailing as I go into the pond with a loud splash.

***

"Zaid!"

My eyes suddenly shoot open, staring right at the face of Salman. His expression is the complete opposite of the jovial one I saw in the dream.

"You were supposed to keep watch. Not fall asleep."

He takes a step back, allowing me to slowly sit up. It's a battle to keep my eyes open. I take a deep yawn. Then another as I rub my eyes. My head feels so heavy. A few late morning rays spill in through the broken window and into the room.

As I shake away the slumber and draw myself back to reality, I take a look around. I was surrounded by shards of glass as I slept. It's a miracle that I didn't get cut. I feel dehydrated. Was I sweating in my sleep? My hair is a mess and I feel dirty.

"What were you thinking, Zaid?"

Should I tell him that I was dreaming of life before all this? But I don't think that's what he means. Looking out the broken window, I have a much better view of Aleppo than before. There's smoke rising from nearly everywhere. Black smoke. It's more than there was yesterday evening. If there is any gunfire, it's too faint to hear. I can see a few buildings ablaze. Even up here, their heat crashes against me.

"I—I'm sorry, Salman. I don't know what happened."

Salman sighs and shakes his head. "C'mon. You need to eat something."

I slowly rise to my feet with Salman's help. *Ouch!* My legs are so sore that it hurts to even stand on them. And moving them is even worse. Salman helps me steady myself by holding me upright with his strong grip. I follow him toward the room's exit and into the corridor.

"Do you know what time it is?"

"Almost noon," Salman replies as he glances back at me. "I tried to wake you up a few times, but you wouldn't stir. Thought it would be best to just leave you be. We stopped Amaan's bleeding."

"Amaan?"

"The wounded boy. His brother—the one we met in the corridor—is Faisal."

That fills the gap.

"I can't believe you slept through it all."

"All the what?"

"Shelling. There have been bombs dropping not too far from here all morning. Two of them were close enough to shake the building. Thank God we were okay."

That explains all the dust and smoke. "Did you find any phones here?"

"None that were working."

My heart sinks upon hearing him utter those words. I follow Salman to another room on the other side of the hallway. The door is open. "You go on inside, Zaid. I need to look for something."

He departs without another word, leaving me to enter the room alone. I stagger inside, still unable to completely walk properly. This room has no windows. A chandelier brightly illuminates the private dining room. Unlike below, unlike the wrecked street outside,

79

everything is just as it would be on a normal day, upright with nothing knocked over.

Fatima sits across from Faisal and another boy—must be Amaan—at a red-clothed dining table that could seat twelve. They each have a handful of dates, some bread, and a glass of water in front of them. At the center of a table is a crystal white fruit basket. It's been emptied.

Their eyes focus on me as I enter. I'm immediately hit with a rush of cool air. This room's A/C must be working. *Alhumdulillah.* Fatima immediately smiles upon seeing me as Amaan speaks up. His voice is a little hoarse but polite. *"Assalam-O-Alaikum.* You must be Zaid."

"Walaikum Assalam." Returning the traditional greeting, I see that his thigh is partially covered in a wrapping. There's a dark red stain on it, but it's been applied perfectly. I look over at Faisal. He smiles and I return the gesture. At least, I mean to.

"I set aside some food for you, Zaid." Fatima motions toward some dates and bread next to her. Her eyes look so alive. Much more than they were yesterday.

I take my seat next to her. As soon as I see the food sitting in front of me, my stomach reminds me how long it's been since I've eaten. My hand is nearly shaking as I grab the bread and tear off a good piece. Faisal and Amaan both stare at me, waiting for me to speak. They're just as nervous as I am. Faisal appears to be seventeen, four years older than me. Amaan is only a year younger than Faisal, at least I think.

"Is it just you two?" I ask as I take a hefty bite of my bread. It's softer than it looks and is easy to chew. I hardly gnaw on it before swallowing it down.

Faisal nods.

Downing the bread in a bulky gulp, I take a sip of my water. It's not cold, but it is the most refreshing thing I've ever tasted. I feel my parched throat thanking me a thousand times over before I speak again. "Where were you when it all began?"

They both exchange glances as if wondering who wants to answer. Finally, Faisal replies. His voice is different than the night before, and it's stronger than Amaan's. "At home. We were sleeping when the shooting began. It came out of nowhere. Our parents got us out the back door. They told us to go a few blocks down and wait for them at the backside of a restaurant that we went to all the time."

I watch him glance down for a moment.

"There was so much shooting. People were…" He pauses before his words grow mellow. "…shouting. We ran there as fast as we could. No matter where we ran, we couldn't escape the chaos. When we finally got there, we hid right where they told us to. We hid there the entire night, amongst the trash bins and rats, waiting for our parents. We could hear everything: the shooting, explosions… and the screams. It must have been hours before the sun rose… but they never came."

As he says each word, I see him replaying it all in his mind. Hiding by a dumpster? I can't imagine that. At least we had a building to hide in.

"By then we knew the truth. We went into that alley as sons. We left as orphans."

His words cause a terror to run up my spine, but I do my best to not show it. For all we know, they may not be the only orphans in this room.

Wordlessly, I bite into one of the dates in front of me. The dry fruit is sweet. Even the blandest ones always get my taste buds excited. I chew on it for a little bit before swallowing. Tasting something this delicious after so long is like a breath of fresh air. For a moment, it feels like I'm sitting at my home's dining table while eating the same dates.

I make sure to take my time eating. There's not much food here. The slower I eat, the fuller it'll make me. My senses gradually awaken with each passing second. After a few more bites, I look over at Amaan. His eyes are still on me.

"How did you get hurt?"

"I was shot by security forces," he replies.

My eyes slightly widen. "…security forces?"

Amaan nods. "When we realized that our parents were… well—we decided to move. Our grandparents don't live far. I was carrying a gun for protection. I found it… on a corpse. The soldiers thought we were rebels. I don't know why. Even when I threw my weapon down, they didn't believe us. They were aiming their guns at us and telling us to get on the ground. So we ran. But they shot at us."

"The army is supposed to protect us. Why would they shoot at you?"

"I don't know."

I try to play it all in my mind, but it just doesn't make any sense. It must have been night time or something. Soldiers wouldn't shoot at civilians, right? Nabeel never would. I know that. I look back up at him. "I'm glad you're fine."

"Thanks to *Allah*, we found you three." He looks over at Fatima. "You truly were a miracle worker."

She politely smiles but doesn't reply.

"Do you know where we are?" I ask.

"Just outside of the New Aleppo District's eastern border."

So we're going in the right direction. We covered more ground than I previously estimated. However, just as Salman told me, we're still far from even being in the vicinity of our home.

"Are your feet hurting, Zaid?" Fatima's sweet voice breaks me out of my thoughts.

I look over at her.

"If you take your shoes off, it helps with your feet."

Nodding, I take her advice and notice that hers are already off. Fatima's fair-skinned feet look just as stiff as mine. Kicking my shoes off, I let them fall onto the floor. I peel my heavy socks back, wincing as I do. Just doing that hurts. I lay them on top of my shoes. My feet look almost swollen and some blisters have formed on their bottoms. My toes are so numb and stiff that it's a battle to just stretch them. I slowly suck in some air as I do.

After a long moment, I look back up at the two brothers.

"It must've been a long walk for you three," Faisal says.

I simply nod. Even after all that sleep, I still feel exhausted. The moment I think I'm awake, drowsiness sweeps back over me. It's as if I will keel over and pass out at any moment. I force myself to plop another date in my mouth and chew it. God-willing, it'll help keep me awake. Thank God it's seedless because I don't think I possess the willpower to spit out a seed.

"At least we found each other," Faisal continues. "They say that true strength lies in numbers."

I mean to echo Jari's words about how true strength comes from the heart and not numbers, but I don't find the strength.

***

Salman quickly enters the room. He's carrying a small radio. Holding it with both hands, he grips it delicately, as if it is a glass vase. His eyes show a flash of excitement. So this is what he was looking for.

"This one works," he says as he sets it on the middle of the table, right by the fruit bowl. "Let's see if we can catch a reception."

It certainly looks old. Wooden with rusting dials, its antenna is a bit bent as well. The top of it is covered in a layer of dust. It reminds me of the one the old *Imam* has at his house. But that one hardly ever worked. I pray this proves to be more useful.

Salman flips the switch to turn it on. A low static hums out of it. Fatima reaches over and wipes the thick dust off of the speakers. Grabbing ahold of one of the two dials, Salman looks over at the rest of us. "What frequency would the news be on?"

Faisal is quick to respond. "*Al Aan*. It's—uh, 96.9."

He slowly turns the dial. We all watch the needle slowly inch along. There's constant, unending static. The needle passes a few stations I recognize, but nothing changes. 95.0... 95.7... 96.4...

Slowly rising to my feet, I lean closer to the radio, pushing my open palms against the table for support.

The static ends. There's a voice. It's faint at first, but it grows clearer as Salman fine tunes the frequency before turning up the volume with one quick rotation of the second dial. It's a man's voice. Even with the static in the background, we can make out most of what he's saying:

"*—rebel forces have continued pushing into—districts of— Haydariya and Sakhour. There has—heavy fighting between the army and rebels. Many residents are being driven to safer areas outside of Aleppo or closer to the city's center. If—not able to evacuate, we—to stay indoors until the situation—calms down.*"

Those two districts are on the opposite side of Aleppo from Salaheddine. They're on the city's north side, right by our home! I thought the fighting was just in this area. However, if the rebels are attacking there, then it must be happening citywide. They're so close to my neighborhood. But...

My eyes widen. This means there's a greater chance that— that—we've got to get back home!

Fatima and I exchange a glance. Her eyes show the same thoughts as mine.

"*The military is continuing to shell rebel-held districts as well as engage them on the ground. Citizens claim that—they are firing indiscriminately even in heavily po—*"

The entire building suddenly tremors.

A deafening explosion erupts, drowning out the radio. My heart-rate spikes. As the ground beneath me trembles, I nearly lose my footing but hang on to the table. Faisal and Amaan dive underneath the table without hesitating. So does Fatima. Salman grabs my shoulder and forces me down under the table with him.

On all fours, I cover my head and tuck it in. The room quivers chaotically. It's like an earthquake. The table shakes, knocking off one of the plates. It breaks. The framed paintings clatter against the wall. For a moment, it's as if the world is ending. But the echo of the blast soon disperses. After a few more moments, the trembling stops as well.

I stay down there. So does everyone else. Nobody dares make a sound or a move. Another explosion detonates, breaking the stillness. It's thunderous, louder and stronger than the last blast. The walls and ground quake. Are they about to give in? The chandelier's lights piercingly clang against one another. A few of them fall and shatter. The lights flicker as the rumbling continues.

My ears are pounding, and my heart beats even faster. I hear a building loudly collapse. Its bricks violently crash against the road. As the chunks of rubble beat against the concrete, I shut my eyes, trying to escape this reality. It feels like the blast is right on top of us—as if I could see it if I looked right outside the doorway.

The blast disperses like the last one. Then the rubble settles. As my ears stop ringing, I hear something else. It's faint but grows louder with every passing moment. What could it—no, it couldn't be that... yes, it is! It's a helicopter! More than one! They sound just like the ones I saw when I visited Nabeel at the military base once. They're military helicopters!

The army is here.

My eyes shoot open and look at Fatima. She's in the same position as me. So are the two brothers. Salman is coming out from under the table, and I hastily follow him. The propellers are so loud now. They must be drawing nearer to us.

"Those are military helicopters!" Excitement fills my voice. "We—we need to flag them—"

Salman stares me dead in the face. I've never seen that look in his eyes before. "No."

What? Did he really just say that? "They can help us."

"I said '*no*', Zaid."

He must be outside his mind. I take a rushed step past him. "I'll do it then if—"

I'm roughly slammed and pinned against the wall. My back has a sharp jolt of pain shoot through it. The wind is knocked out of me. Salman's forearm is pushing up against my chest, keeping me there. His gaze looks... deadly. "We're not flagging anybody down, Zaid. We're staying here."

I glance over at Fatima. Then Faisal and Amaan. None of them make a move to get him off of me. Have they all gone crazy? I look back at Salman. I try to move, but he's too strong. The helicopters are getting fainter now. They've passed us by. We've missed our chance.

Staring at Salman, the same wretched feeling I felt when watching my parents disappear in the distance washes back over me. There's nothing I can do. My heart sinks as something heavy comes onto it. What has Salman done? Within a few moments, the propellers have fallen silent. They're gone now.

He finally lets me go. Without a word, he turns around and leaves.

What has Salman done?

CHAPTER 10
LEGACY

The last blast obliterated the building right across the street from us. When I woke up this morning, I saw it standing tall. Now, it's as if it never existed. It looks like just another pile of meaningless rubble.

Any peace that came over the city at night has vanished. The shells descend from the heavens. They always start off faint, barely audible, but they quickly grow louder until it seems that they'll fall right on top of us. It's followed by the explosion, the thunderous detonation. The buildings and walls tremble so hard that I think they're going to collapse at any moment. How much more can they take? The deafening blast echoes through the street. Sometimes, I hear screams as people outside witness them firsthand. I smell the odor of the eruptions as they kick up so much dirt and leave a cloud of smoke behind.

None of the blasts are as close as the one that hit across the street. Some of them hit the neighborhood, destroying anything they touch. I feel the heat of the closer ones, and when I look out the window, I see the destruction as buildings topple down or go up in flames. There's more black smoke rising. It's an endless barrage. The heavens themselves have begun to rain down bombs and missiles.

After a while, as the day continues to grow longer, I hardly hear the falling shells and blasts. My mind blocks them out. In the end, there's nothing I can do to outrun them. Even if are falls right on top of us, I will not be able to avoid it. We're just sitting here, sitting and listening to the world around us burn down. Sitting and hoping that the next bomb doesn't fall on us.

I remember reading about The Massacre of Ayyadieh during the Third Crusade. I always wondered what it must have felt like for those men, women, and children to be helplessly led outside the city of Acre and to that small hill, knowing that they were walking to their deaths. I suppose I've found the answer. I now know what it is to helplessly sit and know your life and death are in the hands of a stranger.

Outside of the falling bombs and raucous explosions, there is nothing else. I don't hear the beautiful call to prayer ringing through the streets of the city. I don't hear the sounds of merchants and buyers. I don't hear blaring horns or loud engines. I can't even sense the familiar smell of oil that was always soaked into the roads. All the things that made Aleppo feel like home are nowhere to be seen. The city seems naked without them.

If I didn't know where I was, I would not recognize my city.

After the incident in the dining room, we all keep to ourselves. Faisal and Amaan are in one room with Salman. The radio softly plays behind the closed door. Fatima is somewhere else. I know Salman ordered nobody to go near the window, but after being cooped up in a dark room for so long, I am beginning to not care about what he has to say. He may have very well forsaken us by hiding from those helicopters.

The hours pass in solitude. Sometimes I stand by the window and watch the bombs descend. Seeing them fall reminds me of a post-apocalyptic movie, the ones where the world has ended. Any one of those bombs could be the end for us. We'd never even see it coming.

When I'm not by the window, I lock myself away in a room. I keep thinking of what could have happened if those helicopters noticed us. I wouldn't helplessly be watching this destruction. I could have easily flagged them down. They would have taken us. I know it. That was our ticket out, and Salman threw it away! He threw it away like it was his right to do so.

Ever since this nightmare began, Salman has acted as if every call is his to make. From the time Jari walked out those doors until now, Salman's word has been final. But now he's gone too far. Just the thought of it makes my blood begin to boil.

The shelling ceases late in the afternoon. A part of me hopes it is the end, but I know better than to hold on to any hope. I arrive at the broken window I fell asleep in front of. The shattered glass is still there. Looking outside, I see the deserted streets. Countless structures are now piles of debris and smoking ash, overrunning onto the walkways and roads. The neighborhood looks just like any other street I've seen: wrecked. But one thing catches my attention. Right by a scorched vehicle, a pair of still and stiff legs comes into view as they lie on the road. The rest of the body is hidden behind the truck.

Two birds are circling it: vultures. They're going to—

They both swoop down behind the truck and onto the body. I can't see them, but I know what they're doing. The same thing probably happened to Bilal and Jari. I just wasn't there to see it. My grip around the wall tightens as I watch the scene unfold.

For all I know, I may end up like that. All it would take is one bomb or bullet. As terrifying as that image is, there is one that strikes even more fear into me: could that be my family?

***

Leaving the room, I run into Amaan in the hallway. He politely smiles when he sees me. I mean to return the gesture but don't.

"Salman said not to go near the windows, Zaid."

"I don't care."

"Don't be hard on him. You don't know what he saw."

My gaze compels him to explain.

"He went out early morning. You were sleeping at the time. He thought he heard somebody crying. I told him not to go, but he went anyway. I didn't know what he saw, but there was sudden gunfire. When he came back, he was different. It took him an hour to tell us what it was." Amaan glances down for a moment. "He says he saw a rebel take two civilians hostage as they tried to scare the security forces into backing off."

"What happened?"

Amaan pauses. I can tell he's debating whether or not to answer my question. "The soldiers… they just shot through the civilians to hit the rebel. They gunned them all down."

I blink several times. There's another silence as I try to run his words through my mind. I can't imagine this. First Faisal and Amaan were claiming soldiers shot at them. Now Salman.

"Just thought you should know."

As I hear him walk away, I still can't grasp this. It seems impossible. Those soldiers serve the same army as Nabeel. They've taken the same oath. They would never shoot at civilians even for that reason. This can't be the truth…

But the falling bombs. They're the military's. And they're hailing down on this district like they're trying to eradicate every building, road, and gutter. There's no way the military is able to ensure that they're only hitting the rebels and not civilians.

I hear a question in the back of my mind. It starts off as a whisper, but it grows louder as the reality of the situation sets in. Before I know it, it's the only thing I hear: is the military's priority to protect civilians or defeat the rebels?

Deep inside, I'm beginning to realize what the answer is.

***

"Zaid?"

I look back to see Fatima entering the room. She leaves the door open a crack. The ceiling light dimly reflects off her face and

90

dark pink headscarf. She's freshened up a bit, just like I have. Her face is much cleaner than the night before, and her eyes don't seem as weary. She probably got some sleep. At least one of us was able to. I notice what's in her hands: Jari's emerald green rosary beads. "We were all looking for you, Zaid. Salman says we should eat a bit. We'll be heading out in about an hour or two."

My reply is quick. "I'm not hungry."

"Are you sure?"

I turn away from her. "Every explosion I hear is making me sick to my stomach. I don't think I'm in the mood to throw up my dinner."

"You heard about what Salman saw?"

I don't respond.

"I didn't want to be the one to tell you."

-"I would have found out sooner or later."

"Is that why you're by yourself?"

I stay silent, still not meeting her gaze.

She softly takes a seat next to me. We're quiet for a long time as she runs her hands against the prayer beads. Seeing her holding them, a sudden regret grips my heart as I remember what today marks.

"What are you thinking about, Zaid?"

Finally, I look back at her. "Ramadan started today."

Her eyes show that she remembers. As I mention it, I see the longing wash over her face. We both share the same feeling, knowing that the holy month—the holiest and most celebrated month of the year—is upon us, but we are unable to observe it as it begins to slip away right through our fingers. It's like missing a train by a few seconds and watching it pull away, unable to do anything to bring it back.

"We were going to start fasting. Now we may never get the chance."

"Don't talk like that, Zaid."

"The first day of Ramadan is supposed to be a happy time. The entire city is celebrating. Two days ago, Aisha was going to the market and buying supplies. Everyone was. We were getting ready like we do every year. When the sun goes down, there's food everywhere and festive lights reach as far as the eye can see. Aisha was going to prepare a feast for the first day. She was so excited—everyone was so excited. But there'll be none of that this year." I pause, my voice shivering. "Maybe not ever again."

Fatima listens, her gaze staying focused on me.

"There's so much... so much happening, Fatima. I don't know what to think anymore. I don't know..." I take a deep breath, holding back the tears in my eyes. But my voice shows it. "Why do people do it?"

"Do what?"

"Sacrifice their life like Jari did?"

"I don't know, Zaid." She thinks for a long second, glancing down at the rosary beads. "Maybe it's because when we die, we don't take anything with us. Not our wealth. Not our possessions. But what we leave behind are people... a legacy. And if we leave those people better off than we found them, then maybe it amounts to something."

I let her words saturate in my mind for a moment. "What will Jari's legacy be?"

"I'm not sure." Her green eyes lock with mine as she pauses. Reaching out, she lightly puts her hand on my shoulder. Just that simple action brings a sliver of peace to my soul. "But it'll be inside each of us."

CHAPTER 11
PREY

The door swings open, slamming against the wall. Fatima and I immediately look toward it. Faisal stands in the entrance, his eyes filled with terror. "We need to go. Now!"

My eyes widen as we both stumble to our feet. "What's happening?"

"People with guns are outside. They're coming into the building. We need to leave."

In an instant, the calmness I felt disappears. I stuff the rosary beads into my pocket as we nearly run out into the hallway. "Are they soldiers?"

"I couldn't tell. I barely saw them entering, but I don't think they're wearing any kind of uniforms." Faisal spits out his words like rapid fire. "Move quietly. We don't want them to hear the floorboards creaking."

"Do you know how many there are?"

He shakes his head.

Salman and Amaan dash into the hallway from the other room. Salman has all three sacks slung over his shoulder, while Amaan is carrying the radio under his arm.

"Leave that," Salman commands. "It'll slow us down."

Amaan looks over at his brother. Faisal nods, and Amaan sets the radio down lightly enough so it doesn't make a sound.

"There's a back door exit from the second floor," Faisal whispers. "There's a second set of stairs that leads to it. We need to go from there."

Coming to us, Salman hands me and Fatima our respective supply sacks. I hang it on my shoulder like before, immediately feeling its weight. It's heavier than last night, but I ignore the pain as I adjust the strap.

"Which way?" Salman asks Faisal.

"Follow me."

As Faisal leads us down the narrow corridor, I hear the voices below us. They're rowdy and loud. If I didn't know where they were, I would think that they were in the room next to me. The intruders are ripping open cabinets and throwing things onto the hard floor. Those voices sound just like the one that beckoned Jari to his death. It's like we're back in that storage closet again. The ground and walls nearly shake with the rancor.

The hallway is longer now. Narrower too. With every step, I almost hold my breath and pray that I don't make a sound. We're headed toward a crossroads up ahead, but it doesn't seem to be getting any closer. It's only getting further away as the voices below intensify.

Finally arriving at the fork, Faisal leads us down the right path without missing a beat. He's in the front of the pack with his brother, while Salman is in the back. Amaan is moving too fast and is putting too much pressure on his good leg. He needs to slow down. I try to say something—whisper something to him, but I'm not quick enough. A few paces into it, he steps onto a floorboard that echoes a loud creak.

We all freeze. My heart stops. The noise reverberates down the corridor. It seems to last forever... and then some. Amaan slowly turns his head to look back at us, maybe thinking that it wasn't as loud as he thought. But he sees our expressions. The squeak drives a stake into my soul. For a long moment, we just stand there, hoping and praying that—

"You three! Go look upstairs!"

"Move!" Salman hisses.

I see the second staircase, the one we're going for. We're almost there. Faisal and Amaan pick up their pace and we follow right behind them. Almost there.

But then we hear it. Those are... footsteps. They're heavy and fast. And they're coming from the staircase in front of us!

Faisal suddenly whips around. Fear is in his eyes.

"Get out of the corridor." Salman takes a few quick steps back toward the hallway's fork. He can see the other stairwell—the one we came up last night. His eyes widen before he motions toward the nearest room. "In there. Now!"

We rush in, Faisal and Amaan entering first. The room is empty, except for a couple of boxes, a closet, and a broken window. As he hurriedly comes in last, Salman closes the door lightly enough so that it doesn't alert anyone. I recognize the look in his eyes. His mind is working as hard as possible. No sooner does he seal off the room than we hear the footsteps arrive at the top of the stairs. That's two—no three pairs of heavy boots. They abruptly stop.

My breaths are quick. My heart is even faster. Behind the closed door, Salman keeps one hand pressed against it as if that will be able to hold them back. Everyone is paralyzed. My eyes are glued to the door, waiting for any sign that we're safe.

"Did you see anything?" one of the voices asks.

"No. But I'm sure I heard that."

"You stand here." A machine gun is cocked and readied in a quick motion. "I'll start checking the rooms."

A door is violently kicked down. It flies on its hinges before slamming against the wall. Aggressive footsteps charge into it. Salman turns his head to look at the rest of us before turning toward the room's window. He motions for us to go over there.

Faisal and Amaan are in front, followed by the three of us. This time, Amaan holds on to his brother so his bad leg doesn't make another mistake. I move behind Fatima. Slow and soft steps. I put my foot down on the ground gradually, praying to *Allah* that my movements are silent. There's broken glass scattered on the floor. With each step, I slide the glass shards away with my foot before moving forward. Another door swings open. The gunman is slowly making his way to this room.

Faisal outstretches his hand toward Salman. "Give me the gun, Salman."

"Not yet. Is there anything out there?"

Amaan looks out the window before whispering back to the rest of us. Is that hope in his eyes? "There's a fire escape."

Coming to the window, I see the metal stairwell that leads to the sidewalk. Black smoke is everywhere. It's thick, but I can make out the walkway. I barely stop myself from leaping onto the fire escape and making a run for it.

"Move," Salman orders.

Faisal doesn't hesitate. He grabs the fire escape's railing before pulling himself onto it. It wobbles a bit under his weight. He keeps his steps quiet as he hastily makes his way down there. Amaan goes next, only half a step behind his brother. He doesn't even offer anyone else a chance. For a moment, it seems like it'll rattle... but it doesn't. The two of them disappear into the smoke.

Fatima glances back at me. I know what she's about to ask.

"Go." I motion for her to climb on.

Grasping the railing, she climbs onto the metal steps. As she does, her sack taps against it, sounding off a soft echo. She freezes for a moment but then begins to descend toward the street. It doesn't shake as much now. Faisal and Amaan must be on the ground.

"You're next, Zaid."

I look back at Salman. "You go f—"

Another door is busted open before the man charges in. It's one down from us.

96

Salman pushes me forward, nearly shoving me onto the fire escape. Grabbing ahold of the hot railing, I steady myself onto the metal staircase. I ignore the chaos of my soul. There's black smoke all over the street. It's not as thick on the walkway; however, I can still barely even see the bottom of the fire escape.

One hand holds onto my sack, making sure it doesn't hit the railing like Fatima's. It's heavier than hers and will cause a bigger echo. My other hand leans on the railing, keeping most of my weight on it. It'll make my footsteps lighter... God-willing.

Move slowly, Zaid. Too fast and you'll make too much noise. But too slow and—no! Don't think about that.

I'm only three paces behind Fatima. With every step, my heart beats faster and louder. As my foot touches down on each step, I hold my breath. *Don't make a sound; please don't make a sound!* I feel Salman come onto the escape. He's right behind me, not even half a step away. We're out of view within moments.

The room's door violently flies open. The heavy footsteps enter. As I continue to move, I hear the man walking across the floor. I stop myself from speeding up. I can't move any faster without the risk of alerting him.

We're halfway down. I see the others. Fatima is still climbing down, but Faisal and Amaan are already on the street, ducking behind an abandoned and emptied fruit stand. Above us, the man rips open the closet's entrance. He'll look out the window next. I'm nearing the sidewalk now. Salman is still right behind me. I can feel his breath on the back of my head and neck.

Fatima reaches the ground and joins Faisal and Amaan. I hear the heavy footsteps getting louder. The gunman is almost at the window. Coming to the last step, I race onto the sidewalk. Behind me, Salman's hand is on my shoulder, urging me on, as we dash to join the others.

Out of sight from the window, I don't feel any safer. Being surrounded by this smoke and not knowing what is even twenty feet in any direction is no comfort. No sooner do we get to the others than some footsteps arrive onto the sidewalk. They're just as heavy as the men from upstairs. I look through a crack between two of the crates we're hiding behind.

The footsteps are getting louder... louder... and louder. Each step they take injects more fear into my heart. I barely stop myself from trembling. They're heading straight for us. Did they see us? If they did, t—then there's no escape. We're all cramped back here, like sheep waiting for the slaughter.

Salman is to my left and Fatima is crouched down against my right shoulder. I feel her soft hand touching my arm, and I can smell Salman's sweat. Is he trembling too?

I see a pair of dirty, brown boots cut out of the fog and come into view. It's immediately joined by another one. They halt right in front of the fruit stand. I stop breathing. These men are not wearing any kind of uniform, and I see the barrel of one of their rifles aimed at the ground. They're looking right at the fruit stand—no... they're looking up at the window. One of them speaks, his voice shrewd and deadly. "What are you doing?"

Another voice from above us replies. It must be the man at the window. "We heard someone up here."

"Did you find anybody?"

"If I did, my rifle wouldn't be this full."

The other man chuckles. Every syllable of his laughter is filled with wickedness.

"But we found a radio in the hallway. They must be here somewhere."

"Maybe they got out of the building?"

"Let's make a bet." As the man from the window speaks, I hear a sinister smile in his words. "Whoever catches them gets the next bottle of wine we find."

One of the men in front of the fruit stand pulls back the lever on his automatic rifle as he snickers. "It'll be me this time."

My hand curls into a tight fist as I hear their taunts and sneers. Are we just their prey? I feel my blood boil as I watch the two men on the street turn to each other. "You go to the left. I'll swing around to the right. We'll share the prize between us."

They both depart in opposite directions. As I hear their footsteps fading away, I can't get their vile words out of my head. They spoke about shooting us as if it was nothing... as if it was a game. How could they talk about it like that?

I can't hear their footsteps anymore. Are they gone?

Behind me, Salman slowly rises to his feet and checks our surroundings, including the window. He pauses for a long moment before setting his hand on my shoulder. "Run toward the building straight ahead. It'll keep us out of their vantage point."

As I stand up, I notice that Salman is holding his pistol in his free hand. Does he really know how to use that?

"Go now, Zaid."

I don't hesitate. Without a second thought, I'm suddenly dashing across the street and into the thick, black smog. I can barely breathe in it, but it doesn't slow me down as my shoes beat against the ground. I feel them all around me: Salman, Fatima, and the brothers. Salman gets a step ahead of me and Fatima, while the brothers are behind us.

But then I hear a voice, the one from upstairs. "Over there!"

They've spotted us! In the next instant, shrilling gunfire extinguishes the silence.

Rat-at-at-at!

I don't stop. I can't stop. I run faster. Faster. And faster. *Don't look back, Zaid.* My feet barely touch the pavement as I dart through the smoke. My breaths are quick—gasping almost—as I run for my very life. It's just like that night it all started. The gunfire is right on top of us. Its roar drowns out almost any thought. They can't make us out in the smoke, can they?

The gunfire is thunderous. A bullet strikes the ground ahead of me. I hear the piercing collision and feel it bounce off the road. Something flies right by my skull. It brushes my hair with lightning speed, barely missing my head. It's a bullet. Half an inch closer and it would have—can't think about that now!

Keep running, Zaid! Keep going. Don't stop! Don't stop! Don't stop!

I can't see ten feet ahead of me, but I don't slow down. Their heavy footsteps are behind us as the gunfire roars on. They're coming fast. How far are they? I don't dare look back. My eyes suddenly widen right as my foot hits something, sending me stumbling.

Don't fall, Zaid! Catching myself, I regain my balance and keep running forward. I see the corner of the brick building run right by me. Several bullets pelt it, kicking up dust. The footsteps behind are louder than ever! The men call out to one another.

"Keep moving!" Salman yells over the bullets. "Don't stop!"

I'm hardly a step behind him, and I sense the two brothers at my side. I don't think of how I am keeping up with them all.

It's endless—the gunfire. It extinguishes everything else as bullets cut through the fog. My heart frantically beats against my chest, pounding so hard that I hear it ringing in my ears.

The men are getting closer. Their footsteps are growing louder—no, they're growing softer. I—I can't tell! I can't think of anything right now except to keep running. Keep running and don't stop.

We're deep into the thick smoke. It's so hot. I can't breathe. I still can't make out what's even a few feet ahead of me, but I follow the sound of Salman's steps. It's all I can do. The gunfire seems distant now and I can't sense any bullets. I don't know if we're leaving them behind or if I'm just too focused on Salman. It doesn't matter. All that matters is that I keep running.

The sack is lighter than ever as it drags behind me. Scorched buildings are a blur all around. My vision tunnels in on the walkway, ignoring everything else. My heart won't stop pounding. And the terror won't die down. The smoke is suffocating, but I push forward.

"To the left!" Salman suddenly roars. "Behind the wall!"

Where is—catching sight of him through the mist, I see him divert from the sidewalk. I follow Salman and Fatima behind the broken brick wall. Surrounded by rubble, it stands by itself. The wall is just about my height and barely manages to stay upright. A push and it'll topple over. However, it's wide enough for us to all hide behind, and maybe the thick smoke will protect us from being seen from the sides. It's our only hope.

The ground beneath us is scorching. I feel it against the bottoms of my shoes. It would burn my hands if I touched it. The wall is blistering too. There's so much smoke, and it's a struggle just to breathe. My lungs try to let out a desperate cough, but I force it to stay in.

Crouching down, I hesitantly peer over the wall. Everything beyond the sidewalk is shrouded in smog. Are those voices? It takes my mind a second to focus. There are some people—three, no four— on the road. They're just like us, only a few years older than me.

Didn't they hear the gunfire? They need to get off the road. I almost stand up and call them over to us.

But I never get the chance.

The thunderous and deafening bellows of gunfire break the smoky silence. Bullets rip out of the black fog and start flying everywhere with a violent vengeance. I duck behind the wall, shutting

101

my eyes. A few bullets break against the wall, causing it to quiver. I hear them brutally smashing against brick, concrete, and metal.

They've found us.

We can't move. Their rounds are raining everywhere. I stay against the wall, afraid to open my eyes and scarcely able to stop myself from trembling. The shooting goes on. Round after round breaks against our barrier. How many bullets is that? Hundreds? There's no end to them.

Wait… I'm wrong. Almost none of the bullets are hitting the wall. It sounds like they're hitting almost everywhere but here. Are they not aiming at us? I can't tell.

I don't know where the courage comes from, but I find myself peering over the barrier. The whizzing pellets slice in and out of the smog. The bullets aren't intended for us. They're firing at something else. I see somebody in the smoke. It's… a man. Dressed in full military gear, he has his rifle aimed and firing perpendicular to us. He lets it loose as he takes cover behind a burnt vehicle along with another figure. His gun roars, lighting up the smoke in bright flashes as his bullets cut into the fog.

I hear a scream. It's coming from where he shot at. Then another. The cries are as sharp and gut-wrenching as the ones from the night of the attack.

Opposite of the soldier, somebody appears crouched down behind a merchant's shot up cart. I can't make out his clothing. A comrade shoots alongside him as well. They're aiming at the soldiers. Are those AK-47s? Those men raucously snarl as they pull their triggers and spray their bullets all over the soldiers' barrier.

My gaze whips back to the soldiers. They're gone. There's no sign of them anywhere. The fog makes it so hard to see anything. But more bullets fly out from the soldiers' side of the battle.

The shooting is relentless from both sides. Showers of bullets strike against the ground, vehicles, and walls. They destroy everything in their path. Dirt is kicked up on both sides, mixing in with the fog. I can't keep up with any of it. All I can do is watch the street go to ruin—watch shops, vehicles, and stands turn into wreckage. An explosion erupts not far away, causing me to flinch. It's on the soldiers' side. Then a second blast goes off. They're loud enough to put out the gunfire. But it doesn't distract any of the shooting. Above the bombardment, I hear the men's voices. However, mixed with the bullets, it's all a blur.

The city's destruction has again begun. And we're trapped in it.

More soldiers appear out of the smog. As each one appears, it's as if another rebel does too. My ears grow deaf with all the shooting. A bullet catches the top of the wall, forcing me to duck back down. I hear the sound of gunfire tearing into flesh. It's followed by screams. I make out one of the voices. I can't tell which side it's coming from. They're trying to order an airstrike. They're yelling out their orders. However, the two men with radios are down. A different man suddenly screams in anguish. I don't make out his words, but I hear the voice of another one. He's yelling at the others to fall back.

The rest of the group is behind me. They're cowering behind the wall, their gazes aimed at the ground. I don't know what makes me do it: courage or stupidity. But no matter what it is, I find myself again looking over the wall, unable to tear my eyes away as the scene unfolds.

The voracious shooting doesn't end. It intensifies. But now it's lopsided in the rebel's favor. A handful of them step into view, continuing to pull their triggers. Their clothes are dirty, and their faces are merciless. Endless streams of bullets rip through the smoke, and there are just as many screams. Some aren't the cries of men... but of women.

My eyes widen. Where is that group? The one I saw before the shooting? I crouch down behind the barrier. Looking through a crack in the wall, I find them. They're right where I last saw them, but now they're lying in the middle of the street... and they're not moving. They're resting there, just like Jari was. Their clothing holds dark stains... it's blood. For a moment, everything becomes inaudible as I stare at the victims of the battle's crossfire.

The rebels advance. Heavy boots beating against the ground, their weapons stay raised as they keep shooting. Are they firing at the retreating soldiers? I can't see from my angle behind the wall. Why... why is this happening?

The shooting begins to slow down. I hear some footsteps chase after the soldiers. Then the gunfire disappears into the fog, along with the pursuing footsteps. The remaining rebels scatter across the road. One of the rebels stops and towers over one of the people caught in the crossfire. He aims his gun down at the body. What's he doing? There's a moment of peace. Then his gun goes off and the body jumps with a jolt.

I clench my chest. As I horrifically stare at the scene, I can't feel my heartbeat. He... he just shot a body, a corpse. I hear one of their sharp voices cut through the air. "That should be the last of them here."

"We need to get indoors before they start shelling this area." That's one of the men who was chasing us. I recognize his vile, arrogant voice. Keeping my gaze on the defaced corpse, I know where I've heard that voice before. It sounds just like the man who beckoned Jari to his demise.

"I thought you were looking for supplies?"

"We were, but then we found a group. We were trying to catch them."

"Are they here?"

"We chased them up until we saw you battling the soldiers."

"Search for them. We don't know what they saw or know."

Is that why they're after us? They're afraid we know something that can help the military? And based on a hunch, they'd just—just… this can't be happening.

My eyes are wide with horror as I keep staring at the bodies through the crack. My heart is shivering. I feel it. The rebel's footsteps are all around us. Any moment, one of them will step out of the black fog and find us.

I catch sight of something. There's somebody on the opposite side of the road. It's not a soldier… or a rebel. It's a boy. He's no older than me and is hiding behind some wooden crates. I can barely see his eyes and the top of his head as he looks out from between two boxes, but he catches my gaze. His expression is just as terrified as mine. Was he a part of that group? Did he see what happened to his friends?

"Search the buildings too." The arrogant voice speaks above everything else. "They could not have gotten far."

I sense the fear radiating off of everyone behind me. There's no way out. We're trapped here. If we step out, they'll see us. And if we don't, they'll find us sooner or later. Salman quietly pulls out his gun as if preparing to make a final stand. Is… is it really going to end like this?

My gaze again meets the boy's. He's trembling just as much as anybody. Just like me, he witnessed the madness and massacre unfold.

The heavy footsteps are everywhere. They violently kick down doors, call out to one another, and fire into buildings. I almost wince with each sound. There's nothing I can do. Nothing any of us can do. With every step, I start to quiver harder and faster. Because with every step, they're closer to finding us.

This is it. After everything, it will all end like this.

Without thinking, I glance up at the heavens. I can't even see the skies through the smog. Suffocating from the smoke and drenched in my own sweat, I feel tears forming in my eyes. But I offer the prayer of any condemned man or woman… the prayer for salvation.

You didn't answer my prayers for Jari. B—but please… please don't condemn us here.

I lower my head and again lock gazes with the boy. He's whispering something to himself. For a long moment, everything becomes peaceful. It's as if time has stopped. There's a sudden change in his eyes and he does something—something I hardly fathom.

…he smiles.

"Over there! I see one of them!" the arrogant voice cries out.

The boy is on his feet, attracting the attention of every rebel. He's not trembling anymore. He stands there long enough for them to see him.

Without hesitating, he takes off into the thick smoke. Deafening gunfire surrounds us as they try to shoot him down… but they can't. Their bullets strike everything but him.

"After him!"

All the rebels charge and stumble out of the buildings and shops. They dart right past us. In the next instant, they're all pursuing him, blindly firing into the smog as they disappear.

And within moments, we are alone.

CHAPTER 12
FORSAKEN NIGHT

I don't know how long we hide behind the wall. But I can't tear my gaze away from where that boy hid. The scene replays in my head again and again. Just when it all seemed lost, he rescued us. They chased that boy into the smog; they chased him until their gunfire became faint and distant ... and we were saved.

Nothing is spoken. I don't think any of the others saw what happened. They must know I witnessed what the men chased after, but they don't ask me about it. Maybe they can see it on my face, or maybe they're just thankful that the men are gone.

Squeezing the top of the wall with one hand, I can't forget the look in the boy's eyes. It all happened so fast. He knew what would happen. They were looking for us, not him. But he still did it.

My gaze becomes downcast. Was that boy the answer to my desperate prayer? I didn't even know his name—never said a word to him. Yet he risked his life for us. For all I know, he may have *given* his life for us.

Shutting my eyes, I say the prayer I was taught to say whenever we hear of a death. It's the same one I spoke over Jari. The identical gut-wrenching feeling I felt when I recited it beside him again washes over me.

"To God we belong, and to Him we all return."

Feeling a hand on my shoulder, I look back at Salman. He's ready to move on and so are the others. I'm not, but I don't argue. The sun is long gone by the time we leave the wall. If it wasn't for the smoke, I'm sure I would witness the stars popping up in the heavens.

The idea of a starry night seems as distant as the thought of my mother's warm arms.

We start making our way down the desolated street. The bottoms of my shoes feel a little thinner and worn out. I don't know if it is the hot ground or all the walking. Either way, I don't take the time to examine them. I hardly even notice the difference, unable to fully bring my mind into the present.

The boy's eyes… I know where I've seen them before. They reminded me of Jari's. They looked just like Jari's before he stepped out of the shop and faced those vile men.

Are those the eyes of courage?

The odor of burnt wood is mixed in with the same foul stench of death—the same stench that was everywhere last night. It's worse than before. Just the thought of how much death must be surrounding us causes me to shudder.

The smog remains dense. There seem to be more distant explosions tonight. I hear them almost constantly and see some cut through the mist, but they're all far enough that our footsteps drown most of them out.

Salman and Faisal lead the way with Amaan a step behind them. I'm a pace behind Fatima with my heavy sack slung over my already sore shoulder. I pick up the whispers between the brothers and Salman. However, I don't have the energy to decipher what they're saying to one another.

I scarcely keep my mind focused, not even watching where I'm stepping as I follow them. My thoughts keep going back to that boy's and Jari's eyes. This was not the first time I've seen that gleam. I finally remember where I've met that gaze before any of this even began. They were worn by Nabeel.

***

Two days before Nabeel leaves for the last time, I find him standing at the kitchen counter with his friend, Zakariah. I don't know his rank, but Zakariah serves directly under Nabeel in the army and only lives two miles down the road. The two of them always seem to be on leave at the same time.

Their voices are low, almost secretive, but I catch the look in Nabeel's eye. Except back then, I didn't recognize it.

"What are you guys talking about?"

Seeing me enter and hearing my voice, they both look my way before exchanging glances. That gleam in Nabeel's eyes disappears.

I excitedly run up to the two of them. "Tell me!"

Nabeel looks back down at me as he stops leaning against the counter. Reaching down, he ruffles my hair. "You're too young to know about that, Zaid."

"Aww, what's that about? I'm not part of the group now—"

My brother playfully flicks me on the forehead as he crouches down a little. "I'm sorry, buddy. Maybe next time."

"You're always saying that."

Zakariah laughs as he comes closer to me. He puts his hand on my shoulder. "That's just not fair, Nabeel. You're a horrible brother for leaving Zaid out like that."

I see a concerned expression momentarily wash over Nabeel's face.

However, Zakariah glances up at Nabeel and shoots him a quick wink as he continues. "Why don't I just tell you then?"

My eyes light up. "Really! You're the best, Zakariah."

Coming to his knees, he puts his arm around my shoulders and leans close, acting as if he is about to tell me the world's biggest secret. "You see, Zaid, your brother and I were having a discussion about which one of us would win in a wrestling match. We all know that I'm stronger, but he just won't admit it." He sighs and shakes his head as he looks back at Nabeel. "But you agree with me, don't you, Zaid?"

I don't hesitate to respond. "No way!"

He moves his head back in surprise. "Huh?"

"Sure you're pretty strong, but my brother would beat you!"

Zakariah is slow to reply, taken aback by the statement. "C'mon, Zaid. You do realize that I'm older than him—"

"Age has nothing to do with it, Zakariah! My brother was the school's wrestling champion. He wouldn't lose to you." I whip my head to look back at Nabeel. "Right, big brother?"

Nabeel is slightly smiling now.

With a chuckle, Zakariah rises back to his feet. "Alright, alright. Well, I best be off, Nabeel. We can finish our little *discussion* next time."

Nabeel shakes his hand. "Give my greetings to your folks."

"I will." Zakariah grabs my shoulder and gives it a squeeze. "See you, Zaid—no, sorry: *Dr. Zaid*."

Did he really just call me that? How did he know?

Hearing Zakariah's footsteps grow faint, I turn back to Nabeel. He opens the fridge door and rummages through it.

"You told him?" I ask.

Nabeel doesn't look my way. "I tell everyone."

I watch him pull out a pound of chicken meat rolled up in brown paper as he turns back to me.

"Aisha is visiting her parents tonight and *Abbi* and *Ummi* are having dinner with friends. So looks like it'll just be you and me." Nabeel shoots me a wink. "I'm going to make some *shwarma* for dinner. Just the way you like it: tomatoes, lettuce, onions, *lots* of chicken, and even more spices." He starts setting the ingredients on the countertop. "I went by Sohail's shop today. The mangoes he was selling were ripe, so I picked some up. We can have them for dessert. That is if we have room."

110

He looks back at me with a smile, but it fades when he sees my expression.

"What's wrong, Zaid?"

I glance at the ground before replying, "I don't think I want to be a doctor anymore."

"Why not?"

"...I don't think I can."

He takes a few steps toward me before crouching down to come to my eye level, urging me to continue.

"Ms. Farooq said I'm not smart enough."

"She did?"

"I got the lowest score in the class on the last math test. She said I'm not cut out for it."

"I didn't realize Ms. Farooq could tell the future."

I don't respond.

"Did you tell *Abbi* or *Ummi?*"

I shake my head.

He takes a deep breath and glances down at my feet. His eyes look like he's weighing something, wondering if he should say it or not. When he does speak, his voice is different. It's no longer speaking to me as my younger brother but as his friend. "You know, Zaid, Zakariah was joking about what we were talking about."

"Really?"

He nods before his gaze focuses back on me. "Not even a few weeks ago, my soldiers and I were in a bit of a... well, situation."

"What happened?"

"We were in Homs. The people we were fighting—the rebels—had heavy control of some neighborhoods. We were trying to take them back. It was..."

A silence ensues as he searches for the word.

"Difficult." Nabeel pauses. "Some soldiers were pinned. The army tried an airstrike to break the rebel lines. It was a heavy bombardment that leveled entire streets. The cost was high. But we couldn't break their lines."

I don't interrupt him.

"Our intelligence said it was a lost cause. We were ordered to abandon the soldiers. They said we would lose more men than we would save. But even the army's 'intelligence' doesn't know everything." He looks away. "Zakariah and I disobeyed our commanding officer. As did our men. Those soldiers that were pinned weren't just men. They were my friends... my brothers. And I would never abandon them, even if it led to..."

For a moment, his eyes again display that same gleam, but it disappears as quickly as it came.

His gaze again meets mine. It's firmer this time, stronger. "It doesn't matter what people say, Zaid. It doesn't matter what the facts say. All that matters is what *you* say. And, maybe more importantly, what you *do*."

I hang on his words, unable to say anything.

"Why do you want to be a doctor, Zaid?"

"I've always wanted to."

"But why?"

"Because... I don't want to see people suffer. I... I want to be the one to help others. I want to save lives, make a difference and put others before myself. I want to make this world a better place. Just like the *Imam* always talks about."

Nabeel smiles. "Never forget that. And never go back on your word. No matter what happens. Please never forget one thing, Zaid: I love you. No matter the circumstance—no matter if I'm so far from you that you may never see me again, know that I'm with you." He presses his finger against my heart. "I believe in you, Zaid."

The Heart of Aleppo

***

The memory fades, and I'm back in the black smog. There is no Nabeel or Zakariah here. Just us. The warmth of my home is replaced with numb feet, pain-filled ankles, and aching legs. More than anything else, it's replaced with the coldness of the desolate streets. This fog just goes on… and on… and on…

The longer we go, the more my mind slowly focuses on the present. The pain and soreness are only amplified tonight. Unlike before, we hardly see anybody on the roads. I think we're the only ones on these deserted streets. Maybe everyone else was wise enough to just stay put.

I can't distinguish the streets apart. It's hard enough to even make anything out in this darkness. It's all one giant blur now, just one pile of debris to the next with no end in sight. I almost forget that every pile of rubble was once a proud building.

Numb to all this, I don't look left or right. I don't even look straight ahead. Keeping my eyes downcast, I simply watch my feet take one step after another. I'm a zombie. We make it at least a few miles before my feet feel like drenched logs, but I'm used to this battle by now and try to not let it slow me down.

The corpses aren't hard to find. Men, women, and children… some younger than me. But, tonight, I don't feel anything. Maybe the shock is just too much and my mind can't cope with any more of this. Or maybe I've grown numb to the carnage. My mind counts the bodies. I don't know why. I try to stop myself, but I'm powerless to do so. Each time it gets close to fifty, I lose count and start over. How can there be this much death when the city was so alive just a few days ago?

Every step is more difficult than the last. My legs just want to fall off. After a while, I start telling my mind that there are only a few

113

steps left until we stop. I know I'm lying to myself, but I do it anyway. The *Imam* always said lying was not a sin if it is done to protect somebody. I hope that protecting my sanity counts.

Just need to make it to that building. We'll stop and rest in that alley. Only a few more steps to that…

That helps a bit. I don't know how long I do that for. It feels like hours. But I guess it really doesn't matter anymore. All that matters is that we keep moving forward. We ignore the pain, the smog, the destruction, and just take one step after the other. It's all that we can do now.

The trouble I had breathing in all this smoke and fog is gone. I don't know if the smoke is getting any thinner or if I've just adapted to it. The strap grows heavier. It's soaked with my sweat. Every now and again, I switch my sack over to the opposite shoulder in an effort to alleviate the pain. But after a while, either shoulder hurts just as badly as the other.

The two brothers carry almost nothing. They glance back at me from time to time. A couple of times they even call out when I'm falling behind; however, neither make any offer to hold my baggage for me. They keep talking to Salman. I still can't make out their exact words, but it sounds like they're discussing what all they heard on the radio.

Fatima offers to carry the sack more than once. However, I don't let her. She stays alongside me, slowing down when I do. We don't really talk. She seems just as lost in her thoughts as I am.

It's just like the night before, except now the streets are littered with so much more destruction. The sound of silence is louder than ever, reminding us that we're trapped in this desolation and that there won't be any salvation tonight. I try to get it out of my head, but the silence is too loud.

Tonight, my heart bears a heavier weight. Maybe it's because I'm so tired. Maybe it's because of all the death surrounding us. But I think it's something else. I can't forget the boy's courageous eyes, and I will never forget how another stranger gave his life for mine. Two people sacrificed themselves without a second thought. Above all, one question consumes my mind:

Am I worth that?

***

"Get off the road!"

As Salman's cry echoes in my head, I look up to see the yellow headlights breaking through the fog. It's coming fast. And it's headed right for us.

I don't think. I drop the sack. My legs instinctively fall out from under me and I go toppling onto the side of the road. Crashing face first onto the dirty ground, I ignore all the pain ringing through my body. I lay there flat, unmoving. The rest of the group's footsteps dart off somewhere.

The sputtering roar of an engine comes into earshot. It's a jeep. Above the ignition, I pick up the voices of men. They sound like the voices that were chasing us.

The jeep's wheels are crushing down on the road, piercingly crunching whatever they're running over. Is it climbing over something? It sounds like it's running over—no, it can't be.

I'll be in view of those men within seconds now. Where is everyone else? Eyes shut, I can't feel them anywhere. I'm not in the jeep's path, right?

Don't move, Zaid. Whatever you do, don't move a muscle or make a sound. Don't even blink. And don't breathe.

As the crunching wheels and roaring engine grow closer, I feel my heart pounding faster. *Allah*, please make me invisible to them. Please!

The jeep's engine is raucous. It's closer than ever. I smell the stench of diesel. The voices are unruly. Their hoots drive a fear-ridden stake straight through me. They're right on top of me. I hold my breath as I face away from the vehicle. Stopping my hand from forming into a tight fist, I don't move a muscle. I don't know if it's my willpower or if I'm just paralyzed with terror. I feel a light shine on me. The hair on the back of my neck stands up under the warm illumination. It's bright. It stays on me for a long moment. My heart suddenly stops. Did they—

The jeep passes by me and the light leaves me. The engine and the voices begin to fade away.

I stay on the ground for several moments after the jeep disappears into the night. It's over as quickly as it began. Gaining control of myself, I finally open my eyes. I'm back in the desolate night with nothing but the sound of silence around me.

Staggering to my feet, I see the others. They're coming up from behind a wrecked van. Their faces appear relieved as they look at me. Turning away, I pick up my heavy sack with a grunt and sling it back onto my shoulder. With how tired I am, I may as well have picked up a car.

I take a deep breath, regaining my composure. My legs shake a bit as they search for their strength. A part of me wonders if it may not have just been better if those men had seen me.

Maybe that way, I would have escaped this.

***

"Are you okay, Fatima?" We're again trudging through the darkness and desolation when my soft words break the silence. Salman and the two brothers are a bit too far to hear my words, but Fatima walks alongside me.

She turns to meet my gaze. Weakly smiling, her eyes are just as weary as mine. "I'm fine."

"Do you need some water?"

"Not right now, but thank you."

"What are you thinking about?"

"Life." She takes a deep breath. "Only two and a half days ago, we were in school. We were walking to the bus stop. And now... I don't even recognize where we are anymore. It's like we're not even in Aleppo."

I stay silent.

"I keep thinking about them all: my parents, your parents, Bilal, Aisha, and Nabeel. Do you keep seeing their faces?"

"I can't stop myself." I hold back any tears or remorse. "I keep seeing all their faces, hearing all their voices, feeling all their warmth. And the more I do, the more I feel trapped here."

She glances away for a moment, as if worried about saying what she's thinking. "...Zaid?"

"Yes?"

"Will... will we ever see them again?"

I don't reply as my gaze drifts back onto the road.

"Do you think we will, Zaid?"

After a long moment, I look back at her. "God-willing, we will."

God-willing. In the past, I always said those words with hope. Tonight, I say them so I don't have to say what I truly feel. And from the look in her eyes, she knows it.

CHAPTER 13
TRUE INTENTIONS

They stop in front of a run-down shop. It's not nearly as damaged as most of the other buildings we've come across. Still in the back of the pack with Fatima, I watch Salman and Faisal go in first to make sure it's clear. Their flashlights scan the insides for what feels like minutes.

My feet are beyond numb. I've been carrying them like logs for the past few miles. A part of me doesn't want to even wait for them to call us in. It doesn't really matter anyway.

Finally, I hear Salman's voice beckoning us forward.

Amaan heads straight in without hesitating, but I let Fatima go before me. I lug my heavy and stiff legs up the shop's steps. They hit the ground hard with each stride. They're going to be in real pain tomorrow. More than ever before.

I'm exhausted as I enter the building. I want to collapse. However, it doesn't feel like we've been traveling for the entire night. I would guess it's not even midnight yet.

My eyes adjust to the darkness inside. This must have been a pottery store. Clay ceramics line up the shelves and display cases. Even in the dark, I can distinguish their craftsmanship. Wide, tall, slender, and thick, each one is handmade to perfection. A few vases are shattered on the ground, their remnants still scattered across the floor, but this place looks mostly untouched.

I can see the back door from where I stand. It's been ripped wide-open and leads into an alley. God-willing, whoever was inside made it out that way and to safety. I don't know who lived here before, but now standing in their abandoned shop, I can't help but feel a connection with them.

"We'll rest here for an hour." Salman's voice is the same as it's been since everything began: authoritative. He tries one of the lamps in vain. "Then we'll keep moving until dawn."

"Where are we headed?" My cracked lips are so parched that I can hardly speak.

"Still back toward Ballermoun."

I look at Faisal and Amaan "Even you two?"

"We're going with you. We don't have anywhere else to go. Not after our parents…" Faisal pauses as his gaze drifts onto my sack. "Can we have some food, Zaid?"

There's a long silence. None of them want to carry it, none of them offered to hold it, but they all want to eat from it. I don't know why that makes my blood boil. Without a word, I sling the sack off of my shoulder and catch it in my hand. I hurl it between the three of them. It nearly smashes Faisal's foot before he jumps back. Instead, it hits the ground with a loud thud.

"Get it yourself." I turn and leave them.

Their stares burn into the back of my skull, but I ignore them.

The staircase is close to the back door. Just like any other shop and home in this city, it's a narrow stairwell. As I make my way through it, I see several pictures lining the wall. They're hanging perfectly level and are neatly organized. It's just like *Ummi* hangs all of our photos. If I didn't know any better, I would say that I am back home.

I stop at one of the photos. I can't really make it out in the darkness, but I think that the frame is golden. I run my hand over the casing. It's smooth with rigid corners, feeling just like the one that frames Nabeel's photo from his military ceremony.

Staying there for a long moment, I close my eyes and keep my hand on it. I take a deep breath. Then another. For a moment, I'm

119

back in my staircase—back home on those creaky steps and in front of all those photos. I can't feel any of the soreness or pain. If only... if only I could suddenly arrive back there with a wish.

I open my eyes before any tears have the chance to stream down my cheeks. Turning away, I keep going toward the second floor.

Entering the corridor, I stagger toward the first door I see. It's open just a crack. I give it an effortless push, and it swings open to reveal the room on the other side. I try the lamp sitting on a table. I don't have any hope as I do, but it suddenly turns on and breaks the darkness. I stand there for a moment, stunned.

The dim light reflects off everything. This bedroom must have belonged to a child. There's a football in one corner resting next to the dresser. It's dirty with marks all over it. The bed is concealed in a blanket decorated with bright trucks. It seems ruffled, as if somebody occupied it only moments ago.

The closet has no door, revealing a multitude of hanging clothes. There are some traditional *thobes* in a variety of colors. Alongside them are western shorts, jeans, and shirts.

Coming to the bed, I notice the picture sitting on the bedside table. There's a man dressed in a black and gold *thobe*. He's a little bit heavy set. Riding on his shoulders is a boy. The child is six... maybe seven, hardly half my own age. The man holds the boy steady as the boy rests his elbows and chin on the man's head. They're both beaming with joy.

I recognize the backdrop. It's the National Museum. *Abbi* and I went there all the time, and Nabeel promised to take me there last time he visited home.

Weariness washes away the memories. As I fall onto the bed, a breath of fresh air floods my body. Sinking right into the mattress, I imagine that it's mine. It feels just like it: soft but springy. It sucks me right in. My legs hang off, but I don't have the energy left to heave them onto the mattress.

120

Taking a deep breath, I lose myself to the moment. This bed feels just like my own. The same one *Ummi, Abbi,* Aisha, and sometimes Nabeel would read me stories at. The same one I woke up on before being thrown into this...

I can still hear their voices, still feel their warmth. When they were here, when my family was here, I never knew what fear was. I was always safe—they always kept me safe. But now they're gone... maybe forever.

A tear slowly runs down my dirty cheek. I don't wipe it. I can't find the strength.

It doesn't take any effort to close my eyes. There is nobody here to read me stories tonight, no mother to kiss me on the forehead. Instead, my only companion is a mix of weariness, fear, and tears. And so I lay here alone until I cry myself to sleep.

***

I loudly knock on the closed door. My thumps echo down the hallway as my feet impatiently tap on the ground. But the door doesn't open. After a long moment, I beat against the door once more, louder this time as I hope—

"Why are you standing outside of Nabeel's door?"

Whipping around, I see *Ummi* standing behind me. Her arms are lightly crossed as she smiles. How long has she been standing there? "Nabeel promised to take me to the National Museum," I reply. "We're going to see The Hall of Arslan Tash and Tell Ahmar."

"He just arrived last night, Zaid. Let him rest."

"But he promised."

She shakes her head as she takes a step toward me. "Nabeel has a lot to do today, Zaid. You should let him be."

"We talked yesterday on the phone before he came and—"

121

"Come, Zaid."

Is she not even listening to me? "But I haven't seen him since he got back."

"You can see him later. Why don't you go find Bilal?" My mother's hand comes onto my back and ushers me away from Nabeel's door. "He's going to go deliver some rugs at Dr. Farah Khan's office. You can go ask her those questions you were asking last night about being a doctor."

I don't resist as she gently escorts me toward the staircase. Halfway there, I shoot a hopeful glance back at the door. Maybe he'll open the door. Right now. And we'll go to the museum.

But he never does.

***

My eyes are slow to open, eyelids still feeling heavy. As I gradually come to my senses, my mind is even slower to awaken. It clings to the memory like a leech, refusing to let go until forcefully stripped off of it.

The peace of standing right outside Nabeel's room is immediately replaced with reality. I feel just as bad, both inside and out, as I did before I fell asleep. Maybe a bit more so now. The pain is mixed with even more soreness, but at least my feet are not completely numb anymore.

I don't make any effort to get up; instead, I try to let myself get every second of rest possible. I remember when the dream occurred. It was during Nabeel's last visit and a few days before I saw Zakariah and him in the kitchen.

Why do a few months ago feel like another lifetime?

That old life is gone. Staying on my back, I replay all that's happened, everything from the night the attack began until now, as I keep my eyes glued to the ceiling. It's a blur of chaos and violence. *This* is now my reality.

The dim, flickering lamp barely lights up the room. It's just as dark outside as when I fell asleep. For once, it seems almost quiet. There's no distant gunfire, constant explosions, or hungry flames. All that can be heard is an eerie stillness. The silence is scarier than the destruction. We all know it's just a façade. Out there, it's anything but safe. Is this what people mean when they say 'calm before the storm?'

It must be nearing time to go now. As badly as I want to fall back asleep, I know we have to keep on moving. I notice something on the bedside table as I rise up. I blink twice to make sure I'm not hallucinating. It's some bread, a handful of dates, and a sliced up mango on a plate. There's a glass of water next to it.

After staring at it for a moment, my stomach painfully grumbles.

I've never felt this famished before. I don't think. I simply react and snatch the plate. My heart is pounding with excitement. My mouth is watering. Devouring the food, I down it in large gulps. I violently stuff my face full like a demented wolf, trembling as I do.

The dates are thick and soft as I bite into them. Many of them contain seeds, but I swallow most of them. They're so much more filling than they look. So is the bread, dry as it is. I don't bother tearing pieces of the bread off with my hand, instead using my teeth. I attack the food so aggressively that sweat starts running down my face. I don't slow down. The quicker I gobble it all, the more my stomach thanks me.

Gulping down the last of the bread, I seize the sliced mango. The mango is sweet—sweeter than any I've ever tasted. Just one bite into the velvety yellow fruit and I forget everything else as it melts in my mouth. It's still cool, even in his heat. The sugar gives my body a much needed jolt.

A breath of fresh air, air that is pure from all this smoke and fire, flows through me. It takes me back home—back to my mother's kitchen. A part of me is fooled into thinking that I really am home. Unlike before, I dine on the mango slowly, letting each bite sit in my mouth for a long moment. I want to enjoy every second of it. The sweetness drowns out the fear and worries in my soul. Eating it with my hands, I don't worry about the sweet nectar running all over my fingers. I clean off the large seed by sucking it down. After going over it three times to make sure there is nothing left, I drink the juice off of my fingers.

I take a deep breath as the feast ends. My eyes stay on the empty plate. There's not even a crumb left. For a moment, the thought of what my mother would say if she saw me eating like this enters my mind. I've never eaten this way before, devouring it like a savage. Is that what's becoming of us?

Noticing the napkin that was left next to the plate, I wipe my fingers and mouth. I don't know who left that, but I'm sure I could guess. Fatima always knew how much I loved mangos. It's a love we both share.

My gaze stops at the picture frame on the bedside table. Staring at the building in the backdrop, I feel my heart sink for a moment. Nabeel and I never did go to the National Museum like he promised. Now, we may never get the chance.

I stop myself from lying back down. Salman said we'd take a one hour break. It must be well past time. I'm sure Salman will come through the doorway to wake me at any moment now. I'd better beat him to it.

I rise to my feet with a groan. The pain is all still there, but after that feast, I know I'll survive the rest of the night's journey. It was just what I needed.

Stretching my back, I enter the dark corridor. The mango's effects are finally kicking in as they fully wake me up. Without thinking, I let out a light burp. *Alhumdulillah.* That felt good. I look to the left and right. Seems like nobody else is upstairs.

I begin making my way to the staircase. No matter how much rest I get, it seems that I just wake more tired and sore than before. The *Imam* would always say that strength doesn't come from rest but from *Allah.* Even with all the rest in the world, you would have no strength without His will. I always thought that was just a saying he used to make us stay up later and longer at the *masjid,* but I'm finally beginning to understand what he meant.

I don't know why I keep thinking about Nabeel so much. First, it was while trekking here. Then it was the dream. Maybe it's because he always knew what to do, and if he was here, everything wouldn't seem so bleak and uncertain.

He was stationed far from Aleppo, close to the border by the Western Bank. I wonder if he is on his way here now. It's been two nights since the attack. The radio said the army is engaging the rebels. Is he here too? And if he is, is he safe? Those soldiers shot at the rebels even with those people in the middle of the road. They didn't care if they hit or missed them, and they've been bombing the city with no way of knowing if they're hurting civilians. Nabeel wouldn't do that. He would have rescued the civilians before attacking. I know it.

Arriving at the stairs, I start making my way down with one hand tightly grasping the handrail. Walking down the hall was no problem, but going downhill is a different story. My legs are boulders. I have to fight to keep myself from toppling down. Every step is a battle, but I don't make a sound. Just one foot after the other. A few steps down, I hear something. It sounds like a voice… muffled behind a closed door. I stop moving, trying to focus my ears and make out what they're saying.

"I'm sure they're sleeping… saw them. How… longer do we have to do this?"

I take another quiet step, attempting to hear them better. Something stops me from making myself known, as if a chain is holding me back. The voice is distorted, but I recognize it; it belongs to Amaan. His words are followed by another. I can't fully recognize the second voice behind the door, but I know it's not Salman's. It must be Faisal. "Not long now. We just need to go a bit further."

"Are we taking them with us?"

"The girl would be useful. She knew what she was doing when she treated your wound."

What are they talking about? Do they mean Fatima? I inch closer to the bottom of the staircase. Their tones sound so much different than before.

"And the boys?"

"Salman is strong. The other one... he's baggage. And he's weak. He'll slow us down. He's not like Salman. He hasn't been as open to us. I think he may have been on to us from the start."

I stand there, paralyzed. They can't be talking about—

"What if they don't want to come along?"

There's a pause before Faisal's voice breaks it. "Then we'll deal with them."

"Will they take us in?"

"If we approach them the right way, then the resistance will let us join their ranks with open arms. They know the fighting will only get worse from here. With everything that's coming, they'll take all the hands they can get."

My eyes widen. This can't be happening. Faisal's words echo in my head. My mind has to be playing tricks on me. There's no way they could be talking like this.

"Wake the others. It's time we go."

Hearing the door open, I try and hide behind the staircase's wall. Arms at my sides, my back and palms are pressed against the barrier. Their footsteps are softer than normal. I hold my breath as they walk right past me. With just a turn of their heads, they'll see me.

My mind is racing. What do I do? Do I attack them? Do I try and defeat them here or do I wait? Even if I wanted to, I don't think I could. I see the back of their heads as they come into view. They both suddenly stop. They're about to turn around. I know it. *Allah*, please make me invisible. Please protect me…

…they don't catch a whiff of me.

Going out of view, their soft footsteps begin to grow fainter until they're gone. But I don't feel any safer. I remain there for long after they've passed. Everything has changed. After everything they've seen, they would betray us and join the rebels? How could they—

I've got to warn Salman and Fatima.

CHAPTER 14
ESCAPE

They're all awake by the time I reach Salman and Fatima. The storeroom's lamp is illuminated. Salman's back is to me as he rummages through his sack. My mind is going crazy, a complete opposite of this calm room.

Amaan sees me at the doorway. He's standing close to his brother, not too far away from me. He politely nods at me before looking away. Is this the same person who was just speaking so menacingly?

Fatima is wiping her green eyes as she lets out an exasperated yawn. She looks as fresh as ever. Blinking several times to wake herself up, she looks at me before smiling.

I don't return the gesture. I can't think right now.

Salman is still looking through his bag. Bent over, his gun is on display as it hangs from his belt. Faisal's eyes are on it as he prepares his own things a few feet away. He exchanges a quick glance with Amaan.

I've got to tell them. *Think, Zaid, think!* I need to get Salman and Fatima alone. The other two might be armed. I think Faisal or Amaan have a knife, or maybe it was a dagger. They might try something if they realize that their secret is blown. We need to slip away when we get the chance.

"Glad to see you're awake."

Hearing the voice, I turn toward Faisal. He's staring at me and wears a slight smirk. There's a look in his eyes. I can't tell what's behind it. A fearful thought grips my soul: maybe I shouldn't have come straight here from the stairwell. I arrived only a couple of minutes after them.

Before I can say anything, Salman's tired and firm voice breaks the uneasy silence. "Zaid. Come get your sack."

I make my way into the room. My footsteps are heavy. The air is cold in here, and there's complete silence. I feel Faisal's gaze follow me, burning the side of my skull. Does he know?

"Are you okay, Zaid?" Fatima sounds genuinely concerned. Is it that obvious?

Crouching down and picking up my sack, I sling it over my shoulder as I look over at her. "It was a bad dream. Woke me right up. But I'm fine."

Salman walks right by me without a glance and heads toward the door. "Let's get going already."

Faisal is the one to respond. "We're just waiting on Zaid."

His voice sounds like it did behind that closed door. It's completely different from the boy we found in that darkened hallway. However, I don't let his tone rattle me, not missing a beat when I glance back at him. "I'm ready when you are."

***

I can't take my eyes off of the brothers. They're not leaving Salman alone, staying on either side of him. We go down the desolate streets just as before: Salman and the two brothers up front while Fatima stays alongside me in the rear.

This time, I can't see any of the destruction or feel any pain. I can't focus in on any of the misty surroundings, and the smoke isn't bothering me either. All I can do is stare at the brothers' backs as I hear their true intentions echo in my head over and over again.

I'm only a few paces behind them. If Faisal or Amaan are suspicious, they're doing a good job of hiding it. Neither even give me half a glance, keeping their eyes straight ahead or on Salman as they lowly speak to him. Like before, I can't make anything out. Are they trying to influence him? I wish I could hear what they were saying.

My heart won't settle down as it swings between being terrified and angry every few seconds. I can't get their voices out of my head, can't forget how they talked about us as if we were just animals.

I don't even know if Salman will believe me. He's been distant ever since we left Jari's shop, trusting no judgment other than his own. He was angry when I gave that woman food. He didn't trust me to wave down the helicopters. A part of me fears that he won't pay my suspicions any heed.

"What's bothering you, Zaid?"

Hearing Fatima's voice, I'm suddenly yanked back to reality. I look over and meet her inquisitive, green eyes. She looks like she's been staring at me for a while now. "Nothing."

My response comes out as a reaction, not realizing what I'm saying until the word is out of my mouth. Fatima doesn't believe it.

I take a deep breath. She's not taking her gaze off of me. Will she believe me? I move a little closer, leaving only a few inches between us. "Something is happening, Fatima."

"What?"

"They're planning something—Faisal and Amman, I mean." I make sure to keep my voice down. "They're not going with us to Ballermoun."

"But they—"

"They're going to join the rebels."

She falls silent. Her face doesn't show any reaction and she doesn't miss a step, but her eyes urge me to go on.

"I heard them a few minutes before they came to wake you up. They didn't know I was there. They've always intended this. They want to try and get us to go with them. If we don't go along, they're going to... going to get rid of us."

130

"I…" Her soft voice trails off. She glances up at their backs for a long moment before looking back at me. "Are you—?"

"Yes. I'm sure."

"What… what are we going to do?"

I start spitting out what I've been thinking all along. "Salman has a gun. I think they're armed too. I don't have anything and neither do you. If I ask Salman for the gun, it'll look suspicious. I don't think he'd even give it to me. We need to alert Salman without them finding out. But I think Faisal might be on to me."

"What are you thinking?"

"We slip away when they're not looking. We can lose them in the smog. You bandaged up Amaan's leg. How quickly can he run?"

"He can do almost everything with it, but he can't run at full speed. He barely escaped the soldiers earlier today."

"Then all we need to do is somehow warn Salman."

She takes a deep breath. It's all starting to settle in her head now, and she's handling it better than I thought she would. Finally, Fatima nods. The sweetness that is always in her voice is replaced with a determination I didn't know she possessed. "I'll get him away from them."

"How?"

Through her eyes, I see her mind at work. "Your sack. It's been bothering you all night. They all know it. Tell them you need someone to carry it. It won't look suspicious, and they won't offer. They haven't yet. But Salman will."

I nod after soaking in her words. "Okay."

"Don't do it yet." She puts her hand on my arm. "Wait at least an hour. We just started moving, and it'd look suspicious if you were already tired."

"How are we going to warm him when he's taking my sack?"

"Leave that to me. You focus on selling it to them."

"What if he doesn't believe us?"

"He will." Fatima looks straight ahead. "I know it."

***

The hour passes uneasily. All I feel is the pounding of my heart as every second goes by. I can't tell if my stomach is nervous or nauseated. Why do I want to throw up? The longer we go, the more Faisal and Amaan's words sink into my soul. This isn't a dream. They really are willing to kill us.

I don't have a watch and can't tell what time it is, but I know every step is another closer to the moment of truth. If I can get Salman to come back, we have a chance. But if they catch on... I don't even want to think of what could happen then.

"Do it now, Zaid."

Hearing Fatima's whisper and feeling her gently pat my shoulder, I take a deep breath. The other three are still no more than five or six paces ahead of us. I've been playing this out for an hour now with every scenario, both the good and the bad, running circles in my head. Now it's time. For a moment, I can't speak. But then I find my courage.

"Salman!"

My voice is louder than I intend it to be, echoing down the darkened street. At least it gets their attention. He arrives at a gradual halt after a few more steps and turns back to me. So do the other two.

"I can't feel my shoulders." I keep my dry throat from cracking up, but I sell the weariness in my voice. "Could someone carry my sack for a little while?"

"We'll stop soon, Zaid."

"Please, Salman."

"Can't you toughen it out?" One of his hands annoyingly lands on his hip. "We're almost there now."

Keeping my eyes on Salman, I sense all of their gazes. My heart is trembling; however, I ignore the fear and cast away the doubt. I've got to finish this. We may not get another chance.

"No." I sling the bag off of my shoulder and drop it onto the ground. It lands with a thud. "I've been carrying this the whole time, and now it's somebody else's turn."

Letting out an aggravated grunt, he looks at Faisal and Amaan. Neither of them says anything. I don't know why he expects them to offer any help. The moment is long, the silence uneasy. Finally, Salman glances back at me. "Fine."

His eyes are daggers as he makes his way toward us. Faisal and Amaan are not looking away as they watch on in silence. If they catch a whiff of us telling him, this could end badly. What's Fatima planning?

Coming to us, Salman stops and gives me a deadly stare. He bends over to pick the sack off of the ground. As he does, Fatima crouches down, acting as if she's helping him lift it up. With Salman's body in front of her, she's out of view from the brothers.

"We need to get away from them."

Hearing her faint whisper, Salman hesitates for a moment before looking at her face. Her words were so soft that he's trying to figure out if he really heard them. After blinking several times, he looks at me, his expression no longer angry.

Salman nods.

***

"Let's stop here." Salman comes to a halt in front of a building. My gaze comes onto the wrecked store. Like every place we've seen, it's been shot up, but this building is more damaged than any other we've stayed in yet. The windows have been blasted out and the building is riddled with bullets. Chunks of its walls lay scattered on the walkway and road.

"We still have some time left." Faisal puts his hand on Salman's shoulder, encouraging him to continue. "Keep moving."

"It's already starting to get light."

"We need to cover more ground."

"Zaid and Fatima are tired. I'm tired." Salman is selling a mix of annoyance and weariness in his tone. He readjusts my sack and his. "We need to rest."

"No—"

"Zaid, Fatima, and I are the ones who've been carrying the luggage," Salman snaps. "Unless you're about to offer to carry all our bags, we're done for the night."

For a moment, a disgusted expression washes over Faisal and I think he's about to cock back his fist and strike Salman. He stares at Salman for a moment—too long of a moment. But he doesn't make a move.

Salman takes a step toward the entrance, turning away from the brothers. As I come into his view, he sends me a quick wink. "Let's go inside."

Fatima and I follow Salman in without a word. As I pass the brothers, Amaan glances at Faisal. They're hesitating. Only when Faisal nods do the two of them follow us in.

I step over a rugged block of debris to arrive at the store's entrance. The front door is only hanging on one of its hinges. One touch too strong and it'll topple over. I feel the two brothers only a few steps behind me. Is there a reason Faisal was so adamant about continuing on? Maybe they have a plan of their own.

This place was a butcher shop. It's been ransacked. Nearly everything is broken or turned over, leaving it hardly recognizable. But I can make out the meat hooks hanging off of a line. Coming inside, Salman sets both sacks by his feet. Switching on his flashlight, he keeps it aimed at the floor as he turns around to look at Faisal and Amaan. "You guys check upstairs. I'll look around this floor with Zaid and Fatima."

"Chances are that if somebody's here, they'll be upstairs," Faisal begins as he steps closer to Salman. "Can I borrow the gun?"

"You have a knife, don't you?"

"What knife?"

"The one you've been wearing all night."

After a long pause, Faisal reaches under his shirt and toward his waistline. His eyes suddenly change when he touches something. He pulls out the switchblade and pops out the blade. His gaze comes on to me. "That's right. Forgot about that."

"Let's get a move on," Salman orders. "We need to check the place before dawn."

Faisal motions for his brother to follow, and Amaan does as he's told. I watch the two of them start heading toward the stairs. In my peripheral vision, Salman is starting to go through this floor, looking behind one of the closet doors and scanning it with his flashlight. Step by step, the two brothers grow further away. They don't look back.

I turn away when they reach the bottom of the stairs. Acting like I'm headed toward the storeroom, I listen to the wood creak beneath their feet. Their movements are sluggish, unhurried. Why are they moving so slowly? Do they know what's happening? I don't dare look their way, afraid that they'll catch me sneaking the peak. That'll settle any doubts they have.

Arriving at the storeroom, I shove the door open. The sturdy door swings on its hinges before lightly bouncing off of the wall. I glance into the empty room for a few moments, needing to play the part.

135

A presence appears behind me. I swiftly turn around and arrive face-to-face with Salman and Fatima. I didn't even hear them. His gaze is on me while she looks toward the staircase.

"Backdoor," he hisses. "Now."

Salman tosses my sack and I catch it with both hands. I steal one more look at the empty staircase before we quickly make our way toward the back of the shop. I'm in the lead. My heart is excited, mind racing. *Don't run, Zaid. That'll make too much noise. Walk fast but not too quickly.*

Leaving the shop's front room and entering a darkened corridor, we turn the corner and arrive at another hallway. I hear the creaking floorboards above us. Their steps are quick. They're moving much faster than they did up the stairs, but I can't tell exactly which part of the floor they're on.

I ignore all of the closed and open doors we pass. All I can focus on is the creaking floor and my own footsteps. Do they hear us like we hear them? Rounding another bend, the back door comes into view. *We're almost there! Keep moving!* It's wide open. A few early rays of dawn can be seen on the other side. The closer we get to it, the harder my heart pounds. The exit grows with every step as my vision tunnels on it.

"When we get outside, turn right and don't stop. They won't be able to see us from upstairs." Salman's voice sounds nervous. Is he scared? "Fatima, stay between us."

We made it.

Stepping outside, I barely get a glimpse at the desolation around us before a stinging pain pounds into my skull. The world spins chaotically. Next thing I know, I roughly hit the rigid ground on all fours. For a moment, I can't think as the throbbing pain in my head drowns out everything else. My knees get a bit scraped, and the fall leaves my hands aching.

Somebody towers above me. No, it's two people. Their presence is all too familiar.

"Going somewhere?"

CHAPTER 15
COURAGE

Looking up, my gaze falls on Faisal. With one of his hands balled into a tight fist, the other holds his unsheathed switchblade. Amaan stands by his side and is holding a knife too. They're not even five feet away. Salman and Fatima are directly behind me.

"Seems like we're in a dilemma now." Faisal's vile voice matches his gaze. His face is merciless, completely opposite of what it was when we found him in that dark corridor. His focus slowly drifts away from me and onto the others. "I hoped it would not come to this, but now you three have a choice."

A silence falls between us. My mind is racing and my heart is pounding as I remain on all fours. I feel myself trembling, but it's not from fear. Not anymore. Keeping my gaze on Faisal, one thought echoes in my mind above everything else: Salman still has the gun. But he's too close to them. I need to distract them—get their attention on me. I need to say something. Anything. Come on, Zaid.

"If you think we're willingly going to go along with you," I begin.

All eyes come onto me as they hear my words.

"If you think we'll just join the rebels like you." I don't know where I get the courage to speak as I slowly rise up to my knees and then onto my feet. "Then you've got another thing coming."

Amaan and Faisal focus on me. It's just the chance Salman needs.

Salman goes for his gun. He moves with blinding speed, trying to pull it out. But he hardly touches it before Faisal is upon him.

138

Knocking me to the side, Faisal steps up and violently shoves Salman square in the chest. Salman stumbles backward before he crashes into the brick wall.

It happens so fast that I don't get a chance to react. Grabbing Fatima by her shoulder, Faisal coarsely shoves her toward Amaan.

Amaan grabs Fatima's wrist. She lets out a squeal as he drags her to him. His words are cruel. "We don't care about you two. But she's coming with us, even if it's over your rotting corpses."

"Let her go!" Salman roars and whips out the gun. I nearly leap onto Amaan. But we both stop short of making any move.

The tip of Amaan's knife is pressed against Fatima's side. Any more pressure and it'll cut into her skin. Amaan's fist remains clenched around the weapon's hilt. His eyes are on both of us.

I can't believe this. He—he's not bluffing. One wrong move and he'll do it. My gaze locks with Fatima's. Fear courses through her eyes. She's terrified—trembling. These... these people. How could they turn on us like this?

"Drop the gun, Salman." Faisal and Amaan take a big step back as they yank Fatima with them. "Drop it or else."

Salman's pistol is trained on Amaan, but his eyes are glued to his sister. So are mine. My shaking hand curls into a tight fist. After everything we've done, after everything *she* did for him, he's using her as a hostage? These animals! The blood pouring through my veins is sizzling. With each passing second, my vision begins to tunnel around Fatima. I've got to do something.

"I said *drop* it," Faisal repeats.

Salman slowly crouches down and sets the pistol on the ground. I'm helpless. I can't do anything. Even with all the fury running through my veins, I can't make a move. They'll kill her. This can't be happening.

"Kick it over to me," Faisal commands, his words filled with apathy.

Salman hesitates.

"*Now.*"

Putting his toe against the weapon, Salman slides it across the ground.

The gun glides several feet before stopping by Faisal. His gaze doesn't leave Salman as he reaches down and picks it up before shoving it into his belt. He's smiling, maliciously smirking at our helplessness. What kind of a person is he?

Something happens inside, something I've never felt before. Humanity is washed away, and it's replaced by something else. My blood is beyond boiling. My heart is consumed by something far beyond rage as it quivers with an uncontainable tremor. *How dare they! How dare they use her like this!*

Faisal's vile gaze goes from Salman to me. "We're leaving. Try to follow, and you know what happens."

"I—I don't care if you go." Salman takes a deep breath. His voice is petrified. He's pleading—no, begging. I've never heard him like this before. There are tears in his eyes, the helpless tears of a beggar. "Leave her... please, leave her. And I won't stop you."

They don't reply. His words only make Faisal's smirk grow.

"Take whatever you want." Salman is desperate. He's about to break into tears. "Take the food, the supplies, and the gun. *Take me! Take me instead!* But..." Salman is trembling now. "...please... leave my sister alone."

Faisal doesn't even blink, doesn't even hesitate. "No."

...monsters. Both of them. His simple response drives a dagger through my heart. The shaking intensifies, and all I can say is one thing. "Did you lie?"

They both look at me.

"Did you lie about what happened the night of the attack?"

140

Amaan looks me dead in the eyes. There is no compassion behind his gaze. There is no remorse. There is only a void. "Yes. Our parents were never killed by any soldiers."

His voice is hollow as he utters those words. He doesn't even flinch. The lie doesn't bother him. I don't even recognize this boy anymore.

"We were orphans long before the attack. This rebellion. It's finally the chance for our lives to mean something."

"You—you're mad."

"No." He smiles. "We're patriots. Look around you. Look at all this destruction. This city is in ruins. The rebels may have invaded the city, but every bomb dropped—every shell aimed at this city has the military's name written on it. Is that where your loyalties are? To that dictator Assad? To that criminal? To the people who would throw every life in this city away for their own power?"

"I'm not loyal to any party." My voice rises with every word. "I'm loyal to my friends. To my family. To my fellow citizens of this city who are just as scared as the rest of us!"

"You're a coward." Amaan's words are sneering. "Both of you. You hide it behind your so-called righteousness. But people like us, we're the ones who are going to bring about change. You two will just die like the rest of the people cowering in fear."

They really believe that. They believe every word. I watch them both begin to leave, dragging Fatima with them as they take a few steps back. Her eyes are horrified. She's looking back at us as they take her away. Every step echoes loudly and slowly. And with each one, my heart begins to quiver with an unrelenting rage.

Far enough, they turn their backs to us and begin to depart. I can't move. Neither can Salman. If we try anything, they'll kill her. If we don't, we'll never see her again. What do I do? I can't think. I can't feel anything.

When the masses are against you, when fear is on every side, and when it seems like you're alone, that is when you should stand the tallest. That is when you plant yourself like a mountain, and you do what your heart knows is right. Even if death will be your only reward.

Jari's words echo in my head. They flood out all the fear. With them, I hear the oath I took standing over my friends in his storage closet: I will protect them with my life. And I never go back on my word.

I charge.

My feet beat against the ground as I race toward them. I'm running faster than I ever thought possible. Salman follows me. My heart feels no fear, no terror, and no hesitation. Only rage. I'm nearly upon them. They haven't sensed me yet.

A few steps away, I lower my head. Amaan suddenly whips around. Then his brother. But it's too late. I crash into Amaan. As my shoulder leads into his stomach, I hear him groan with pain. We both go tumbling and hit the ground.

He's on his back, and I'm on his chest. I don't think. Roaring, I pin him beneath me. I raise my fist before bringing it down on his face. It slams into his cheek. Pain shoots through my knuckles and arm, but I don't stop. I pummel him again. Harder than I've ever hit before. I don't know where this strength is coming from, but I don't care.

A deafening gunshot blasts behind me. It shakes the very ground. But I don't flinch or look back. Not even when I hear Salman violently snarl as his limbs slam against Faisal's.

Eyes locked on Amaan's face, my fist comes down on him again. It's going right for his temple. He powerfully catches it midflight, stopping the blow. As blood drips out of his mouth, Amaan's gaze locks with mine. His eyes look wild.

His free hand brutally backhands me. My head jerks to the side. I spit something out. I can't stop myself from toppling onto the

142

ground right beside him. The pain stings. Landing on my side, my stomach fiercely caves in as he kicks it. I roll onto my back as I cough.

I'm losing—at his mercy. I need to move.

He stomps on my chest, knocking the breath out of me. Then again. My lungs and chest are quivering. All the air is gone. I can't even think straight. Another gunshot is ringing in my ears. Why can't I focus? Amaan towers above me, his face crueler than ever. There is no mercy.

I take another breath, trying to find the strength to move. Amaan's boot stomps right above my heart. He strikes me with all his weight, numbing my chest. I can't do anything. With my wind knocked out, he is upon me.

Amaan's knife is cocked back in his hand. His knee pushes into my upper chest, sharply pressing into my bruises. The jagged ground stabs my spine. I'm pinned, unable to breathe. Something's on my throat—it's his other hand. He's crushing down on it.

He—he's trying to strangle me! My mind screams. I need to breathe. I need to get him off. I'm struggling for air, desperately gasping. But his grip is too strong. Air rushes into my mouth but won't go any further. Crushing my throat with one hand, his free hand plunges his knife toward me. I grab Amaan's hand, stopping his blade a few inches from my chest. It's shaking as he keeps pressing it forward. My other hand grabs his hand that's choking me. I need to break his grip! I'm losing air!

Spit is running out of his clenched jaw. He's pulsating with anger, looking like a rabid dog. He's so strong. I can't get him to budge. And I can't get any air. With every passing second, the tip of the blade inches closer to my chest. My hand is shivering as it desperately tries to hold the knife back. I can't break his grip from my neck. My throat is beyond crushed. I frantically struggle for air; every breath is harder than the last. But there is none to find.

My heart is pounding. The edges of my vision turn black. I barely hear our grunts above my heart's growing drumbeat. With each passing second, I feel my mouth foaming as my groans become more desperate. My eyes are locked with his. Mine are desperate. His are wild.

I can't feel my fingers. Or my toes. He forces his weight into me. Any air that leaks in is kept out of my lungs as he keeps his knee pressed into my chest. My body screams in pain. *Get him off, Zaid! Get him off!* I'm shaking with desperation as I hold off his blade and frantically claw at his grip. His dagger won't stop inching forward. It's about to cut into my shirt. My grunts are hysterical. I can't overpower him. I can't break his grip. He—he's too strong. My heartbeat is growing louder. It drowns out our grunts and struggle. *Fight him, Zaid!*

Everything is black now—everything except his vile face. My heart deafeningly pounds in my ear. It keeps growing louder with each beat until my head is about to explode. My body grows numb. He is strangling me harder. I can't feel either of my hands. But I don't give in. The blade is at my shirt. It's inching closer... and closer...

His eyes. They look just like the rebels'. They look like those of a killer and—

Amaan suddenly jolts to the side, falling to the ground. Loudly coughing, I roll in the opposite direction. I gasp for air. I can't think of anything else. Lying there on my back, I helplessly keep my eyes aimed at the heavens as the blackness leaves my vision.

Life breaths back into me. Sensation suddenly floods through my limbs. Crawling to all fours, I feel color returning to my body as the numbness disappears. I shake my head in an effort to regain my senses before looking back up. Fatima stands with a brick in her hands. Amaan is rising back to his feet, still holding his knife. A bit of blood runs down the side of his face, but his eyes are just as merciless.

I stagger to my feet, joining Fatima. I nearly topple over right away, still desperately regaining my breath and the feeling in my legs. I

144

hear Salman behind us. There's another gunshot. *Don't look back now, Zaid.* Keeping my focus on Amaan, my hand curls into a tight fist.

With a roar, Amaan rushes at us. He wildly slashes down with his knife. Fatima and I step in opposite directions and he passes between us, harmlessly cutting the air. He doesn't miss a step. Twirling around, he comes at me. His eyes are blood red. I leap back. His knife again misses, but I feel the wave of air it sends at me.

I keep my hands out in front of me. One wrong move, one misstep, and it's over. *Keep focused, Zaid.* Letting out a roar, he lunges at me again and attacks with the blade. I sidestep to the left. An intense pain suddenly engulfs my hand. I instinctively let out a shrieking yelp as he passes me. A burning sensation consumes my right palm. Now it's wet. Is that blood? It is. The red liquid is leaking out of a long cut on my hand. It feels cold.

I leap back, barely dodging his knife. It misses me by mere inches. I feel it run right by my stomach, cutting a few threads of my shirt. *Ignore the blood. Keep him distracted, Zaid. But don't get too close. You can't beat him with that knife.* I keep moving backward. He comes at me again. I sidestep the brutish hack. He doesn't relent, almost immediately taking another swing. His knife slices nothing but air.

There's a loud cry from behind us. Amaan whips around just in time to see Fatima charging at him with her brick in hand. She sends it right for his head. But he's too quick. He dodges her, and she stumbles right by him. As she does, he viciously shoves her in the back with his free hand. She crashes face-first right at his feet, kicking up dirt.

Without hesitating, he swiftly kicks her side. Fatima yelps as she is rolled over. He kicks her again, harder this time—in the stomach. She groans in pain as her body buckles down.

He raises his knife.

No! I don't think—can't think. My bloody hand grabs the brick lying by me. His back is to me. I leap at him. There's no mercy in my eyes. He brings the dagger down on her. My brick slams against the back of his skull. It vociferously cracks. Amaan's head jolts before he collapses straight down.

Standing over the fallen boy, I don't have time to help Fatima up. There's a roar behind us. I whip around and see Salman. He's… limping. There's a dark stain on his jeans, right above his knee, as he rises back to his feet. His fists are clenched. A few feet away, Faisal is rising back up as well. Blood is running down the side of his skull. His eyes look just like Amaan's.

Where's the gun? I see it. It's right between the two of them.

There's a moment of peace as they both stare each other down. It's like a standoff. Faisal's eyes drift down from Salman and onto the pistol. But Salman's gaze doesn't waver from his foe.

The tranquility ends. I suddenly charge at Faisal, brick still in my bloodied hand. Faisal goes for the gun. Salman goes for him. It all happens so fast. Tackling him with a loud collision, Salman drives Faisal several feet back before slamming him onto the ground. Faisal lets out a groan as his back hits the jagged ground.

Salman raises his fist, keeping Faisal pinned beneath him. He doesn't hesitate. His fist smashes Faisal's face.

"Salman!"

Whipping his head, Salman sees me toss the brick his way. He catches it with both hands before turning back to his stunned opponent. He raises the brick high above his head. Salman lets out a roar, one louder than any I've ever heard.

I turn away as he brings it down.

Crack!

The thunderous collision erupts for a split second before dying away. When I turn back, I don't look down at Faisal. Instead, I see Salman slowly staggering up to his feet. I've never seen him like this before. He's wincing with pain, barely able to stand on his injured leg.

146

I grab him underneath his shoulder just in time to keep him from collapsing. Holding him upright, I turn my head and see Fatima dashing toward us. She's wearing all three of our sacks.

Reaching out, I take two of the bags from her before slinging them over the same shoulder. I don't feel their heaviness right now. My heart is still pounding like a drum. I can't even think straight.

Fatima gets on the other side of her brother, helping keep him upright. I feel him shift some of his weight over to her.

"We need to go," Salman speaks through a clenched jaw. "It'll be light soon. We need to make it at least three blocks."

"But your leg—" Fatima starts

"Forget about it."

Without another word, we leave.

CHAPTER 16
ALWAYS BY YOUR SIDE

Salman grows paler with every fleeting moment. I've never seen him like this before. Only one block down the road and he can barely move. Fatima and I are nearly dragging him along with us. We can't afford to slow down. The longer we take, the more chances of us being spotted.

My mind is racing, still half-trapped in the battle. I still see Amaan's eyes, still smell his breath as he tried to strangle me. *Can't think about that now, Zaid.* With every passing second, my breaths become quicker and my grip around Salman tightens. *Keep moving. Don't stop. Don't slow down.*

I hear something. It's not far away. There's a vehicle coming down the road. It sounds like the jeep from last night. The sputtering engine is growing louder. Any moment, it'll turn the corner and come into view.

"...inside... get... ins..." Salman's words are not even a whisper.

Dragging him a few more steps, we arrive at the entrance of a building. Thank God the door is already open. Fatima and I don't say anything as we disappear into it.

It's an electronics store. At least it used to be. Just like the butcher shop, it's been completely ransacked and is hardly recognizable now.

We need to set Salman down somewhere. There's a counter. But it's too out in the open. Anybody passing by will see us. *Come on, Zaid. Think*

Stepping over a fallen rack, I lift Salman over it. I see a storage room. There's a table inside. My eyes light up, and I look over at Fatima. She sees it too. Without a word, we begin hauling Salman across the store's floor and toward the closet.

We reach there right as the jeep, or whatever it is, passes by the building. It doesn't stop or even slow down. I think that means we're safe, but neither of us glance back as we arrive at the table. There are a few wires and cables on it. Looks like somebody was repairing them.

"Hold him."

Hearing my command, Fatima grabs both sides of him as I let go. I clear the table off with one quick swipe. The cords loudly clatter on the floor. Turing back to Salman, I grab one side of him. His shirt's sleeve is soaked by my bleeding hand. Laying him on the table, I realize that his eyes are barely open.

With him set, Fatima hurries to his head and begins checking his eyes for something. I don't know what to do. I stare at her face, trying to read her expression.

"Zaid." Fatima's voice is authoritative as she runs some test by moving her finger further and closer to his pupils. "Put pressure on the wound."

With my bloody hand on top of my other one, I press down on his thigh's bullet wound. His jeans are drenched in blood. They feel like a soaked towel. As soon as I push down on it, I feel blood squirting out onto my hand. It oozes between my fingers and across my palm. My heart squirms at the sight and thought, but I apply and keep as much pressure as humanly possible, putting all my weight into it.

Salman groans in pain. His voice is weak, so weak, and every syllable is filled with ache. He sounds ready to pass out. I keep my eyes on his face. His gaze is aimed at the ceiling, and he's muttering something to himself again and again. Does Fatima know what she's doing? She is no longer checking his eyes. Instead, she hastily digs through her sack before pulling out some sort of bottle and some wrapping. She throws the rest of the bag to the side as she races to me.

"Move over."

I do as commanded. She takes my place, completely focused on the wound. I can do nothing but watch. Blood runs down my hand, dripping off of my fingers. My own cut is still bleeding. I can't tell how badly, and I'm starting to feel a bit more lightheaded. However, I don't dare tell her. She needs to worry about Salman first.

"Wipe his blood off of your hand."

Finding a towel on one of the racks, I do as I'm told while keeping my eyes on her. She squirts a liquid onto a cotton ball, nearly drenching it. Fatima uses both hands to press it onto the wound. Salman groans again, more painfully than before. However, she ignores it and keeps it pressed there for a long moment. She turns to me. I catch the look in her eyes. Fatima is terrified, but she won't let it stop her.

"Zaid. Go get some water. I need to keep him from falling unconscious."

With a quick nod, I depart. Water—where would that be? If this place is like any other building or shop, the kitchen will be on the second or third floor. The first one will just be the store. The hallway is filled with clutter. I ignore it all. Dashing through the corridor, I nearly slip and hit the wall as I make a quick turn. My eyes widen when I spot the staircase.

Racing up the stairs, I move with all my strength, jumping two steps at a time. The adrenaline isn't as strong as before, but I still feel it pumping through my veins.

My feet hit the second floor's corridor. The kitchen should be here somewhere. There's a closed door to my right. I instinctively grab the beat-down doorknob. It hardly moves and the door won't budge.

150

I dart to the room across from it. This one is unlocked. Swinging it open, I am met with a ransacked storage room.

Where could it be? I race to the next room. The door's already open just a crack. Lowering my shoulder, I ram into it. The door flies on its hinges before colliding against the wall. It's the kitchen!

The fridge if only a few steps away. I rip open its doors. A rush of cool air hits my face. Is the electricity still on here? No time to think. There's a bottle of water at the edge of a rack. Without thinking, I grab it with my wounded hand and slam the fridge door shut as I race back down.

I'm in the corridor. Then on the stairs. Finally, I hit the ground floor and race toward the storage closet.

Fatima is bandaging the leg. She already rolled up his jeans to fully reveal the wound and has finished a couple layers of the wrapping. The wrapping over the wound is stained with a dark red color. Hearing me enter, she turns and looks at me.

"Help him drink it," she orders.

With a nod, I pop off the cap and let it fall to the floor as I run to Salman. My blood is starting to run down the bottle's side, but I can't help it. His eyes are still barely open. I don't know where he's finding the strength. My free, unwounded hand goes onto the back of his head. I help him lift it up a bit and I bring the bottle to his lips.

He's weakly staring at me with a gaze of gratitude. It looks like he'll pass out at any moment.

"Drink it, Salman. Please."

Some of the water flows into his mouth, but a bit spills onto his chin. He feebly gulps down as much as he can.

"Don't pass out. Whatever you do, don't pass out." I feel my eyes beginning to water as I look at his weak state. *God, don't take him from us. Not him too. Not him too...* I give him more water. Again, he takes most of it, while the rest runs down his face. "Don't leave us."

"Keep giving it to him, Zaid."

151

I do.

The first few gulps do nothing. He drinks as much as possible, the remainder streaking down his cheeks and chin. I encourage him on as I try to not give him more than he can take at one time. But then I see it in his eyes. They leave the edge of unconsciousness. Life starts to return to them. They grow a little stronger with each gulp, as if I'm pouring more life into them with each sip I give him.

I don't stop. I keep helping my friend, keep trying to lure him to stay awake. I witness the color slowly return to his pale face. It's as if I'm giving him an elixir. I don't know if it's the prayers or water that is saving him, but I don't stop either.

The bottle is half empty. He doesn't stop drinking. More color returns to him. There's only a quarter left. I keep my eyes locked with his. Finally, I tilt the bottle's bottom toward the ceiling, feeding him the last drop. He takes it.

Feeling a hand come onto my shoulder, I turn to face Fatima's gaze. She sees the empty bottle. "I think that's good Zaid."

Stepping aside, I allow her to clean off the spilled water from her brother's face. She whispers something in his ear. It's a prayer I think: *Ayatul Kursi.*

I take a few deep breaths. Does this mean he's safe? She's saying something else to him. I think Fatima's telling him that she needs him to stay awake for a little while. I don't understand why she's making him do that, but she knows what she's doing.

Fatima finally looks back at me. Relief fills her eyes. I feel it in mine too. Her gaze goes from my face and onto my injured hand. "Let me see your hand, Zaid."

"It's fine."

"Zaid."

I've never seen her look this stern. Not daring to argue, I stretch out my open palm and reveal my wounded hand.

152

With a clean cloth, she lightly wipes all the blood away from my palm and fingers. It stings a little, but I don't move. Seeing the cut clearly for the first time, her eyes soften. She looks back at me as she pulls out the same bottle of liquid as before along with a clean cotton ball. "I didn't know it was this long."

"I don't think it's too deep. The bleeding has slowed down."

"How are you feeling? Lightheaded?"

"Only a little," I reply.

"Can you still use your hand? Move it around like normal?"

"So far, *Alhumdulillah*."

She keeps her gaze on my hand, and I keep mine on her. Pouring the liquid onto the cotton ball just like she did for Salman, she prepares to rub it onto the wound. Her free hand comes under mine, holding it in place. It's cold and soft.

I know what's coming. I look away, unable to bear the sight of it. A burning sensation suddenly overtakes my wound. I try and jerk my hand back, but she doesn't let me. "Ahh!"

"I'm sorry."

"It's… fine." The sensation dies away as quickly as it came.

She keeps the cotton ball pressed down on the cut for a little bit. My gaze travels back and forth between it and her green eyes, but she stays focused on the wound as blood soaks into the cotton ball.

"You're right, Zaid. The wound isn't too deep. Thank God."

I nod without saying anything.

"Are you sure you're not too light-headed?"

"Yes." I pause for a moment. "You're not hurt, are you?"

She slightly smiles as she discards the cotton ball and grabs the wrapping. "I'm fine, Zaid. *Alhumdulillah*." Fatima remains focused on the task at hand, not looking up at me. "Thank you for what you did. You saved me. You were… brave."

Hearing her call me that feels like a dream. Unable to take my eyes off of her face, I watch her start to position the wrapping around my hand. I don't like her seeing me this way: in need of help. "You don't need to do this, Fatima. I'm sure it'll be fine. You can save the supplies for when we really need them."

Ignoring my words, she starts to bandage the cut. Her gaze rises to meet mine. "Don't act tough and try to hide your wounds. I'm always watching you, Zaid."

Fatima begins to delicately wrap the wound. She really does have the gentle hands of a nurse. As soon as she puts on the first layer, I sense the blood oozing into the cloth, but it doesn't bother me as I keep looking at her face.

"You promised you would one day become a doctor and make this world a better place, Zaid." She again smiles at me, her eyes gleaming. "I believe you'll do it—I know that you are destined for great things. That's why I'm sticking by your side and watching over you." Fatima pauses, her next words softer. "I will *always* be at your side."

Fatima's voice is sweeter than I've ever heard before. They're a breath of fresh air, and each syllable flows directly into my heart.

"Even before all this, you were always watching out for me. But now, you've been my protector. Even for complete strangers, like that woman you gave food to. I've seen how brave you've been. You're always putting me and Salman before yourself. I want you to know that you're never alone. I care about you too. I… I want you to know that."

The third layer of wrapping is done. She did it all without even looking down at her work, keeping her green eyes locked with mine. She reaches for the scissors to cut it off from the rest.

"I often used to think about the world. With everything being as it is, is there really any hope for change. After seeing you—being with you—I know the answer to that. It lies within people like you."

She briefly pauses.

"The last thing Jari told us was to never forget this city as it was—to be the light and hope of it, to keep the heart of Aleppo inside of us. And every time I see you, every time I watch you, I know that this city's light lives inside of you." Fatima's smile grows. "So show me, Zaid, show me how you will change the world. I know you will because... because I believe in you, Zaid. I always have, and I always will."

As I hear her words, I don't feel my bloodied hands or aches. There is nothing else but her. It's just like all those times growing up when we would be sitting under a tree, trying to play pranks on Nabeel, or studying for school. I only focus on Fatima. Glowing like never before, she looks more beautiful, more pure, than I've ever seen her.

She cuts the wrapping and clips it together. Finally, her gaze looks down at my hand. "How does that feel?"

All I can do is smile.

***

I don't know how long it is before Fatima goes to sleep. She keeps Salman up for at least an hour or so. She says it's to make sure he's falling asleep from fatigue and not from blood loss. He fights to stay awake for that hour, but Salman has always been strong and pulls through.

Fatima falls asleep half an hour after her brother. I physically see the adrenaline abandon her, leaving her with a huge crash. She lays down right next to the table he's on, turning the floor into her bed.

They both look so peaceful. I watch over the two of them for a bit. My body is worn out. My eyelids are drooping. My heart rate is calm. I finally feel the rush wearing off, allowing the pain and soreness to settle in. I want nothing more than to slip away from this reality.

But my mind won't shut off.

155

I hear distant explosions, but I don't focus on them today. Looking over Salman and Fatima, I remember the last time I was in this situation. It was in Jari's shop when I took an oath to protect them, to watch over them with my life. Thanks to God, I upheld that oath today.

How long has it been since this nightmare began? I can't even recall if it's been three days or four? It feels like a lifetime. I don't know what our closest call has been. Was it Jari's shop? The men who chased us through the smog? All the explosions that have nearly fallen directly upon us? Or was it Faisal and Amaan's betrayal? It seems like one wrong step in any of those situations would have been the end of it all. To think that the three of us made this far is a miracle. Just the thought of losing either of my friends terrifies me. I don't know how I would be able to go on.

My mind drifts toward the two brothers. I can't fathom how quickly they went from friends to vile enemies. One second they were on our side, journeying through the abyss and dangers with us. In the next moment, Amaan is trying to strangle me without an ounce of mercy in his eyes. He nearly succeeded. The bruises on my neck remind me of that. A shudder travels up my spine.

What would make them do that? They were boys born and raised in Aleppo, just like me and Salman. Did this ordeal drive them mad, or were they that way from the start? A part of me wonders whether we would've been friends if I had met them before all this happened. Would they have been skipping stones with us in the park and playing football in the field? I think only God will ever know the answer to that.

For all I know, I may have ended their lives. I smashed the brick against Amaan's skull. I can still feel the rough brick in my bloodied hand. I attacked him without any hesitation, without holding anything back. My inhibitions vanished when I saw him standing over

156

Fatima. And after I struck him down, I did not even give him a second glance.

Then, with Faisal, I gave Salman the weapon that ended him. The blow was so loud. There is no way that Faisal survived. *I* did those things. Me. The same boy who could never win a wrestling match, who was always picked last every time we played in the field. Was that… murder? I did not even realize what I was doing when it happened. It was all instinct.

I close my eyes for a moment as a wave of guilt flows through me. What have I done? Was it right? Or have I become the person that the *Imam* always warned us about. Maybe it doesn't matter anymore.

Slumber begins to finally overtake me. As I pass into sleep, the last things I see are my friends: safe.

***

The memory floods in. This one is only months old. The day after I failed a test, *Abbi* took me out from school early to bring me here.

"Why are we here, *Abbi*?"

"I come here often, Zaid, to imagine something."

I've only ever seen this place from afar. I never knew that beyond its walls—beyond the words "University of Aleppo"—was such a massive institute. But now we're here. Sitting on a bench right outside the doors to the campus's main building, I watch my *Abbi* as his eyes stay trained on it. There's a look my father wears that I don't recognize.

"*Abbi*?"

He takes a deep breath before looking down at me. "Do you know what I see when I look at this university's doors?"

I shake my head.

"I see you, Zaid. I see you walking in and out of them, surrounded by your peers. I see you laughing. I see you studying. I see you belonging here."

I stay silent as my gaze drifts away from him. Just off of the university's main road, we can see the countless buildings that make up the campus. There's a faculty for engineering. One for agriculture. And one for medicine. Some of the massive buildings climb six or seven stories high. The buildings are surrounded by beautiful greenery. The trees, hedges, and grass are perfectly trimmed and decorate the grounds.

The nation's proud flag is high above everything else. The black, green, and white stripes look bold under the afternoon sun. The red triangle and white star draw the eye of any viewer. Up in the clear, azure skies, it moves with the slight breeze.

Countless men and women walk in and out of the main building's doors. Going up and down the steps, they're all smiling as they speak to one another. They seem so happy. It's a constant sea of people. Their excited and joyful voices drown out everything else. Textbooks and notebooks in hand, they go right past us without a second glance. I see their faces clearly, and they're no different than me.

"Do you know when the Faculty of Medicine was established here?"

I shake my head.

"1967. Since then, tens of thousands of men and women came here as students and left here as doctors. Surgeons, physicians, radiologists... everything, Zaid. Tens of thousands." He pauses. "Now tell me, Zaid, are you going to claim that every single one of them came from a wealthy family?"

I don't respond.

"Are you going to tell me that every single one of them was naturally gifted?"

Again, I stay silent.

"Are you going to tell me that every single one of them was smarter than you?"

"...no."

"Then why do you not think you can make it here. Just because a person says you're not cut out and you failed a test?" He glances at the doors again before his gaze returns to me. "There is one common thing I can tell you about every person who has done something meaningful with their lives, Zaid, whether it be a general, astronaut, author, or businessman. It's that they were dreamers. Just like you, they were not afraid to dream." My father pauses. "And a dream is something that's more valuable than all the money and gold in the world."

I've never heard him speak like this. A part of me can't fathom the words coming out of his mouth.

He looks down for a moment. "When I was a little older than you, I made perhaps the biggest mistake of my life. It was a mistake that most people make: I sold my dream." Again, he pauses. "I sold it... and I have to live with that forever."

Abbi's gaze comes back to me. He puts a fatherly hand on the back of my neck.

"Never sell your dreams for anything, especially money. They print more money every day. But dreams..." His strong hand leaves my neck and comes onto my shoulder. "You only have one of those. Don't let them steal that from you... ever. When you know something is right, when your heart tells you to stand for something, never listen to the voice of fear. Let your dream—let your life—be the light that this world desperately needs."

"What if I never make it, *Abbi*?"

He shakes his head and smiles. "When you take a leap of faith, the question is not whether you'll fall, Zaid. Instead, the question is: how high will you soar?"

159

Chapter 17
An Unpleasant Truth

Waking up, I'm no longer at The University of Aleppo. Instead, I'm back in the storage room. As my eyes slowly open, I can't tell if I'm sore or rested. My mind feels a little solace, but my body is weary. One thing I know for sure is that my heart is still restless.

Coming to my senses, I feel the bruises on my throat. Amaan's grip left its mark. I thought it was painful before, but now it's a whole new story. I instinctively cough a couple of quick times. Reaching over to rub my neck, I wince with pain.

My entire body is sore beyond measure. But what really gets my attention is my bandaged hand. It hurts. Looking down at the wrapping that goes around my palm and the back of my hand, I stare at it for a moment. The burning sensation is long gone, leaving behind the ache. I try stretching it out. It's suddenly engulfed in pain. I try balling it into a fist. I cringe again.

I don't think it hurt that much before I went to sleep. My backside is numb, having slept against the cold, rough wall. There's a crick in my neck too. Before all this began, I could never sleep anywhere besides a mattress. Now, I can make anything into a bed.

Rubbing my eyes with my unhurt hand, I finally look at where my friends were. Salman is sitting up! I blink a couple of times to make sure I'm still not hallucinating. Sitting on the table, his back is to me. He's testing out his injured leg, slowly lifting it up and down. Salman grimaces each time, but his leg is moving perfectly.

I stagger to my feet, using the wall for support. My legs are so sore that I'm trembling when I do finally stand. I don't know if it's

160

just my mind playing tricks on me, but standing seems harder than ever before.

Salman turns his head to see me. He smiles. "*Assalam-O-Alaikum*, Zaid."

"You're alright. *Alhumdulillah.*"

Hearing me instinctively thank God, Salman shifts himself so he can get a better look at me. "Thanks to you, Zaid. You were incredible."

All the harshness that's been in his voice these past couple of days has vanished. I've never heard him this grateful before. That thankful look in his eyes is… strange. "Fatima did all the work," I reply. "I just did as she said. Where is she?"

As if on cue, I hear footsteps entering the room. I know it's her before I even look. My eyes widen as I get a look at her. Fatima has freshened up, and she's found new clothes. She seems to be glowing. Wearing a loose, full-sleeved yellow tunic over a pair of emerald green trousers, her pink headscarf has been replaced by a green one that's a little darker than her trousers. It brings out her eyes. "I'm glad to see you're awake, Zaid," she warmly says.

After finding myself speechless for a moment, I finally respond. "Thank you."

"I found some clothes upstairs in one of the bedrooms. There was some boys clothing too. I think they have things in your and Salman's sizes."

"Really?"

She nods.

Turning to look at Salman, I speak again. "When I went to the fridge, it was working. I think the electricity is still on here."

"It is," Fatima replies. "The water is running too. I was able to rinse off in the shower not even twenty minutes ago."

…am I hearing that right? "The shower is working?"

"You should take one before something happens to it. It's on the third floor."

"I will—but what about the wrapping?" I hold up my injured hand.

"The wrapping will be fine if you're just using water and don't scrub it."

Fatima does not have to tell me twice. I take a step before stopping and glancing over at Salman. "You should go first, Salman. You should probably clean the blood off of your leg."

Smiling, he gestures for me to go. "You go on ahead, buddy. It may take me a while to climb the steps, and it'll take even longer to get cleaned off."

With a nod, I depart.

***

Like Fatima said, I find the shower on the third floor. While the first floor is ransacked, this one doesn't seem to have been touched by looters. The looters must have been forced to leave before they could get to it.

The door is open when I get to the room, but the light is switched off. The bathroom has nearly the same setup as my home. The only difference is that this one appears older and more worn down. There's a window on the wall to the right, but it's blocked out by a curtain. However, there are some bullet holes that have ripped through it.

I close the door. It's probably best to not switch the light on. I walk across the off-white, tiled floor and pull back the thin and damp shower curtain. The tub is relatively clean. It's still wet from Fatima's use, and there are a couple of towels set on the corner of the sink. The bath itself has a few cracks, as do the white walls, but it's nothing serious.

162

Quickly slipping off my shoes before undressing, I step into the tub and draw the curtain forward. My eyes focus on the shower faucet. Is this really going to work? I turn the knob. In the next instant, a rush of water crashes against my body. I stand there for a moment, unable to believe that it's really happening. The water is lukewarm, neither hot nor cold, but I don't care.

The streams that miss me beat against the tub's hard floor like fast-falling rain. Feeling the water rain down and wash all the dirt and dust off of my skin, I slump onto the ground. My head hangs low, allowing my hair to become drenched as I run my hand through it a few times. The shower sputters, increasing and decreasing without any notice. Splashing against me, streams of water drip off of my chest and flow down my back.

How long has it been since I've cleaned myself? I don't even know. I've been covered in sweat, dirt, and blood for so long that I forgot what it felt like to be cleaned. My wrapping grows wet, but nothing comes of it.

The downpour seems to be changing temperatures. Sometimes it warms up before cooling down. For a moment, I think I'm out in the middle of the storm. I remember the last time a storm hit us. Aisha took me out to our home's roof and we danced in the rain. It feels just like that. Without thinking, I put my palms together and form a bowl. I watch it collect water. Raising the bowl up to my face, I take a sip out of it. The last shower I took was at my home. Unlike the cracked tub, it was immaculate. The water was constant and warm. A part of me wonders if I'll ever be there again. For all I know, it may not be standing anymore.

I shiver at the thought. It's not from fear but from longing.

Sitting in the tub, hunched over with my arms wrapped around my legs, I shut my eyes. Tuning into the rhythmic sound of the falling water, I let my thoughts escape this place and go back to a time when I did not even know what true fear or desperation was. Back then, I

163

had everything. I didn't realize it, I never thought it, but now I know. I used to live like a king, but that life is long gone.

I don't know how long the shower lasts when I shut off the water.

Using the towel, I quickly dry myself off. The towel is a bit crusty and rough, but that doesn't faze me. I take my time, not knowing the next time I may get this chance.

Wrapping the towel around my waistline, I step out of the tub and onto the cracked floor. The shower wasn't hot enough to create any steam. Nonetheless, I'm immediately hit with a wave of cool air. I see my reflection in the mirror. My frame looks skinnier than before this whole ordeal began. The bruises on my stomach, chest, and neck are clearly visible. So are the ones on my hands and arms. My hair is disheveled. I try and fix it with my fingers, but it doesn't do much to help. I almost don't even recognize my eyes. They look so much… older.

Looking down, my eyes come onto a toothbrush sitting on the sink. It's a used one, some of its brushes a bit discolored. A thought suddenly enters my mind, saying that I haven't brushed my teeth since this ordeal began. *Ummi* never let me miss a day. For a moment, I feel the urge to use this toothbrush. Thankfully, I resist.

My gaze goes back to my reflection. Catching something in the mirror, I turn my head around and see some clothes hanging on the doorknob. There's a thin, blue collared shirt, a pair of jeans, and socks. They look to be in my size.

Who could have…

Realizing who put them there, I slightly smile.

I change into the clothes, and they fit perfectly. I take a deep breath. I've been stuck in those dirty clothes for so long that I'd forgotten how filthy they were.

Before leaving, I pat down my old shorts and feel something in the pocket. I reach in and pull out the folded note. It's Jari's letter—

164

the one he left for me and instructed me to open when I need it most. I completely forgot about it.

Staring at it for a long moment, I wonder if now is the time to read it. But I decide not to. I feel fresh after this shower, and reading it would only make me nostalgic. Instead, I stuff it into my pocket before leaving to join the others.

***

Not long after I freshen up and return downstairs, Salman goes up to the shower. He's able to move on his own, even climbing the stairs without help. Even so, I walk behind him to make sure he doesn't fall. Fatima says that the bullet didn't hit any bone or cut into any muscles. Hearing those words brings a deluge of relief to me.

By the time I hear him descending back down the stairs, Fatima and I have set up a meal in the kitchen. Finding some plates in the cabinet, we set three of them up on the small, circular table. It's far enough from the window to keep us safe from being spotted. Staying away from windows is so ingrained in us now that we do it without even thinking.

The meal is just like the rest we've eaten: a bit of bread and dates. We find some mangoes but decide to save them for later. Mangoes are one of Syria's gems, sold in nearly every other shop. Now they have become a luxury. However, for the first time since this ordeal began, we all drink cold water after finding it in the fridge.

Salman staggers into the kitchen. He's not putting much weight on his hurt leg and moves a bit slower, but he seems to be walking just fine. Just like me, Salman wears a new set of clean clothes.

He takes his seat at the empty spot between me and Fatima. Without thinking, I whisper a quick prayer, thanking *Allah* for providing us with the provision. But I do it all on instinct, not even thinking about the words.

Ripping off a large piece of the bread, I stuff it in my mouth. I hardly bother chewing it before gulping it down. Salman attacks his food the same way as me, while Fatima eats with a bit more decency.

Swallowing the bread, I pick up a date. It's a big one. Probably has a seed inside. I bite off half of it, feeling my teeth rub against the seed. As I chew, I pluck the seed out of the remaining half before casting it aside. Hearing Fatima's voice, my gaze meets hers.

"Do we have any idea where we are?" She nicely bites into a piece of bread as she finishes her question.

I quickly reply before eating the second half of the date. "Before I came down, I looked out the window. I think I saw Sabeel Park in the distance. It was very far though, so I couldn't be sure."

"What makes you say it was Sabeel Park?" Salman asks, taking a sip of water.

"The Statue of Sayf al-Dawla. I think I saw it."

"Which way was the park?"

"Opposite of where the sun is setting."

"The complete opposite way?"

I think for a moment. "Maybe about 90 degrees to the right."

"That'll make it toward the east then—the northeast." Salman pauses. "More or less at least. This time of year, I think the sun sets toward the northwest."

"Are you sure?" Fatima asks.

Salman nods. "We've been traveling north. Or, at least, that's what I've been trying to do. It's hard to tell which way we're going at night with all the destruction on the roads. But if you could see the park, then that means we've been traveling in the right direction."

He says those words as if they're a relief. Was he not sure if we were going in the right direction this whole time?

I take a sip of my water. I haven't tasted cold water in so long that it's foreign to me. It leaves me stunned for a moment before I'm able to speak. "How far do you think it'll be now?"

Salman looks my way as he swallows a bite. "You mean until we reach Ballermoun?"

I nod.

"It's tough to say. I don't know exactly how much distance we've covered, and I don't know how the roads up ahead will be. Some of them could be too wrecked or too dangerous to travel on." He thinks for a moment. "If I had to take a guess, I'd say no more than four days."

Four days? Those words drive a stake through my heart. He must be mistaken. All along, I've been thinking that we'd be arriving home soon. But now Salman is guessing that we're not even halfway there. The longer we take, the higher the chances are that our home will be deserted by the time we get there and it'll all be for nothing. Worse yet, we'll find our homes as nothing more than piles of rubble.

"Is it worth going further?" I ask without thinking. As soon as those words leave my mouth, I regret saying them.

"What do you mean, Zaid?"

"After all this time, we finally find a place that's safe. We have electricity and running water. Is it worth pushing forward? What if we just stayed here until it all ends?"

"Sure, it's safe now," Salman begins. "But only God knows if it'll still be safe tomorrow. At any moment, looters, rebels, or soldiers can come barging in through that door." He takes a deep breath as he looks at Fatima and then me. "I don't want to say this. Only God knows best. But I don't think it'll be ending anytime soon, Zaid. There are more bombs dropping on the city each day, and even if it all did suddenly end, I don't know what situation the city would be in."

Fatima speaks up, looking at her brother. "Won't help be arriving soon?"

"We've seen what the army—"

"Not the army," she interjects. "But other countries. The United Nations. Our country's allies. Won't they see what's happening? Won't they send help?"

Salman is silent at first, glancing down at his lap. I know what he's thinking. By now, I've come to realize the truth as well. It's the unspoken fact that has lingered on my mind for a while. Finally, he looks back at his sister. His words are soft, barely above a whisper. "Nobody is coming, Fatima."

Her eyes widen.

"Syria… it's nothing more to the world than a political strategy. Russia backs Assad. America backs the rebels. It's a power struggle for them. Just a minor endnote in their larger goals. None of them truly cared when Assad's father took over forty years ago. Nobody lifted a finger then, and nobody is going to care now. Sure, they may talk about it. They may watch videos. They may give speeches. But nobody is going to do anything, Fatima. It's just us now."

"B… but the news. They'll be showing—"

"People all over the world will see the reports." Salman's voice grows more solemn, more hopeless, with every word. "It'll be on the five o'clock news as they're eating dinner. They'll see the destruction and maybe some corpses. And do you know what they'll do?"

Fatima is silent.

"They'll say 'that is horrible'. Then… they'll change the channel and go right on with their meal."

I can't read Fatima's expression as she digests her brother's words. Maybe she's known the truth all along, but it took this for her to finally accept it. For a moment, it looks like she'll cry. She looks down. She probably just lost her appetite. I think all of us have. Finally, her gaze sets back on Salman and then me. "When's the last time we prayed? Formally, I mean?"

We're both silent for a moment.

"It was at Jari's house when he led it." As I say those words, I feel shame wash over me. Since my earliest days, I've hardly ever missed any of the five daily prayers. But since we left Jari's home, I haven't performed a single one. I didn't even realize it until Fatima asked.

"I think we should start doing them just like we used to. That should be a priority."

I slightly nod. "It's *Asr* time right now."

Hearing me say the name of the afternoon prayer, Salman takes a deep breath before he slowly rises to his feet. "Let's all make ablution. I'll lead us. We can finish eating later."

CHAPTER 18
SMALL MEASURE OF HOPE

It's not hard to find a few prayer rugs. They're seemingly everywhere in Aleppo, even in all this carnage. I stumble across some in the sitting room's closet on the second floor. We set three of them up: Salman in the front, me a step behind him and to his right, and Fatima a few feet behind me. The rug I'm on is red with gold embroidery. There's an image of the Holy Kaaba on it, reminding us of what we're praying toward.

Salman asks me to do the call to prayer. I know it by heart, having heard it multiple times every day since birth. However, I've never recited it formally. I always dreamed of one day being asked to do so by our *masjid's Imam*. He would sometimes let one of the boys do it, but he always seemed to pick everyone else but me.

I never thought I would finally do it under these circumstances.

With my hands cupping the back of either ear, I recite the words that used to echo through every street of Aleppo. I speak it loud enough to consume the room but soft enough so that my voice doesn't spill outside. Even now when I get to recite it at long last, I can't fully raise my voice, as we were taught, while reciting it.

As I make the call to prayer, each verse echoes in my head. It feels like I've heard these words but never listened to them before. I feel my heart tremor as the words leave my tongue. *God is greater than all things. He is above all. He is one. There is nobody worth turning to except Him.*

I've never truly understood what that meant—until now.

Come to prayer. Come to betterment. As I say those words, I realize what they mean. It's not about the worship. Instead, it's about becoming a better person. It's about learning discipline not only in worship but in all things. And the discipline will make us better.

In the last two verses, I again proclaim that God is greater than all things. And I once again declare that in both good times and in bad—in misery and in triumph—there is nobody worth turning to or thanking other than Him.

My voice is cracking up as I come to an end. Salman soon begins the prayer. We're facing southeast, the direction of Mecca. Standing at attention, my hands are clasped over my stomach as I look at the ground in front of me. I lowly recite the words to myself. I've heard and uttered them thousands of times. But now, just like with the call to prayer, I'm finally beginning to comprehend them.

It begins with a supplication asking God to guide us on the right path and help us stay on the course of righteousness. As I hear my own words, I begin to tremble. I can't stop it. I feel ashamed— ashamed that ever since this ordeal began, I have not truly turned back to ask Him for guidance. Maybe that's why I've been so confused and scared.

Another chapter from the Qur'an comes to mind. It's one all of us learned together at the *masjid* and is the one that Salman and Fatima are likely reciting as well: *Surah Rahman*. All three of us know it by heart. The title itself is a reference to God's compassion. I recite it perfectly, not missing a single note or beat. Just the rhythm of the verses is intense, striking a chord deep within my soul. One line is repeated over and over again in nearly every other verse:

Then which of the blessings of your Lord will you deny?

I now know what it truly means. That line is repeated after God mentions something of His majesty or His blessings. He is asking us that after everything we've seen, everything we know, everything we've experienced, what will we claim to have achieved through our sheer power alone? What is it that we have without His help?

Finally, I begin to comprehend the truth. I begin to realize that it is not me who has survived this ordeal. It is not me who beat down Amaan when he was strangling me. It is not me who hid from the men searching for us in the smog or outside of Jari's shop. It is not me who survived every explosion and bomb dropped on Aleppo. I did none of that by myself.

My heart bursts into tears. My head bows a little lower.

I can't stop shaking. As we go from standing to bowing, from bowing to prostration, and from prostration to sitting, I am unable to control the trembling. Halfway through, I close my eyes. I haven't truly gone back to God once during all this time, even after all of my parents' teachings. However, He has still not forsaken me. He has not left me on my own, even after having every right to do so. I could have gone up in smoke with any of the blasts. Amaan could have succeeded in his attack. Or I could have been out on the street, injured with no shelter.

But the three of us are alive. We're together. We are able to keep pushing forward through this abyss, and we have a better shelter than most people in the city. Yet, I never thanked Him.

And for that, I am ashamed.

I hear Salman end the prayer. Next, we each make a personal supplication just between us and Him. We can ask for anything. They say that directly after prayer is the best time to ask for any favors and blessings.

I don't know what Salman and Fatima ask for, but I ask for nothing. I can't contain the tears anymore. As they roll down my cheeks, I do nothing but thank Him. Looking into my outstretched palms, I barely see anything through my tear-filled eyes. I can hardly even whisper without breaking into sobs. However, as I thank Him, it doesn't matter. None of it does, except for one thing:

For the first time in a long time, I feel some small measure of true peace.

***

It won't be long until it's time for us to leave.

The A/C seems to be switching on and off out of its own free will. The droughts grow longer as the day draws on. Maybe Salman was right about this shop soon becoming as desolate as the rest of the city. If that's the case, then it's a good thing we won't be staying here.

It's been an hour since the prayer ended. I haven't spoken a word since then. The little bit of solace I felt in my soul is still there. I don't know what it means, but I take the peace as some kind of a sign that things won't stay this bleak forever.

The sun is only about an hour and a half from the horizon. The thought of leaving the serenity of this place and going back into the abyss makes my stomach churn a little. I know we don't have a choice, but I also don't know if I'll be able to stand another night filled with the sound of silence. It's not the exhaustion that scares me. I'm too used to that by now. It's something else.

Fatima is upstairs, searching for any first aid supplies she can rummage up. I already refilled my food sack a few minutes after the prayer. Before I could offer to go up with her, she ordered Salman and me to relax and rest ourselves for the evening. With the sternness in which she uttered those words, even Salman did not have the audacity to argue with her.

Sitting next to Salman in the second floor's corridor, I hear her footsteps coming from the third floor. The floors are just as creaky as anywhere else in the city. With our backs against the wall, Salman's and my legs are stretched out in front of us. The evening light spills into the hallway from the open doors. It's visibly waning with every second, but I do my best not to pay attention to it.

Salman's voice breaks the serenity. "I can't believe that we found a place like this. Working electricity, running water, supplies— what more could we ask for?"

I nod without saying anything.

"I think it was a good idea," he continues. "Praying was, I mean."

Looking over at him, I reply, "Fatima's ideas always are."

"She tends to have better ideas than us, but I guess that's not saying much."

The two of us laugh.

After a moment of silence falls over us, he lets out a sigh. "I miss it, Zaid."

I know what he means.

"What I would give to be at the park again." He closes his eyes, his words filled with a nostalgic longing. "Feel the shade of the old tree as we stand at the lake's bank. Hear the laughter all around us. See the stones gliding across the water like they'll go on forever."

With my eyes shut, I see it all too. The breeze is cool, the park peaceful. Salman's laughter is triumphant, and Fatima's green eyes are so caring. It's as if it was all yesterday. Yet, it feels like a lifetime ago. I keep myself from breaking down as the memories flood in.

"We may see it yet," I whisper. Opening my eyes, my gaze again meets Salman's. I slightly smile. "You still owe me a rematch."

He returns the gesture. "You never could stay down. Always a fighter. It must run in your family."

As soon as he says those words, I think of Nabeel. I... I miss him. So much.

"Still planning on attending The University of Aleppo after this all ends, *Dr.* Zaid?" Salman's lighthearted question brings me back to reality.

I pause before replying, "I don't even know if it's still standing."

"I wouldn't count anything out. Not after what we've seen. Are you ready for tonight?"

"More or less I guess. I feel better now than I did a few hours ago. How's your leg?"

"I want to say it's fine. But I guess we'll know the answer tonight." He looks over at me with a grin. "Worst case scenario, I'll have you carry me on your back."

A light chuckle escapes me.

Salman again falls silent before his voice grows a bit more somber. "I'm sorry, Zaid."

"Sorry? For what?"

He glances down. "How I've been acting since this entire thing began. I know I've been hard and distant. I just… just wanted to protect you the way your parents trusted I would."

Simply hearing him utter those words dissolves all the frustration he's caused these past few days. In this moment, as his words sink in, I feel closer to him than I ever have. I gently pat him on the shoulder and give it a light squeeze. "I know, Salman."

He smiles. "Is your hand alright?"

I raise up my bandaged hand. The wrapping has held up perfectly, even with the shower and everything. "I think Fatima was right when she said the cut wasn't deep. I can move it and use it just fine."

"Good." He thinks for a long moment as he looks away, hesitant to say his next words. But when he speaks, his voice holds a tenderness in it, a brotherly love. "Fatima thinks highly of you. She… cares for you."

"I think we all care for each other."

Salman's gaze returns to me. "That's not what I mean."

There's a look in his eyes. I've never seen it before. Does… does it mean what I think it does?

"I am glad, Zaid. I've always thought of you as a brother—the younger brother I never had. Maybe when this is all over and we get some semblance of our lives back, something will come out of it. I... I hope it does." He pauses. "You're an amazing boy, Zaid—an amazing person. You've proven it more every day. When I froze and was unable to move as they tried to take Fatima with them, it was your lead that I followed. You gave me the courage to fight back. I never thought it'd be you—the boy who could never do anything right— that I would be following into battle. You've become something else, Zaid. I think you're as brave as Nabeel ever was."

There's another brief silence.

"And..." He puts his hand on my shoulder, wearing the most genuine smile I've ever seen. "I'm glad you're with me. I'm glad to be at your side, Zaid Kadir, even if this will be the end of all things."

CHAPTER 19
NO TURNING BACK

It's far less than an hour until we leave. I've gone searching for any last-minute supplies. One last room, then I'll go join the others. Opening the door, I enter a desolate bedroom. At first glance, I can't tell if it was a boy or girl's room based on the green wallpaper and white bed sheets, but then I see some pictures hanging on the wall. It's a progression of a girl from birth to young adulthood. She looks to be thirteen in the last picture. My age.

Turning away, I scan the rest of the room. First the table. Then the bed. Then the—

I do a double take. What's that? It can't be. Without thinking, I rush over to the bed before crouching down and yanking it out. It's a radio! Holding the black, plastic, portable device, my hands are trembling with excitement. I instinctively elongate the rusting antenna. God, please let this work.

The others! I've got to show this to them! Clenching it with both hands, I race through the corridor, keeping my eyes on the radio. I nearly slip on the floor, stumbling a few steps. But I don't slow down. Bounding down the stairs, my steps are quick and heavy as I go two steps at a time.

My feet hit the second floor with a loud thud. They must have heard me coming because I find Fatima entering the hallway and looking my way as I dash toward her. Seeing what's in my hands, her eyes light up.

Turning into the sitting room, Salman's gaze is immediately on me. "Zaid, what is—"

He stops mid-sentence, catching sight of the radio. Fatima is a step behind me as she enters the room. Scampering over to Salman, I set it down between the three of us.

"Switch it on!" Fatima's words are ecstatic.

Salman hits a switch. Loud, wrenching static immediately pours out of it. Fatima and I impulsively cover our ears before he lowers the volume. After waiting a moment to make sure it's gone, Fatima and I exchange a quick glance. Salman begins to play with both dials, searching for a signal. I turn my gaze to him. "Do you think it'll work?"

"God-willing," Salman replies. Even as he tries to control it, his voice is flowing with excitement.

There's nothing but static. It's unending. Is this really all there is? Without realizing it, my fist starts to impatiently beat against my thigh as I keep watching Salman fine-tune both dials.

The static fades down a little and… then there's a voice. My eyes widen. It's in the background and can barely be heard at first. But then the voice grows louder, and I know it's not just my imagination. Soon, the words flood out the static. It sounds like a reporter—a woman.

"…*reports of heavy bombing continue to pour in. The military is still… failing to comment on whether they are actively avoiding civilians in their targeting. City… government officials still advise citizens to stay indoors… not possible to evacuate the city. There is a temporary camp being set up in Mansoura for civilian refugees. All refugees who arrive there within the next few days will be taken someplace else. The military… security forces are continuing to heavily engage… rebels on foot in the districts of…*"

I can't hear whatever else is said on the report. My mind is trapped in one sentence—on one thing that it said. Mansoura… that's west of the city. I visualize an overhead view of Aleppo. If we started in Salaheddine, the southwest part of Aleppo, and are working our way toward Ballermoun in the north, then Mansoura would not be too far west from wherever we are. Am I picturing this right? I run through it again. Then a third time. That's correct! It can't be too far away!

My eyes perk up at the thought of safety. Now my heart is more excited than before we switched the radio on. I look at Fatima and then Salman. Neither of them seems to be having the same thoughts as me as they both continue listening to the radio.

"Salman?"

He doesn't respond.

"Salman."

"Quiet, Zaid." He holds up his finger, keeping his attention focused on the radio.

"Salman!"

His eyes finally focus on me. After a moment, he reaches over and switches off the radio.

"We need to figure out how far we are from Mansoura," I excitedly state.

Why does his gaze seem puzzled? Did he not just hear what the report said?

"Are you listening, Salman?"

His reply is as confused as his expression. "Why do we need to do that?"

"To figure out how to get there."

"We're going back home, Zaid. Not to Mansoura."

Is he serious? I glance over at Fatima. She seems to share his conviction. Am I going insane?

"Are you seriously wanting to go to Mansoura, Zaid?" Salman sounds like he can't believe I even entertained the thought. "Because of what the report just said?"

"Salman, we have a chance to get out of the city." I start blurting things out without even thinking. "We've been asking God for help. I think this is our solution. He's put in right in front of us. It won't take long to—"

"Stop it, Zaid. We're staying the course."

I don't know why, but those words make my blood start boiling. He's doing it again, just like with any other initiative I've had since this chaos began. How can he discard my idea like this?

His eyes seem unwavering. I don't want to say what I'm really thinking, but I won't relent easily. Not this time. "We don't know how long it'll take to get back to Ballermoun," I reply. "You said that yourself. We don't know what's down that path or waiting for us at the end. But we know what's to the west: safety!"

"And we know what's to the north too: our families."

My voice suddenly spikes as I shoot up to my feet and say what I've been holding back for far too long. "Our families!? Our homes!? Do you hear yourself? It's been days—closer to a week than not. By now, they're long gone and our houses have been reduced to rubble just like the rest of this city! You're going to lead us all there to find nothing but a pile of ashes. And God knows that the only way we'll find our families is if we find them—them d…"

I stop myself from saying the last word. I'm trembling. My yelling shakes the very walls. Salman rises to his feet. He looks calm. I can't tell if my words had any effect on him. "We're not turning away from our homes, Zaid. We did not come this far just to turn our backs at the first sight of any kind of sanctuary. Do you really think any camp is safe from being shelled into oblivion? There are no more rules in Aleppo anymore, Zaid. There is no safety."

"How do you know any of that? How can you lead us on when you don't know what's waiting for us even one block away?"

He doesn't respond. At least not right away. Salman glances toward Fatima and then back to me. The more riled I get, the calmer he becomes. He takes in a deep breath before replying, "Because… I have faith."

180

Those words douse out my flames. I lose any response I might have had, so I wordlessly watch as he looks away before walking right by me and into the corridor.

"We will be leaving in half an hour. We should all get ready."

***

There's a gut-wrenching feeling in my stomach as we meet at the bottom of the stairs. Maybe it's because I know what we're leaving behind. With every step we take, we're abandoning a God-sent salvation and willingly walking into the abyss that is Aleppo. Is there truly no way to change Salman's mind?

I'm the last one to arrive. With a refilled sack of food slung over my shoulder, I find Fatima and Salman already set to go. They both watch me descend the last few steps. My baggage is more of a nuisance than a burden today. Outside of the strap cutting into my bruised shoulder, I don't pay it much heed. All I really feel is the pit in my stomach.

The light outside is nearly non-existent. I think the sun's already behind the skyline—at least whatever is left of it. It'll be dark soon, and we'll be walking through the smog left behind by the endless bombings. Throughout the day, I hardly heard any explosions and even less gunfire. I don't think it's because there weren't any. I'm just too used to the chaos. It's a part of me—a part of all of us. I think I'd only notice if the destruction wasn't there.

"Are we all set?" Salman looks directly at me.

I nod without saying anything, hardly even giving him a glance.

"Then let's go."

Head hanging low, I follow Salman through the foyer and outside. It's so… silent right now. It's almost scary. As I step onto the dirt, I lift my gaze. I did not pay attention to the road when we arrived, but I can't ignore it now. Completely engulfed by the thin smog, I see the hazed scene all around me. A bomb must have hit this road before we ever came here. A crater is smoldering just down the street. It's wide and looks deep. Chunks of concrete rubble surround it like shattered glass. A few of the buildings on this street are utterly demolished. Some are still smoking. Any one of those could have easily been us. With everything that's happening, I'm starting to wonder if there'll be any landmarks left for us to recognize if we ever do get home.

Salman and Fatima are looking at the crater. Maybe they're having the same thought. Turning toward them, I break the eerie silence. "Which way are we going?"

"North." Salman tears his gaze off of the scene and motions in the direction. "We'll be trying to stay along Highway 214. It'll just about take us right where we need to go."

I almost say that I hope 'where we need to go' is still standing when we get there, but I stop myself. Tugging on my sack's strap in a vain effort to realign it, I send Salman a slight nod. He knows what I mean and makes the first move, walking in the direction we're headed.

Keeping Fatima between us, I fall in line behind her. I feel all the soreness settling in within the first few steps. This is how it always begins. Within a couple of hours, my feet will be begging for rest, but I won't be able to give it to—

I stop. So do the others.

There's a whistling sound. I instinctively look toward the heavens. Is it coming from up above? It's faint, barely audible. It sounds so far away, but… it's growing louder. The noise seems to be headed for—my eyes widen.

"Take cover!" I roar.

It's too late. The bomb falls right on top of us.

CHAPTER 20
RAINING FIRE

Smog surrounds me. I can't breathe. The smoke is too thick. Dust is everywhere. Stumbling down the road, I violently cough. My gaze is wild. Where is Salman? Where is Fatima? I can't sense their presence.

I don't remember anything—the last thing I heard was the whistling. Then there was an impact. After that—it all happened so fast. Everything became a daze. Next thing I know, I was sent sprawling onto the ground. I scarcely even remember the explosion. The piercing ringing is echoing in my head, and I can't think straight. My breaths are quick. So is my heartbeat. My mind is so stunned that I almost can't even keep my legs under me.

I madly look to the left and right, trying to cut through the smoke and ash raining down. There are people everywhere. I didn't see any before, but now they're coming out of the woodwork. I hardly see anything more than their outlines in this smog, but I hear their screams. However, over the cries, I sense their panicked steps as they race right by me. Were there this many people here the whole time?

There's no sign of my friends anywhere. They just disappeared. I keep staggering through the smog, praying to find the end of it. The ground beneath my feet is hot, and the ashes fall like snow.

What's that sound? It—it's more bombs. Even through all the chaos and confusion, my heart begins panicking like never before. They're just faint whistles at first. But they're growing louder. Sudden gunfire breaks out behind me. It's relentless. The bullets are shrilling. It's close—no, it's distant, but not too far behind me.

My mind screams one thing above the rest: *Run, Zaid, run!*

Catching control of my feet, I break out of my stumbling and into a jog. Then a sprint. My feet beat against the ground like madmen. Tearing through the mist and into a clearing, I arrive only to see the sky raining fire. It showers down on Aleppo.

The heavens are blacker than any night. Crowds of people flee from the shooting, their yells echoing through the street. Gunfire roars from all around me. It's everywhere. It's closer than I thought. A bullet whizzes out of the smoke and rushes right by me before clanging against a burned vehicle. Another inch and—don't think about that now, Zaid.

Dashing through the street, I hear bombs falling from the sky. How can there be so many of them? They grow louder with every passing second.

Then it starts again. Deafening explosions rock the city. Men and women topple over as the bombs and missiles erupt. Buildings go up in smoke. Chunks of debris are blown into the air before spilling down on the city, crushing anything in their path. I feel the heat of the blasts crash against my skin. I witness walls and entire buildings ferociously collapse, kicking up enough dust and smoke to rival a sandstorm.

A building's wall creaks as I run under its shadow. It breaks off in the next instant. Avoiding the falling debris as I leap over rubble, I witness the city that I call home—the city I grew up in—again turn to ashes. But I can do nothing. Like the rest of them, I can do nothing but flee. Some flee to shelter. Others flee away from the battle. However, there is no escape from this. My mind continues to scream one thing through all the madness: *run! Run and don't stop! Run until your feet fall out from under you!*

The Judgment Day that the *Imam* always spoke of is upon us. It is the end.

I hear nothing but the ringing of the earsplitting destruction all around, sense nothing but the insurmountable heat. Black ash covers me. I wipe my eyes of the dust, desperate to clear my sight. My vision is tunneled ahead as I try to escape the bombs. My feet are numb, but I don't stop. My heart pounds against my chest like a mad drummer, threatening to burst out at any moment. But I don't slow down. I can't.

It's chaos. Madness. The rockets are plummeting onto the street at random. Homes and shops go up in a blinding blaze. The explosions are everywhere: in front, behind, and on either side. There's just chaos as the bombs strike the city. Blackness shrouds the heavens. I can't see ten feet ahead of me. There's so much thick, toxic smog. I w—

I'm suddenly sent lurching forward before crashing on my side. My head is spinning. The ringing is louder than ever before. I lay there a moment longer, unable to muster any strength. What just happened?

My thoughts still in disarray, I stagger to my feet. I almost topple over immediately, but I maintain my balance. The ground is shaky, but I somehow keep it under my feet. Was that a bomb? It almost hit me. A few more feet to the left and I would have been caught in the eruption. Instead, a truck was set ablaze. The fire is scorching. That could have been me in it.

A man dashes right by me. Then a boy who's nearly my age. Neither one gives me a second glance. *Keep running, Zaid. Don't stop!*

The explosions aren't slowing down. Neither is the gunfire. Continuing to retreat from the bullets, I shake my head in an effort to diminish the disarray. The endless barrage almost drowns out the screams. Some are of the people—my fellow civilians—being engulfed by the explosions and debris. I hear their thunderous cries before they are cut short. Others are of those like me, those fleeing their homes in terror. People run right over one another.

The gunfire grows closer with every second. A bullet shoots right by me. Then another. Followed by a third. *Don't slow down, Zaid.*

Keep running! The smoke is so thick now that I can barely even see where I'm stepping. However, it only makes me run faster.

But the firefight is moving too quickly. It's catching up. I can't outrun it. Vehicles are riddled with bullets before their engines catch fire. The bombs continue rocking the street, leveling anything or anyone they hit. Shockwaves and heat crash against me from every side. Black smoke keeps rising up to the heavens.

My foot hits something, causing me to stumble. I hardly pay any attention to what it is: a corpse, a woman. Catching my footing, I keep dashing for my very life. I can't slow down. Not even two steps later, I run right over another body. A third is to my right, but I don't even look at it.

A rocket slams into a high-rise building directly in front of me. The scorching explosion cuts through the smoke. I react on instinct. Shielding my face from the blast and the dust, I take cover behind a broken-down car. There's another figure hiding on all fours. It's a man. His head is pressed against the concrete and his hands cover the back of his skull. He's cowering, too scared to even move.

The roar of the blast dies off. By the time I look back up, the building's wall breaks off and falls toward the road. I leap back to my feet. But then I stop. Hearing a cry above the destruction, I whip my head around and see a woman. Her foot is trapped under a chunk of debris.

I don't think—I can't think. Not now. Sprinting to her in a frantic dash, I crouch down beside her. The debris has her left foot and calf pinned. Her gaze locks with mine, eyes consumed by a fearful terror. It's the same terror I've now seen too many times. They're begging for any help.

What can I do? Will she even be able to walk after this? Don't think about that now, Zaid.

Her foot might be shattered under the concrete. But it doesn't matter. I have to try something. There's a gap between the slab of

186

concrete and the ground, and I find a place to grab the debris from underneath.

They're almost here. The gunfire is closing in.

The concrete debris is thick and appears heavy, but I don't let it sway me. I can't leave her here to die. With a deep breath, I try raising it up. The weight doesn't move. Squatting down, I lift up with all my might. Using my back and legs, I pull with every ounce of strength I can muster.

The fighting is drawing closer. The gunfire sounds louder than ever.

I can't lift the debris, but I don't give in. I feel my veins showing as I try to move it. All I need is a few inches, just enough for her to move her foot out from under it. My arms are shaking. My body trembles. My ears go deaf as another explosion erupts on the other side of the street. Its heat crashes against my back, but I don't waver. The concrete is still not moving.

The shooting is nearly on us.

I look up at the scorching heavens. With a roar, I give it everything I have. I muster all that I can rally. I don't stop. My fingers are in pain and feel like they're going to break off, and I cannot feel my arms. But the concrete doesn't move an inch.

A bullet strikes the debris directly to my left. They're upon us. It's too late.

CHAPTER 21
A PROMISE

Sitting on the swing, my head hangs low as I hold on to one of the chains with both hands. A few tears leave my cheeks wet as they roll onto my chin. I hear all the boys playing in the distance. With Salman sick, there were an odd number of us today when we were picking teams. Guess who was left out. None of the boys even looked my way when deciding who'd play. They just picked the teams and started without me as if I didn't exist.

The school's back wall is not even twenty feet away from me. Ms. Farooq is grading today's exams right now, but I already know what my result is. We already got yesterday's test's results back. Everyone in the class passed... everyone except for one person. She read the scores out in front of the class. Ms. Farooq said my score the loudest, going on to say that scores like mine don't make it into art school, let alone medical school. Why does she do that?

The tree's shade does very little to protect me from the endless heat. This tree is just like the one in the park—the one Nabeel and I stand under when we are skipping stones. It's been so long. I miss him... *so much.* I don't know if he thinks of me, but I can't think of anything but my brother these days. Wherever I go, Nabeel is on my mind. I can't shake him off. I can't—

"Zaid, are you alright?"

Recognizing her voice as it comes from behind me, I quickly wipe away the tears with my shirt's sleeve. Can't let her see me like this. Can't let anybody see me like this.

Her footsteps grow closer. Taking a deep breath in an effort to hide my state, I slowly turn around to face Fatima.

She's standing by the tree's trunk. Her pretty, emerald eyes are on me. They seem... caring. "Why are you by yourself, Zaid?"

"I was... I was trying to—" I can't even think of an excuse.

"It's okay, Zaid." Fatima takes a seat on the swing next to mine and gently takes ahold of either chain. Her gaze focuses on the ground in front of her. "It's okay to want to be alone sometimes."

"You're never alone."

"Sometimes... sometimes we're all alone." Fatima looks back at me. "Are you thinking about Nabeel?"

My gaze leaves her. "He's everything I want to be. He's everything anybody wants to be: brave, smart, fearless. I want to be like him—want to be *just* like him. I want nothing more than for him to be proud of me. I want to be all of those things... but I'm not. I'm last place in everything. Sports, school... I'm..."

"No, you're not, Zaid." Fatima pauses. "There's one thing I know you have that nobody else does. Something I always see in your eyes."

"What?" I meet her gaze.

"Hope." She smiles. "Hope, Zaid. I see you dream bigger dreams than anybody else. No matter what, your hope never dies. People try and take it away from you. Sometimes it's our teacher. Sometimes it's the other boys. But you never let them. And hope is worth everything. It's worth more than everything else combined. I've never met a bigger dreamer than you, and I don't think I ever will."

I don't reply.

"You always talk about being a doctor—the best doctor ever. You always speak about changing the world, Zaid. Promise me you'll never lose that. No matter what happens or what anybody else says, promise me you'll never forget that."

There's a silence. A long one. Our gazes remain locked, and in that moment I feel a connection with Fatima that I've never felt before. There is a light in the darkness, a sliver of hope I never truly sensed until now: her. A smile creeps onto my face. "I promise."

CHAPTER 22
CROSSROADS

My body awakes with a jolt. But when it does, I'm no longer in the middle of the street. What am I on? It feels like… a bed? My eyes shoot open, finding themselves staring at a ceiling. It all hits me: the explosions, gunfire, screams, and helplessness. Instinctively trying to sit upright, a heavy hand on my chest keeps me down.

"Whoa there, kid. Take it easy."

The words are Arabic, but the accent isn't Syrian. I look at the strong hand. Then at the face it belongs to. It's a fair-skinned man with black hair and green eyes—a darker shade of green.

"You took a nasty hit." His face is a little grizzled, but he gives off a warm presence. He's wearing a pair of rugged jeans and a black shirt over his well-built frame. The man keeps me pressed down for a long moment before lifting his hand off of me and relaxing back in his chair. "How are you feeling?"

I blink a few times without answering, trying to decipher if this is reality or not. One moment, I'm out in the middle of a battlefield. Then, I'm suddenly here with this stranger. I know it all really happened, still feeling all the pain of being thrown around by the blasts. I look down at the bed I'm on. It's up against the wall with him on the other side. Outside of a small table, there's no other furniture in the room. A blanket covers me from below my waist. The room is warm. I slowly sit up, wincing as I do. "…fine. I feel fine."

"No lightheadedness or dizziness?"

"Just… soreness."

He nods. "There are worse things than that."

My eyes widen as more memories flood in. "There was a woman. She—"

"She's safe. Her name is Saba."

Hearing his reassurance, I calm down. "...what happened?"

"I saw you trying to save the woman. Some debris hit your head. You were unconscious by the time I arrived. I got Saba's foot out from under there, but it was injured. She couldn't walk. I carried the two of you over my shoulders and got you here." He pauses. "Fortune was on our side. Two minutes slower and things would have ended much differently."

"There was shooting. I thought we were going to get caught in it."

"We lucked out."

I look away, grimacing a bit.

"Hey, don't worry, kid." He pats my shoulder. "Everything is just fine."

As silence falls between us, the entire ordeal replays in my head. I see it all as clearly as when it occurred, and the thing that races to the forefront of my mind is the explosion that started it all. My heart starts to race. Salman and Fatima were by my side. But, in the next instant, they were nowhere to be seen, and I was stumbling through the sickening, toxic fog. They disappeared. I didn't even feel them anywhere. They're...

"What's wrong?" The man's question breaks my thoughts.

"My friends... they were with me. They've been with me since this entire thing began. We were caught in a blast, and I—I couldn't find them anywhere." Uttering those words, I'm surprised that I don't burst into tears. Maybe I'm still in denial. "Now, I'm afraid that they might be—"

"Don't talk like that, kid. I'm sure your friends are someplace safe. They're probably just as worried about you as you are for them."

I don't think even he believes his own words. Another awkward silence falls between us. Looking away from him, my eyes are drawn to the corner of the room. My supply sack is resting up against the wall. It seems untouched and exactly as I last saw it. There's a window not far from it, showing the dead of night outside.

"What's your name?" the man asks, bringing my gaze back to him.

"Zaid."

The man slightly smiles. "I'm Ethan."

I've never met an 'Ethan' before. A silence befalls us before I break it, but my next words are more of a statement and less of a question. "You're not from Aleppo."

"No. I'm a long way from home."

"What brought you here?"

"Humanitarian work." His expression is hard to read, making it difficult to understand just what he means. However, after a moment, he continues. "I've been helping distribute supplies to a lot of the civil war's refugees. I was on my way to the airport to collect a shipment of supplies. But then the attack began and everything in this city went to…" Ethan pauses. "I was here with my sister. I lost her in all this chaos and have been searching for her."

"Where were you when it all started?"

"In the southwest."

"Do you know where she might be?" I reply. "Your sister, I mean?"

"If she's able to move, she'll be headed toward the camp in Mansoura. Where were you and your friends headed?"

I remember my final words with Salman and the determination in his eyes. "Back home. Ballermoun."

"We're still a good ways away from there."

"I know."

"I'm taking Saba with me to the camp. She thinks her brother and sister will be headed there as well. She can barely walk, so I'll need to help her. I'm praying that I'll find my sister there as well." He falls silent for a brief second. "Are you still planning on going on alone?"

My next move? I don't think I've even yet come to terms with the fact that I survived that battle. I look away from him. "I... don't know. I don't think I really know anything anymore."

"You're welcome to come with us. The more people we are in a group, the better off we'll be."

I don't reply.

Ethan sits motionless for a long moment before nodding. Can he sense the uncertainty that I'm feeling right now? "Right. You've gone through a lot. It's too early to decide what you need to do next." He rises up out of his chair. "Rest up, Zaid. I'll bring you some food later."

***

After Ethan closes the door and leaves, an eerie silence settles into the room. The only thing I see through the window is darkness. No matter how long I lay my head against the pillow, I can't rest. The silence is only broken by the occasional eruption. I don't witness any blast cut through the night, but I hear them well enough.

How many times do I relive the nightmare? The bomb came out of nowhere. Then the chaos ensued, and I was alone. There was no Salman and Fatima by my side. Every time I close my eyes, I see the destruction surround me. It's like I'm back at Jari's shop, unable to fathom what just occurred.

I don't know when it finally hits me. But when the realization settles in that my friends are long gone, any and all restraint dissolves. Clenching myself, I curl into a fetal position and weep like never before. I can't fight the tears or the shivers as my body violently convulses with every sob.

I remember all the times we skipped stones at the lake. I remember walking back from school every day. I remember Salman giving me his new football for its first use. I remember sitting next to Fatima on the swings when the world seemed so cold and cruel.

One moment, they were by my side. We were continuing our journey home. Salman was so... so sure that we would see our families. Even with my disbelief, he never doubted that this would all pass.

Now it's all gone. There's nothing left.

I've forgotten that I'm nothing but a boy—nothing but a thirteen-year-old boy trying to pretend that I'm strong enough to survive in this chaos. I have no place in a city like this. If anybody should have died in that blast, it should have been me. Salman and Fatima were the strong ones. What have I got to offer? Why did I live when they did not?

Their faces are etched into my skull. Salman and Fatima both stare back at me. Salman is strong, his gaze unwavering, just like Nabeel's. Fatima is staring at me with those beautiful green eyes. I never told her how I felt. Now, I never will.

It's not just them. There's Bilal and Jari. They gave their lives for me.

Abbi. Ummi. Aisha. I see them too. Their gazes are... hollow, lifeless. I never truly said goodbye to any of them, never got to tell them how much I loved each and every one of them. They're gone. All of them. It's just me. It's like—it's like the punch line of some twisted joke.

The weeping intensifies. The more I think of them—the more I relive the warm memories I will never again experience—the faster the tears come. I can't stop thinking about them. Their voices are all mixed in my head, calling to me over and over again.

I'm back in Bilal's car right before we pull away from my home. My family is still close enough for me to reach out and touch. Reliving the scene, I am screaming in my head—screaming to stay. However, I can say and do nothing. I can only watch it all unfold. I see the look in their eyes. They don't want me to leave. Why don't I grab on to them and refuse to let go? Why don't I *stay?* Everything is screaming for me to stop, pleading for me to step out of the vehicle. But I do nothing.

Don't let me leave! Don't let me go! Keep me there! Abbi! Ummi! Aisha! Please! Don't let me leave!

My fist is clenched so tight that my nails start digging into my palm. The car begins to pull away. I'm drifting away from my family, going down a path that they cannot follow. Why don't I stay?

It's not too late! Don't let me leave, Abbi! Don't let me leave! Please! Don't send me into this nightmare! Say something! Stop the car! Do something!

We grow further and further away. I'm condemning my family. My mind is begging me to end this—to somehow change what happens, but I am powerless. I can't change anything. Again, I leave them standing there and disappear into the abyss.

Why did I go! I should have stayed! I should have never gotten in that forsaken car! Never left! I would have rather died at my house than survive in this nightmare! You—you idiot! You stupid boy! Why didn't you stay! Why did you leave them all to die!?

Tears continue streaking down my cheeks. They leave my face damp as they roll off my face and soak the bed sheets. I thought I was brave. But now I know it was only because I was with Salman and Fatima. I'm alone. For once in my life, I am truly alone. Why is this happening to me? Is God really watching this all unfold? I've lost everything to faceless monsters: my home, family, and friends. Now they've stolen any childhood that remained inside of me. Even if I possessed the courage to fight and seek vengeance, I wouldn't know where to swing.

If You are watching, why don't You do anything? Why—why don't You stop this all from happening! What have I done—what have any of us done to deserve this!?

"I don't... understand." My feeble words are not even a whimper. "I—I can't hear You. What do You want from us... from me..."

These monsters left me with nothing. I don't know where to go. I don't know what to do when the sun rises. Days ago, I was a boy with everything in the world. I just never knew it. Now, I am nothing more than an orphaned boy left to fend for himself in a city that has forgotten what it used to be.

I finally know what destitution is.

CHAPTER 23
A FINAL MEAL

My tears finally run dry. The night is dark, the silence unsettling. Staying in the fetal position, I feel the moist sheets beneath me. My face remains wet, and I don't possess the willpower to wipe away the tears.

How long has it been since Ethan left? Two hours? Three? My tired gaze stays focused on the closed door. I can't stop thinking about all I've lost—how I've been stripped of everything I ever held dear. The more I do, the further I lose any will to ever step out of that door. I just want it all to end.

Some conversation spills in from the next room every now and then. It sounds like a woman's voice. It's more than likely Saba and Ethan. I can't make out their words, but Saba seems… seems just like me. Her voice is tired and fearful. However, Ethan remains the same: confident. Doesn't he see what's happening?

This is the first night in a long time that I've been given the chance to rest. It feels… wrong. The part of me that doesn't want this suffering to end thinks I should be out there on the move. Where should I be going? I have no clue. As the night passes, a guilty pit forms in my stomach.

I keep replaying the blast in my head. The moment before the bomb hit, Salman and Fatima were a step away. I could reach out and touch them. But then everything went ablaze. They disappeared as if they never existed. After everything we survived, everything we endured, they went out like that.

Even through the chaos in my mind, I know what is going to happen soon. I have to make a choice. I can keep trekking to the north… alone. Or I can go west with Ethan and Saba, perhaps the last two friendly faces I will ever meet. North to more destruction. West to a sanctuary.

What am I supposed to do? The more I think, the more painful that pit in my gut grows. Keep trudging toward Ballermourn alone? I'm no Salman or Nabeel. I can't survive out there on my own. I barely survived with my friends. Out there are enemies on every side: soldiers, rebels, people like Faisal and Amaan. I can't even tell friend from foe. It's a fool's dream. Maybe it always was. Why couldn't Salman see it? Why was he so set on going north? If we had left toward Mansoura, maybe he'd still be…

I let out an aggravated groan. My fist trembles and is clenched so tightly that it hurts. There's no use in speculating. It doesn't matter anymore, none of it does. Salman and Fatima are gone. That's the fact, and I need to accept it no matter how hard it is.

Shutting my eyes, I take a deep breath, trying to calm myself down. I know what I must do. It's not even a choice. I can't keep heading north. There's nothing there for me. Nothing but misery. I have to go with Ethan and Saba. It's my only chance. I think it's what Salman would want me to—

A knock on my door diverts my attention. It opens and Ethan steps inside with a plate in his hands. Is that… chicken! And rice. I stare at them as if they're foreign dishes. Where did he get that from? As he comes halfway to the bed, I finally rip my gaze off of the plate and on to him. His face is gentle as he moves across the floor.

"Hope you're hungry, Zaid."

I sit upright as he arrives. Taking the plate into my hands, I set it on my lap. Looking down at the food, I blink several times. My mind isn't playing tricks. I smell the aroma of the warm meat and rice.

"You feeling okay, kid?"

My gaze looks back at him. "I'm fine."

He glances down at my injured hand. "That bandaging was done pretty well. I checked it over when I found you. Was it your friend?"

I nod.

"They must've really cared about you. It's good that you were with people you loved when all this began. Many weren't so lucky."

"They were... the best thing I could have asked for. More than I deserved."

Ethan is silent for a moment. "Make sure you eat up. You'll need your strength."

I almost ask him where he found the food, but I stop myself. It doesn't really matter.

He takes a step back, preparing to leave. "Try and get some rest tonight, Zaid."

"Ethan?"

"Yes."

"I..." Reliving the blast that took my friends, reliving the chaos, my voice and eyes start to tremble. "I don't want to die."

Uttering those words drives a spear right through my soul. Tears begin welling in my eyes as all the losses flood back. Ethan's hand gently comes onto my shoulder. His eyes grow more genuine. "I know you're scared, Zaid. Everybody is. But don't let that control you."

I can't reply.

"You're missing your friends and your family. I heard you after I left. I want to tell you that... it's okay. But you have to be strong. If for nothing else, do it to honor their memory. If you can't be strong for yourself, do it for them, Zaid. That's what they'd want. I know it."

My gaze leaves him as I slowly nod. He's trying to console me the only way he can, but his words do little to help. I don't think what

I'm facing is something that anybody can take away with just a few words.

Ethan starts to head back toward the corridor. He moves slowly, as if contemplating whether or not he should stay with me. When he's halfway to the door, my voice cuts into the air. "Why would you do that, Ethan?"

He stops and turns around. "Do what?"

"Come to a place like this?"

Ethan glances away for a moment. His eyes seem distant as he replies, "Because there are things more important than my own life. And if I can save one life, I may have just as well saved humanity."

I watch his eyes as he speaks. There's a gleam in them, the same one I saw in Jari, Nabeel, and that boy who rescued us from the rebels. It lasts a moment after his words end before disappearing.

"Get some rest, Zaid. Whatever you decide, it'll be a long day tomorrow."

***

I'd forgotten what chicken tastes like—forgotten what delicacy a warm and ripe chicken leg offers. It's like I've never eaten it before. Smelling the warm, inviting aroma, I lose all control and go after the food with my hands, stuffing my mouth full of it. The meat's slick juices dribble all over my fingers as I clench the chicken leg. Any dining etiquette *Ummi* taught me is long gone.

The meat is tender. It nearly melts in my mouth. I treat each bite as if it'll be my last. I eat the chicken right off the bone, not leaving a scrap. *Abbi* always said to leave a little meat on the bones, but I ignore his voice when it rings in my head.

As for the rice, it's mostly plain with a just tang of flavor to it. It's like something Aisha would have made. Just like the chicken, I don't need any utensil for it. Taking handfuls, I eat it with more vigor than any sane boy should. The more I eat, the more my stomach urges me on, not wanting me to relent. I could live off of this—I *wish* I could live off of this.

I devour the food as any condemned man would eat his last meal. I don't know the next time I'll dine on anything other than stale bread and old dates. This could very well be the final warm meal I have.

But I know what comes after this. I'll have to make a decision, and it may perhaps be the last meaningful decision I ever make.

***

I've lost the ability to sleep at night. It's become as foreign as the security of my own bed. With slumber keeping itself well out of reach, I am left with my own thoughts. I don't know if it's the battle raging in my mind, the tears, or if I'm just too exhausted to fall asleep. I know it's not the distant fighting raging in Aleppo. I've grown too accustomed to the bombs and gunfire that are ripping my city apart.

But whatever it is, my mind is nothing but restless.

Where do I begin to answer my questions? I don't know what to do. How did I survive that blast? The bomb fell right on top of us. Better yet, how did I survive *any* of this? I am no stronger than any of those who have become victims of this battle.

The sun will show itself soon enough. It can't be more than a few hours until dawn. When the rays break over the horizon, I'll have to choose which path to take. My mind wants to go along with Ethan. It's not just because he's going in the safer direction. At least, that's what I tell myself. Being in his presence feels… it feels like being around Jari, Salman, or Nabeel.

Taking the other road seems like nothing but folly. Going on—continuing toward Ballermourn—is a lost cause. The entire city is being razed to the ground. Thousands of buildings are now piles of wreckage and ash. Who am I to think that my home is safe and still standing?

I don't know what *Abbi, Ummi,* and Aisha would have done when this all began. A part of me thinks they may have come searching for me. But where would they have begun? They wouldn't know where to find me any more than I know where to find them. The better part of my mind asserts that they likely evacuated after realizing that they would soon be overrun. They were already packing when I left, weren't they? Maybe they are trusting me to do the same thing and not go running into a war zone looking for them.

To the north, there is nothing. But to the west is salvation. I don't have a choice. This isn't a crossroads because there is no other path. There is only one option.

I was following Salman out of friendship and loyalty. He and Fatima are gone now. My eyes again water at the thought, but I hold back any tears. There is no time for that. I've shed too many tears since this all began. First Bilal. Then Jari. Now my two best friends. They've all given their lives so that I can live. I have to honor them by surviving. What good will come out of my demise? It'll make their sacrifices mean nothing. I have to go west.

I sit up on the bed and swing my legs over the side. Taking a deep breath, I stare at the ground in front of me. I've made my choice.

…but why does it feel so wrong?

Sticking my hands into my pockets, I feel something in them. It's a folded up paper. My eyes suddenly widen as I remember what it is. I'd all but forgotten about it after everything that's happened. Taking a gulp, I slowly reveal it.

The note is just as I found it on Jari's shelf, only a bit more worn out. The corners are a little beat down and folded, while the edges are starting to become discolored. However, the words on the exterior remain the same: *Read this when you need it the most.*

I thought so many times that I needed to read Jari's words. But out of all the times I've needed direction or any sort of inspiration, this trumps them all. There is no shadow of doubt in my heart about that. With a deep breath, I slowly open the note. My hands are trembling. I unfold it once. Then again, revealing the words written by my long lost guardian. Unlike any time before, the words are not jumbled as I read them. They're the clearest any written words have ever been, and each one goes directly into my heart:

The moment I saw you, Zaid, I was reminded of someone: myself. You wear the same eyes I did as a child. You often feel inept as I did. You often compare your failures to the success of others as I did. Your admiration for your brother and friends makes you feel as if you must be something that you're not.

Learn the truth, Zaid. There is none who may rule over you unless you allow them. You are the captain of your soul. You are the king of your destiny. When you are at a crossroads, always follow your heart. When the masses are against you, when fear is on every side, and when it seems like you're alone, that is when you should stand the tallest. That is when you plant yourself like a mountain, and you do what your heart knows is right. Even if death will be your only reward.

Be the heart of Aleppo. Be the light of hope.

CHAPTER 24
SEARCH OF HOPE

Not long after reading that note, I'm out of bed. I can't sit or lay down anymore. Jari's words echo in my brain, drowning out every other fear-filled thought that has consumed me since waking up in this room. The longer I listen to his words and let them into my soul, the lighter the weight on my chest becomes.

I read the note more times than I can count. I was right all along about one thing: this isn't a crossroads. There is only one path to take. I just couldn't see it clearly enough.

The first light soon breaks through the darkness outside. Won't be long now before the sun shows itself. Instead of fear for what this day may hold, something else takes root in my soul, something that I haven't felt for a long time.

With the sack slung over my shoulder, I quickly tighten up my shoelaces before heading toward the bottom floor. This building was once a shop just like any other I've seen. Lining up the walls are family portraits. A family of five used to live here: a father, mother, and three daughters. There are countless pictures of them that were taken in various parts of Aleppo. There's one photo from the citadel, another from the Great Mosque, and a third from the National Museum.

They once lived in this house as a family. I hope to one day thank them for unknowingly giving me and the others shelter here.

Arriving at the bottom floor, I walk to the shop's broken window and stare outside at the brightening heavens. I'm not afraid to go by windows anymore. There are only a handful of clouds visible. Gazing at the streaks of white and yellow light breaking through the sky's darkness, I can't help but stare at their beauty. I haven't really seen the sky this clearly since this entire ordeal began. This sunrise appears different. More… aesthetic. I don't know why. I've seen countless sunrises before, but this one puts them all to shame.

I soak it all in with a deep breath. I finally feel as calm as I did when praying yesterday afternoon. I don't truly know what is out there; however, I know what hope I am holding dear to.

Feeling a presence, I turn around. Ethan stands a few feet behind me. I didn't even hear him arrive. Our eyes lock for a brief moment before he breaks the silence. "You're heading out?"

"Continuing north."

Ethan slightly nods. "Deciding to continue your friends' journey?"

"No. I'm going to find them."

One of his eyebrows rises a bit. "Find them?"

"They're still alive. I know it. If I survived the blast, then I know they did too. I believe that. I believe that with every fiber of my being. I believe that I'll find them and my family. One way or another, we'll all be together again. I promised to look after them, to protect them." Jari's and Nabeel's words repeat in my head. "And I never go back on my word."

"How do you know that they're still alive?"

Salman's statement—one of the last ones he said to me—echoes in my head, and I repeat it with a smile. "Because I have faith."

After a long moment, Ethan displays a small smirk. Taking a step toward me, he puts his hand on my shoulder and gives it a gentle squeeze. "If circumstances were different, I would have followed you, Zaid."

"I know. I hope that your sister is safe. I know that you will find her, God-willing. Thank you, Ethan, for everything."

206

He nods in appreciation. "I once heard that it's during the darkest hours when the courage of humanity burns brightest. Being here in this city, I understand that more than I ever have before."

"Where did you hear that?"

"My grandfather, David, always used to say that. I see that in you now." Ethan glances outside. "It's daytime now. Are you sure it's safe to travel out in the light?"

I take a deep breath. "I've been hiding in the shadows for far too long. It's about time I remember what bathing in *my* city's sun feels like."

"When I found you yesterday, you were a scared boy, Zaid. Now… you're something else. Never forget the hope you feel right now, and let it guide you." Ethan takes a small step back. His smile grows. "Aleppo is a spirit, not a place. And now you have it in you. You've become the heart of the city—the heart of Aleppo."

***

The sun soon appears behind Aleppo's desolated skyline. It's brighter than any I've seen as it continues to slowly ascend into the sky. With every passing minute, the streets start warming up as they emerge out of the night's darkness.

To be out here while the sun is rising instead of setting feels foreign. There's nobody on the roads—not a single soul visible other than myself. There isn't even much smog to conceal any people. Are they all just hiding indoors like before?

I don't recognize the street, not that I'd expect myself to. It looks just like any other one I've seen so far. The buildings once stood three or four stories high. Now, most of them are wrecked or utterly demolished. The stubs of some of the structure's bases still remain standing, surrounded by bricks and mortar. Many buildings have been knocked right over like fallen trees, crashing onto one another or the road. Others have had a wall blown apart, their remains spilling onto the pavement. The handful that still stand have been shot up beyond repair.

The road itself is in no better shape. Burned and wrecked vehicles—cars, trucks, and vans—dot the street. Several of them are still smoldering under the morning skies. There are even several police vehicles, although the majority of them are unrecognizable now. Most were riddled by gunfire before and after going up in smoke. Shards of glass are everywhere, much of it melted into the pavement. A lot of the glass is long and sharp enough to cut right through my shoes and into my feet if I'm not careful. Much of the road itself has been blasted away, leaving holes everywhere, while chunks of concrete lay spread out amongst the vehicles. Some of the pits are nothing more than potholes, but others take up the entire width of the street.

Just like every single street in Aleppo, this place was once a bustling neighborhood. It was vibrant. It was alive. If I close my eyes, I can still sense it all: the animated voices of merchants, the aroma of the street food mixed with the smell of diesel, and the feeling of walking down the crowded street. It was chaos… but it was my city, my home.

That scene seems like another world. Now they've turned it into a ghost town, one that even the people who lived here would never recognize.

However, I don't let that get me down today. Because no matter what I face, I won't lose that hope I felt when reading Jari's note. I pat my pocket, feeling the letter safely tucked away. God-willing, I *will* find my friends.

I know it.

The fighting seems distant. I hear blasts in the far north and witness smoke get kicked up into the air. If I squint my eyes, I can see shells raining down from the heavens, but I'm too far to feel any of their blasts.

There are helicopters to the distant east, close to the city's center. They're out of earshot, but they hover above Aleppo's downtown skyline—at least what's left of it. I think they're military. The fighting would be heaviest there as rebels and soldiers fight for control of the city's core. We always read that whenever an invader came into a city, they tried to take over the media. I wonder if that's what the rebels are trying to do.

I remember the last thing Salman said before the bomb hit. They were going to keep along the highway to follow it back home. After the chaos began yesterday evening, Salman and Fatima would have taken shelter until it all died down. They likely spent an hour or so looking for me. Not finding me or my body anywhere, they would have been forced to move on. There wouldn't be any other choice but to follow through with the plan. When dawn came, they may have very well taken some sort of shelter. However, I have a feeling that they would only rest up a couple of hours before continuing to trudge forward.

All that boils down to one thing: I can't be too far behind them.

There's something different about today. It's not the absence of pain or soreness. It's not the lack of destruction or wreckage—there's plenty around me as always, although I try not to pay it any attention. At first, I can't put my finger on what is different. But then I realize what it is. The sound of silence—the one that I've heard every night as I journeyed through this city—is nowhere to be heard.

It's... an odd feeling, as is the sensation of walking out here by myself.

I pass by some bodies, no corpses, as I trek on. Most are older, while a few are younger than me. Some are scorched beyond recognition, but I do my best to not look at any of them, even going out of my way to not really go near them. I can't afford any second thoughts.

However, I can't avoid them all. Many of the corpses were shot, the bullet wounds still visible. Others must've died in explosions. Some of them are… missing limbs. I don't know why seeing it doesn't stop me. Maybe I've grown immune to it all. Even the sight and stench of decaying corpses doesn't slow me down one step as I simply continue walking by them.

My slow footsteps are the only sound in this desolate place. A part of me wants to move quickly as I search for my friends, but I remind myself that this is a marathon and not a sprint. I don't know how long it may be until I see them, and I need to keep my strength because I don't know for sure what may be out here.

As I move along, I remember something *Ummi* once told me. She said that when she was growing up, Aleppo was the safest city in the world. The biggest threat they ever faced was a purse-snatcher. But even then, there would be ten people chasing after the thief moments after he tried anything.

I would never dare call my mother a liar, but I'm starting to wonder if she was really talking about the same Aleppo I'm now in. How can a place as peaceful as that become a war zone?

The thoughts dissipate as I suddenly find myself at the edge of a crater. Stepping onto a loose block of rubble, I look down into the hole. It's about eight feet deep. Maybe more. The slope goes straight down, exposing some busted water pipes and jagged concrete, before coming to a halt at the pit. The other side of the crater is just as steep before returning to the road. The pit seems to still be smoking a bit.

I instinctively look away and cough a couple of quick times. There's no other way around the crater unless I'm willing to backtrack, but I can't afford to lose any time. Finding my courage, I step forward and onto the descent.

The slope is covered in loose rocks and rubble. I stay low, trying to keep myself steady. The ground is more unstable than it looks, many pieces of it threatening to tear off as I step on them. It's hot, too hot for me to dare touch the ground. The heat permeates through my shoe's now thin soles.

My steps are slow, each one a few inches further than the last. I hesitate after each stride, trying to ensure that the ground is steady before I keep moving. Arms outstretched, I try to keep my balance. My gaze stays glued to my feet as I watch each step unfold. I can't feel anything as I make my descent, can't hear anything except the loose rocks plummeting down below with each step I take. I'm halfway there now. Just keep—

The slab of concrete under my left foot suddenly breaks off and slides away, sending me tumbling onto the ground. It happens fast—too fast for me to do anything. Losing my balance as I lurch forward, I try to reach out and grab something. But it's all in vain. I roughly crash on my side before rolling down the slope. I cover my face on impulse. Each bounce sends pain coursing through my veins. But there's nothing I can do except helplessly fall down the pit.

Stopping at the bottom of the crater with a loud thud, I lay there for a long moment. Is it over? Letting out a groan, I mentally relive the tumble several times. My body is aching. The elbow I fell on is banged up as pain stings it, and my forearms are throbbing. However, everything else is fine... I think.

Taking a deep breath, I do my best to block out the pain. I shake my head, trying to brush off the ache and clear my mind. It's not as hot as I thought it'd be down here. Some relief at last. I run my hands over either arm, checking to make sure that nothing is bleeding badly. My fingers come out covered in some dust, but there is no blood.

Crawling onto all fours before rising to my feet, I readjust the supply sack. It's a little worse for the wear, but it seems fine too. With another deep breath, I turn away from where I fell and face forward. The climb out looks steeper from down here than from up above.

211

Nonetheless, I don't let it discourage me because on the other side of that are my friends—on the other side of that is hope.

The incline begins not even three steps away. Moving to it with a running start, I immediately begin to claw my way out of the pit. Grabbing anything that I can hold on to, I pull myself out of here inch by inch. I stay low, using my feet as leverage.

One step at a time, Zaid. Look out for anything sharp. Look where you're reaching and stepping before you do.

As I claw like a man possessed, I send down countless pieces of loose concrete and rubble. I feel and hear it break off and tumble down below just as rashly as I did, but I stay focused. The farther up I go, the steeper the climb becomes until it's as if I'm scaling a wall instead of a slope. I'm halfway there. The sun is suddenly in my eyes, blinding me. But I don't stop. And I don't slow down.

For a moment, I lose my footing as my foot slips off of an edge, but I quickly regain it. Holding on to a jutting steel pipe as some water leaks out of it and runs onto my arm, I come to a halt. I don't see anything else I can grab to move forward. But I'm close enough now—close enough to be able to grab the edge of the pit with one good leap.

Holding my position, I take a deep breath. Then another. There's only one shot at this. Otherwise, I'll be tumbling back to the bottom. I cock my body back, eyes focused on where I need to land.

With a thrust from my feet and yank from my arms, I let out a roar as I leap forward with every ounce of energy I have. I hang in the air for a moment. My hands reach out over the edge, instinctively grabbing on to a piece of the road's concrete. My body roughly slams against the slope, face banging against something hard, but I hold on to the concrete as if it is life itself. After my head spins for a moment, I regain my senses. Eyes shut, I begin to wildly scramble, trying to throw myself over the edge and onto the road. I don't stop moving and kicking as I madly attempt to pull myself up. First my elbows

212

come across. I feel them hit the steady ground. Then my chest makes it over the edge. Finally, my legs and feet follow.

I lay there under the hot sun, taking a moment to recompose myself. As the excitement wears off, the place where my face hit the wall begins throbbing. I sense all the dirt and dust covering me and in my hair. Staggering up to my knees, I dust it all off the best I can before wiping my hands on my pants. I take a deep breath... then another. My eyes turn to look straight ahead.

Keep moving, Zaid.

***

Turning from one street to the next, I keep crossing the same scene of desolation. My city—a place seemed forgotten by the outside world—looks no different than any war zone. I remember pictures of Berlin during World War II. I don't think anybody would be able to tell this Aleppo and that Berlin apart.

Going from neighborhood to neighborhood, street to street, they all become a blur. It's just wreckage after wreckage and debris after debris. The amount of destruction on each street seems to be increasing the longer this battle goes on. Either that or we've just been marching deeper and deeper into the heart of this war. By the end, when both armies have had their fill of fighting, there may be nothing left standing.

A few people cross my path every now and then, but they don't pay me much heed. They're civilians of Aleppo, people like me. Sometimes, it's a group; other times, it's an individual. However, they simply go their way and I go mine.

Judging from the sun, it's late morning by now. Trekking between two burnt cars, one of which is still seething, I hear something from above. A pair of beady eyes are looking down at me. Then another. And a third. Vultures are perched up everywhere, some even soaring in the sky. The large, black birds are appearing out of the woodwork. I'm unable to tell if they're watching me or the scene in general. However, a couple of them seem to be keeping up with me, even making circles around me. Are they thinking that I'll be keeling over soon?

Paying attention to them, I fail to notice a pile of rubble blocking the road until I nearly run into it. It's a toppled building. The debris is a mixture of concrete, bricks, and glass. I look to the left and then the right. There's no way around it unless I'm willing to go back the way I came, but that'll cost valuable time and daylight. I let out a groan.

The wreckage is about eight meters high. The last time I climbed something like this, Salman helped pull me up. It's up to me now. Observing the ascent, I notice plenty of jagged edges and sharp shards of glass sticking out. It's like a minefield. My heart sinks for a moment. I can't see any way up without the risk of injuring myself. Even if I don't fall, I'll likely cut myself on any of those landmines. Without Fatima, I don't have any medical supplies or expertise at my side.

Before the thought of turning away and retreading my steps takes root, another enters my mind. It's what *Abbi* said to me on the steps of the university: *When you take a leap of faith, the question is not whether you'll fall, Zaid. It's how high will you soar.*

No turning back, Zaid. You took an oath to look after your friends, to keep them safe no matter what. You never go back on your word.

I start looking at all the dirt-covered debris lying on the ground. There's a can, an empty pack of cigarettes, a broken jar, and—there's a shirt! Quickly picking it up and dusting it off, I rummage through my sack and pull out a small cutting knife. It should be sharp enough. I hastily cut off a bit of each sleeve, careful to try and tear through the garment in a way that makes them come out as two long and wide strips.

The cloth is pretty sturdy and thick, thicker than the shirt I'm wearing at least. I wrap each strip around either palm, making them go around four times. I double check to make sure that they're both thick enough. Wearing these will make it harder to hold on to things, but my hands will be safe from anything sharp.

After looking over my makeshift protection one more time, I finally approach the mountain and stop at its base. I reach deep down and muster all the courage I find. Just take it one step at a time. Pretend you're climbing a tree out in the park.

Finding a place to start, I firmly place my right foot on a small piece of rubble that's jutting out. I press some weight onto it, making sure it'll stay steady. It moves a little, but not enough to be alarming. I push off of it as I reach up high to grab a small ledge that's barely big enough to hold on to. It's a little sharp, but the cloth covering my palm keeps my hand protected. My right foot is on its toes now, and my left foot hangs off the ground as I stretch to keep my grip on the ledge

I nearly reach out to grab another place with my free hand but stop myself. *Foot, hand, foot, hand. That's the order.* My left foot finds a place to settle, only a little higher than my right one. The ground it lands on is a bit shaky, but it holds up. My right hand grabs a ledge as my breaths become a bit quicker.

It's just like climbing a tree, Zaid. Just a tree that has some really sharp edges. Don't look directly down and don't over think. Only look where you're grabbing and stepping. But, most importantly, don't stop until you're at the top.

I move one foot or hand at a time. As I use my injured left hand to tightly grip pieces of rough debris and pull myself up, I feel it putting some strain on the healing cut. The back of my mind starts screaming that I'll reopen the wound, but I ignore the cries. It doesn't matter now.

215

Right foot. Left hand. Left foot. Right hand. I follow that order as if my life depends on it. With each step, I climb higher and higher. I don't hesitate between each movement, but I don't move too fast either. Resisting the urge to look down or up, I keep my eyes focused on where I'm grabbing or stepping next. There's glass everywhere. I feel small pieces of glass cutting into my shoe, pants, or protected hands, but no skin gets sliced open.

Reaching out, I grab ahold of another ledge. As soon as my fingers touch the top of it, I feel them pressing against the flat side of some glass. Longer than any of the others I've seen, the shard is set alongside the ridge with its edge sticking out into my palm. With every ounce of pressure I put onto my hand as I bring my foot up, I sense strands of the wrapping's cloth being cut. Is the glass going to make it to my palm? I hesitate for a moment, but the glass barely cuts into the cloth as I hold on to the ledge. Getting my left foot placed on a ridge, the ground beneath it is too shaky for comfort. Should I move it? No… it'll hold up.

I'm halfway there now. Something to my left catches my eye. I whip my head in that direction only to see one of the vultures who was following me land on top of the rubble. Its hollow eyes are locked on me, as if it's waiting for somethi—

No! The debris under my left foot suddenly gives in. In the next instant, the ledge beneath my right foot breaks off.

My body goes lurching downward. I stop with an abrupt jolt, barely hanging on to the ledges with my hands. My eyes are wide as my legs dangle in the air. Breaths are quick. Heart stopped. The glass at my left hand cuts through more of the cloth. I feel its jagged edge nearly touching my palm. Is it cutting into me? I can't tell.

Hands trembling and legs flailing, I barely hold myself from falling below. My mind panics. *Get a grip, Zaid! How far up am I? Four meters, maybe five. If I let go, that won't kill me. Wait—why am I thinking like that? A fall from up here will injure my foot. Get ahold of yourself. Find another place to set a foot.*

Unable to take my gaze off of my quivering hands, I blindly start running and kicking my feet against the debris, searching for a level place to step on. My fingers are strained as my hands tremble harder and faster with each passing second.

Don't let go, Zaid. Don't you dare let go.

I see the vulture through my peripheral vision. It's—it's inching closer. And it's no longer alone. Two more come out of nowhere, landing on either side of the first. They're waiting for a moment to swoop in and do to me what I saw them do to that body in the middle of the street.

Inhaling a calming breath, I look down at my feet. I see a place to set my foot on. I'll have to reach, but it's not too far. I shut my eyes for a moment, trying to regain any composure that I can. Stretching out my right leg, I place my foot on the ridge and press down on it. With the pressure off of my hands, I hastily move my left hand off of the ledge covered with glass and on to a safer one. I tightly grab it before looking down and finding a place to settle my last foot.

I stay there, taking a deep breath and then another. My senses settle down a bit. Shutting my eyes, I lean my forehead against the rigged debris. That was too close. I hold my position until my heart finally accepts that the danger is passed.

Opening my eyes, I turn my gaze toward the three vultures. They're still looking at me from several feet away. The thought crosses my mind that they could swarm me and try to force me to let go. I'd be helpless against them. However, I don't have any choice but to keep moving forward.

Looking upward, I map out my path step-by-step. I should be there in no time. With a clenched jaw, I push forward and yank any fear or hesitation to the back of my mind. My vision tunnels on my destination, my thoughts becoming focused on it.

217

Right foot. Left hand. Left foot. Right hand. Those are the only words that echo through my mind as I slowly claw my way toward the top of the mountain. *Right foot. Left hand. Left foot. Right hand.*

It doesn't take long. Either that or I get too caught up in my movement and lose track of time. Arriving at the top of the summit, I victoriously look ahead as the vultures abruptly leave. But my eyes lose their enthusiasm. Up ahead, there's another mountain like this one waiting for me to climb.

CHAPTER 25
FINDING THE LIGHT

The memory of Nabeel—one of the last times I saw him before he again left for deployment—flashes through my mind.

I've been waiting in the kitchen for nearly half an hour, though it feels much longer. I recognize the heavier footsteps descending toward the second floor. Leaving my bowl of *halwa*, I excitedly scurry into the corridor just as Nabeel arrives into view. He doesn't look my way and is just about to step onto the next flight of steps to go down to the shop when my words stop him.

"Are you ready?"

Hearing my voice, Nabeel turns around and smiles at me. He looks more dressed for a lunch than for the park. "Ready for what?"

I start making my way toward him. "You said you'd take me to the park."

He hesitates for a moment, his grin diminishing. "Was that today?"

"You're leaving tomorrow for deployment, aren't you?" I stop right in front of him. "You said we'd go the day before you leave."

Nabeel takes a deep breath as an apologetic expression washes over him. "Sorry, buddy. Looks like I'm going to have to take a rain check. I have to go take care of some things before I leave."

I knew he'd say that. Something always comes up. My heart sinks. Without a word, I look down.

"But I promise, when I get back, we'll spend a whole day at the best park or garden we can find."

"You always say that." My words are barely audible.

"This time, I'm telling the truth." Bending down a bit, he playfully flicks me on my forehead, forcing me to look back up at his smiling face and genuine, caring eyes. "Just wait and see, Dr. Zaid... just wait and see."

***

As the memory of my brother fades, I find myself standing over a fallen fence and looking into a garden. My eyes are on the Turkey Oak. The last time I saw one of these was when my two best friends and I were walking back from school. It was only hours before this wicked battle began. Why does that seem like a different lifetime?

Thinking back even further, I remember Nabeel taking me out to a tree just like this one for my ninth birthday. He taught me how to climb it. I was terrified, but his conviction was so strong that I couldn't say 'no'. A few steps into it, I fell straight down and he caught me like it was nothing. He'd always catch me when I needed it, was always there for me in one way or another.

That was all a long time ago.

My ears pick up some high-pitched noise. What's that sound? It's coming from the tree. I hear it again before seeing the source. Surrounded by green leaves, the bird is so small that I have to squint to make out its features. It's the Palestinian Sunbird. No more than ten centimeters long, I recognize its black and navy feathers. It chirps again as it hops along the branch.

How did I not recognize a chirp when I heard it? Have I really not heard one in so long? The more I think about it, the more the realization dawns: I haven't seen any animal outside of vultures since this entire ordeal began. Is that why the city has been so silent?

220

The Sunbird looks at me. Our gazes lock, and I feel a moment of peace as a bit of reassurance washes over me. It loudly and almost cheerfully chirps again, breaking the stillness. And then once more. Not a moment later, it stretches out its wings and flies into the air, as if it is heading straight toward the sun.

The bird disappears into the blue sky. I take a deep breath before turning away from the scene.

I push all the memories away and keep moving forward. I know that I'm going along the highway. Every now and then, I can see it between the buildings to my left. The only trouble will be finding Salman and Fatima in all this. If they're sleeping or resting in a building, I could very well go right by them and never know it.

No, don't think like that, Zaid. Hold on to that hope you felt.

Trudging forward, I don't look back at the garden. Instead, I keep my gaze focused on the destruction ahead of me. The sun is at its highest point now as it looks down upon a city I don't think even it recognizes. It's hotter than ever. The dry heat I grew up in seems to be permeating right through me. Has it always been this hot during the summer? Or has this battle and destruction only made it so much worse?

Just as before, I come across a handful of people every now and then. I usually hear their footsteps a few moments before I see them. Almost all of them are in pairs or small groups. Most of them don't give me more than a glance. They seem to be headed west, probably going toward Mansoura.

I'm so used to all the carnage now that I don't take the time to observe any of it. Instead, I move on while holding on to the dim hope that I will catch a sign of my friends. The rational part of me knows the odds. I have a better chance to run into a thousand different things before catching a whiff of them. However, the part of me that felt solace during prayer or while reading the letter, the piece of my soul that felt hope as it watched the dawn break the night, continues to clench on to the faith that I will be reunited with them.

And so I move on. I continue to trek upon the desolate roads that are littered with wreckage and blown to bits. I continue to march between the debris that was once a bustling city. When there are no distant bombs going off, all I hear is a smoldering pile of ash or my wearying footsteps as they echo up and down the abandoned street.

I wonder if Salman and Fatima are thinking about me as I am of them. Maybe they—

Gunfire.

***

The shrilling bullets rock the street. The barrage came from one street over. Before I can even fully grasp the situation, my feet whisk me away. I've hardly even registered what's happening when I'm dashing through an alley and toward the chaos.

"Come out!" The bullets end and a voice cuts through the still air. It sounds vile—just like the one that shot Jari. "Come out now and maybe I won't shoot you!"

The laughter of another malevolent voice fills the air.

Why am I heading toward it? I've barely asked myself that question by the time I emerge on the other end of the alley.

In the next instant, the machine gun goes off again. I hear the endless bullets violently break against concrete as I catch sight of the scene. There are two men. They're not wearing any kind of uniform. Not even thirty yards away, their backs are turned toward me as they shoot at a slab of concrete. The lank man leans a rifle over his shoulder, while the burly one fires away at their target. The gunfire is so deafening that I can't hear my own thoughts.

The bullets are sprayed onto the barrier with nothing held back. I quickly register what's happening. Those men—they're trying to shoot whoever is behind it, not even giving them a chance to defend themselves.

The burly man's gun runs dry with a loud click. As he effortlessly reloads it, the lank man lets out a snicker before his loud words echo once more. Every syllable is filled with a vile arrogance. "If you refuse to be with us, then you don't deserve to live. You're no better than Assad himself!"

Eyes wide, my mind screams to turn and run. I try to flee back from where I came… but my heart doesn't let me. Not this time. Not anymore.

What do I do? I don't have a weapon. I can't attack two men head-on. Finished reloading, the burly man begins firing at the concrete again. I look to the right. Then the left. My eyes see the answer. Will it work? I don't know. I don't care. I can't abandon whoever is being shot at.

Without another thought, I take off, my footsteps silenced by the roaring gunfire. As soon as I enter the building, I hear the gun go dry. The burly man again reloads it, and the lank man's cruel voice cuts through the air once more.

"Quit cowering like sniveling dogs. We gave a choice to you and your si—"

I can't hear the rest of his words as I hurriedly fly up the flight of stairs. Stepping onto the second floor, I falter for a moment. Do I keep going higher? No, too high and I might miss. I only have one shot.

Sprinting to the end of the hallway, I arrive at a large opening in the wall. No doubt the hole was created by a bomb or missile. The floor beneath me is shaky, threatening to crumble at any moment. But I don't care. Standing at the edge, I face the situation down below. The lank and burly gunmen are directly below me, not even ten feet from the base of the building. I see the tops of their heads.

My eyes look toward the slab of concrete. It's thick and holds up against the streams of bullets raining down on it. I tear my gaze off of it and focus on the men.

Will this really work? I don't know. It doesn't matter. People are pinned behind that slab of rock, and those two gunmen won't stop until they've shot them. I take a step back, preparing to do what I never imagined I ever would before.

I hesitate. A twinge of fear finally surfaces above all the adrenaline coursing through my veins. Its voice reminds me that if I jump, there's no turning back. I'll likely miss and be at the mercy of those two men. The promise I made to Fatima echoes through my head—the promise that I would become a doctor and change the world. There's still hope for that, isn't there?

I remember the words of my father: *never give up your dreams; never surrender them no matter what.* If I take this leap to my certain doom, I'll condemn all that I ever dreamed of. My life is worth something, isn't it?

Shaking my head, I put an end to that voice. That isn't the voice of my dreams. It's my fear using my own father's and friend's words against me. As I ball my hand into a fist, another voice suddenly echoes through my head.

My true voice drowns out everything else. It reminds me of my dream, my real one. It's to make the world a better place, to save the world and help those suffering. And if I save one life, then I may have very well saved humanity.

My name is Zaid Kadir. This is my city. My home. These monsters can take away everything, but they will never take my courage. And I am willing to sacrifice everything if that's what it takes to save a life, if that's what it takes to keep hope burning in the darkness.

There's no more hesitation. Without thinking, I close my eyes and leap out of the building. My body curls into a ball as my forearms shield my face. I hang in the air for an eternity. I feel the rush of it blow right past me. Everything seems to freeze, even my own mind. But just when I think it won't end, there's an abrupt jolt.

I go feet-first into something—no, somebody. The impact painfully shoots right through me. My whole body suddenly rings with agony. As my legs hit something hard, I hear a loud crack. I don't get a moment to digest it. I crash headfirst into the concrete, my skull protected by my arms.

Everything goes black.

***

It's all numb: my body and mind. I'm lying on the concrete ground. I don't feel anything. My eyes won't open.

When sensation does finally flood my limbs, the first thing I feel is the excruciating pain echoing through my limbs and body. It's nothing I've ever felt before. My forearms and hands are scraped up. My head is spinning worse than it was after being knocked unconscious. I'm bleeding, but I can't tell from where. Everything in my body feels broken or torn. For a long moment, I can't move a muscle no matter how hard I try.

What... what happened? I hit something. Was it him?

Each and every fiber inside me is throbbing. But I slowly force my eyes open. Not far away, the lank man is sprawled on the ground. He's just lying there, not moving a muscle. There's... there's blood on his face. Did it... work?

My gaze tears away as something else catches my attention. I slightly turn my head to look, only amplifying the pain. The burly man collapses with a loud thud right next to his comrade, falling down like a sack of bricks. There's somebody standing above him. No, there are two figures.

Now they're standing over me. I can barely move, but I force myself to look at them, squinting my eyes in an attempt to make them out. My heart stops. The world stops. It... it can't be. It's...

Salman.

Fatima is by his side. My anguish is extinguished. Their wide eyes are filled with as much disbelief as mine. Without a word, Salman grabs my shoulder and slowly pulls me to my feet. He's strong enough to bring me upright in one haul. The legs under me are wobbly, but he keeps me steady. Salman's grip is tight, as if I'll disappear if he lets go.

My eyes go from him to Fatima and then back to him. Is this really happening? I can't speak, can't utter a word.

...and I never get the chance.

In the next moment, the ground violently shakes as if it's an earthquake. I fall backward, away from my friends. Landing roughly on my side, I try staggering back up, but my legs give in and I collapse onto my stomach.

An explosion erupts down the road. Then another. Dust and bricks are blown into the air as the thunderous detonations explode. The deafening blasts ring in my ears. I crawl onto all fours, barely keep myself up as the road tremors.

Salman and Fatima are only a few feet away from me. They're under the shadow of the building I leapt out of. The structure quivers with every detonation, threatening to collapse. The shop behind me goes up in smoke. My ears fall deaf with the eruption. The force and heat of the blast beat against my back.

But then I see it.

Neither of them do. Their backs are toward it, blinding them from the danger. A chunk of the building's wall is ripping off. It suddenly breaks free, plummeting below. And—and the debris is falling straight at Salman! They can't hear it. Not above the barrage.

The pain disappears. So do any inhibitions. I don't think. I don't hesitate. With strength that I don't have, I kick off of the ground

226

and leap toward him with every ounce of force I can muster. My arms are outstretched.

Salman senses me coming and whips his head around. Time seems to stop. Everything falls silent. My vision is tunneled. There's nothing but me and Salman. No war, no chaos. Just us. I can't move fast enough. Our eyes lock. I'm not going to make it. He's too far. The wall is going to topple right on top of him. I'm too slow!

No! Not my friend! I can't lose him again!

My eyes shut. Arm still outstretched, I desperately reach for my friend—desperately reach to push him out of the way. The debris is nearly upon us. At that moment, I sense nothing, think of nothing, except Salman.

But then it happens. I feel something on my arm—feel something grabbing me and pulling me toward my friend. Strength suddenly rushes through my veins—strength that I've never felt before. At the last moment, my palms touch something. It's him.

And the world ends.

***

Did I get him? Did I save my friend?

There's nothing but an abyss around me. Blackness is on every side. I can't see or sense anything at all.

The abyss ends when I hear Salman's voice. And Fatima's. They're… they're calling out to me. My eyes open slowly. There's not an ounce of strength left in me. My vision is a blur, the edges all black. The first things I see are Fatima's green eyes. Then his. I… I can't move my legs. I can hardly feel them either. I finally sense it. There's something heavy on them, keeping me pinned on my back. It's the wall. My legs are crushed under it, completely numb and unable to even twitch.

But it doesn't matter.

All I can think is that I got to him in time. I did it… I saved him. Staring at Salman, I care for nothing except that I saved my friend—my brother.

Bombs are falling all around us. Blasts erupt up and down the street. The heavens are blocked by the dust and dirt, but Salman and Fatima don't move. They don't even wince. I see the look in their eyes. They… they're scared for… me. I've seen them scared before, but never like this. They're saying something, but I can't make out either of their words.

I feel Fatima's hand holding mine. It's… soft, just like I always imagined it'd be. Her clasp is so tight, and she's quivering. As the ringing in my ears disperses, I hear her sweet voice. It's cracking up with every word she utters.

"Z—Zaid! What did you do!?"

"Oh, God! No!" Salman's hand grips my shoulder as it trembles. His other hand is holding his own head.

Behind them, the heavens continue turning black as the missiles shower upon the city. The blue sky and sun are long gone, but I can only see my friends' faces.

"What did you do, Zaid?" Fatima's voice is in hysterics, swinging from terrified to sorrowful in each syllable as she repeats the same question again and again. "What did you do?"

A coldness washes over my feet and begins to crawl up my legs.

Even with the destruction, even with all the chaos, my voice is weak and calm. I don't feel any fear in my soul. Not today. Not right now. "…I… I took an oath. After Jari died… I took an oath to protect you… both of you with my life."

Their trembling gazes stay locked with mine.

"I swore to honor that oath. When I thought I'd lost you… I promised myself that if God gave me another chance, I would fulfill that oath… even if it cost me my own life." My eyes lock with

228

Fatima's. "Do you remember what I told you... long ago when we sat on those swings... when the world felt so cruel?"

She nods as tears fill her green eyes.

"I... I swore to you that one I day I would change the world. One day I would save it... one day I would save *my* world... so I saved you..."

Fatima clenches my hand tighter. Her whole body is shivering more than I've ever seen before. Her voice is just the same. "Please don't go, Zaid. I'm... I'm so scared without you."

"Don't be afraid, Fatima. Never be afraid. I will always be with you. Both of you."

"Zaid..." Tears stream down Salman's face. He firmly grips my free hand. "Don't leave us. We need you. *I* need you."

My eyes link with Salman's. "I'm sorry, my friend... it was the only way to save you. A lot more suffering awaits you, but don't ever change. Don't ever lose your strength... or hope. Be the best of us, the light that this city needs... my brother..."

With each word I utter, I feel myself losing strength. The numb coldness is at my torso. They see it too. It's reflected in their eyes.

You were right, father, you were right. It's as you told me. I didn't listen to the voice of fear. Not today. Instead, I listened to my heart, my dream—I did what it told me was right, and maybe it will keep the flame of hope burning in all this darkness...

"Carry it with you... carry the bravery, carry the heart of the city." My gaze slowly drifts between them. "Look after each other. Remember the courage that's allowed us to get this far. Jari... the boy in the street... carry the same courage for our people."

"I will." Salman's tears grow worse. He clasps my hand between both of his. "I promise."

My eyes lock with Fatima's beautiful green eyes one more time. All the dreams I once wished for... all the prayers I made for a future

I once hoped for will never come to pass. But perhaps something better may. Perhaps one day something will…

In Fatima's eyes, I can see the same dreams. All this time we shared them, but I never truly realized it. I kept her safe. I saved Fatima and Salman. I swore to change the world one day… Nabeel believed I would do something great… and maybe I have.

"I will see you, Zaid," she softly says. "Soon… I—I know it. And we will have the life you always dreamed of."

The coldness is at my neck now, but I'm not afraid. I faced death… and I didn't blink.

Fatima leans forward, touching her forehead against mine. Her trembling is stronger now. Salman's voice is in my ear. He's uttering something—a prayer, the same one he spoke over Jari.

I couldn't save Jari… but I saved them. I saved my friends.

In this moment, in this final moment, I finally understand. I truly realize why Jari gave his life for ours. I know why that boy in the street rescued us from the soldiers. I know why Ethan carried me unconscious on his back when death was closing in on all sides. I understand what the gleam in their eyes was.

It was the fire of hope. It was selflessness. It was bravery in their darkest hour. It was knowing that the world is much bigger than them and having the courage to look out for their fellow humans.

So this… is what it feels like… this is what they felt like…

There's somebody standing tall behind my friends. My eyes come onto the figure, while Salman and Fatima dearly hold onto me.

Nabeel… he's here.

Can it be? My brother is finally here after all this time? Nabeel is smiling down on me. He's wearing his military uniform. Can't they see him too? Can't they sense him?

He reaches down, taking my hand. His grip is as strong as ever. No, it's *stronger.* With just one heave, he effortlessly pulls me upright.

230

My legs are now working and the debris doesn't hold me down. How is this possible?

Nabeel wraps his arm around me, preventing me from looking back. But even if I could, I wouldn't. I can't take my gaze off of him. It's really him. It's really my brother.

His smile is as gentle as ever. So are his eyes. It's the look that made me admire him all my life. Without a word, he begins to lead me away from all this. I don't hear the explosions. I don't hear the bombs raining down on the city. I don't even sense my friends anymore.

There's just Nabeel.

"You did good, kid. You did good." His words are the way I've always wanted to hear them: proud. Walking alongside me, he keeps his arm around my shoulder.

I don't utter a word, leaning my head against his powerful frame. There is no more fear. No more pain. No more anguish. There is just peace.

His embrace is warm. Walking side-by-side, he leads me away from everything. "Zaid, what do you say we spend some time alone for a while? Just like you always wanted."

My smile is greater than any I've ever worn. "Are you taking me to the park?"

"No, a garden. And I think you'll really enjoy this one."

It's peace. Complete peace. Together, Nabeel and I walk away from the destruction, away from the war and suffering, and step into the light.

January 23, 2013

To My Friend, Zaid:

Zaid Kadir never knew it, but he was always a hero, a believer. He gave his life not for gain, but for an ideal. He did it so that Fatima and I would live the life that he never could, a life that clung to the hope of one day being free from this war.

Now sitting far from Aleppo—far from Syria—as I write these words, I know that Zaid did not perish. None truly ever do. I will see Zaid one day. I will see the boy who thought he'd lost everything but became the candle of hope in the darkness. Everything he believed came true. Fatima and I found our family… and Zaid was reunited with his.

But in his sacrifice, he will live on. Zaid became what Jari said. He became the light of courage, the heart of Aleppo.

Zaid became the motto that Jari lived by. When the masses are against you, when fear is on every side, and when it seems like you're alone, that is when you should stand the tallest. That is when you plant yourself like a mountain, and you do what your heart knows is right. Even if death will be your only reward.

What did Zaid feel in those final moments? I don't know for sure. Nobody does. However, I believe he may have at last found some small measure of peace, that we all seek, but few of us ever find.

Signed,
Salman

AS OF THIS NOVEL'S PUBLICATION, THE BRAVE PEOPLE OF SYRIA—ALONG WITH MANY OTHERS AROUND THE GLOBE—ARE CONTINUING TO FACE THE ATROCITIES OF WAR WITHOUT ANY END IN SIGHT.

A Nomad's Muse

A land once mine is lost and abandoned
A city once mine is smoke and fire
I built my home with my own two hands
Now it is nothing but piles of sand

A war I do not understand
Politics far beyond my command
They have left me tired and hungry
They have left me a refugee

The city I once loved is ash
My entire life was stolen in a dash
To one side, rebels mercilessly gun down children
To the other, the Syrian army slays civilian after civilian

Gunfire, bombs, blood, and pain
The world I once knew turned insane
Aleppo stood for seven thousand years
Now it is a place for children's screams and tears

The world promises relief, but none will show
Politicians speak, but their words remain hollow
In my country, I am called forsaken
In foreign lands, I am labeled a burden

All this destruction comes at a cost
My place in this world is lost
I am an unwanted wanderer, a nomad
I am one of the faceless masses without a homeland

I now stand alone
I find myself on my own

No friends, no family, no country
Nothing is left but my city's memory

A remembrance of a life I once knew
The recollections slowly become askew
But in it all, I see some semblance of hope
Some slight light in this dark scope

Perhaps this is not the end
Maybe from all this, a higher purpose will ascend
Something will rise from Aleppo's ashes
And a light will shine for the masses

I do not know what the future will bestow
I cannot predict what this all will show
But I have nothing left except tear-filled supplication
And I raise my hands clenching on to the hope for God's salvation

-Ammar Habib

ABOUT THE AUTHOR

Ammar Habib is a bestselling and award-winning author who was born in Lake Jackson, Texas in 1993. Ammar enjoys crafting stories that are not only entertaining but will also stay with the reader for a long time. Ammar presently resides in his hometown with his family, all of whom are his biggest fans.

His list of published novels include:
Memories Of My Future
Ana Rocha: Shadows of Justice
Dark Guardian
Dark Guardian: A New Dawn
Dark Guardian: Legends

Printed in Great Britain
by Amazon